BATTLESTAR
GALACTICA

A NOVEL BY
Jeffrey A. Carver
BASED ON THE TELEPLAY BY
Ronald D. Moore
AND
Christopher Eric James
BASED ON A TELEPLAY BY
Glen A. Larson

First published in Great Britain in 2006 by
Gollancz
An imprint of the Orion Publishing Group
Orion House, 5 Upper St Martin's Lane,
London WC2H 9EA

1 3 5 7 9 10 8 6 4 2

A CIP catalogue record for this book
is available from the British Library

ISBN-13: 978 0 57507 965 6
ISBN-10: 0 57507 965 7

Typeset at The Spartan Press Ltd,
Lymington, Hants

Printed and bound at Mackays of Chatham plc,
Chatham, Kent

The Orion Publishing Group's policy is to use papers that
are natural, renewable and recyclable products and made
from wood grown in sustainable forests. The logging and
manufacturing processes are expected to conform to the
environmental regulations of the country of origin.

www.orionbooks.co.uk

For Julia and Alexandra,
hot on my heels and gaining fast

ACKNOWLEDGMENTS

This book took my life by storm, in a way. I had seen the SciFi Channel's *Battlestar Galactica* miniseries and enjoyed it very much. But it wasn't until the chance to write a novel based on the show came along that I became immersed in the *Galactica* world. The opportunity arrived just as I had completed the first draft of a long-delayed novel in my Chaos series, and it seemed the perfect way to ventilate the mind and experience a complete change of pace for a little while. Thanks go to Jim Frenkel, my editor, for introducing me to the whirlwind – and to my family for welcoming the whirlwind into the house and supporting my crazy work schedule while I tamed it. (And a special familial thanks to Julia, who helped me brainstorm it.)

This novel is my interpretation of a story created by others. It's a *good* story, and one I enjoyed working with. For that, I thank the creators of the show, Ron Moore and David Eick, and the marvelous actors and crew who so vividly brought the story to life on the screen. I'd also like to thank Cindy Chang at Universal for being so ready to find answers to the smallest questions.

A novel is a different beast from a movie, and there are special challenges in telling a story that's satisfying to readers while remaining faithful to the original show. For help with that, I thank Craig Gardner, Richard Bowker, Victoria Bolles, and Mary Aldridge for their willingness to read many pages fast, and for their helpful and insightful comments.

Finally, I'd like to thank you, my readers, for your patience and interest – especially those of you who have been waiting so long for another book from me. Here's one I hope you'll enjoy!

BATTLESTAR
GALACTICA

PROLOGUE

*The Cylons were created by Man. Created to make life easier
on the Twelve Colonies. They began as simple robots — toys
for the amusement of the wealthy and the young — but it was
not long before they became useful, and then indispensable,
workers. As their sophistication grew, the Cylons were used
for the difficult and dangerous work that humans preferred
to avoid: mining, heavy industry, deep space construction.*

*And finally, perhaps inevitably, they were used for war.
Not against enemies from without, but by human against
human, as the Twelve Colonies found reason to wage war
against one another. The Cylons were the greatest soldiers in
the history of warfare. They were smart, fast, and deadly.
Successive models had become increasingly independent,
capable of making decisions without human orders. And
they were utterly without conscience. Killing, to the Cylons,
was simply one of the functions for which they had been
superbly designed.*

*In hindsight, perhaps it should not have been a surprise
that the day would come when the Cylons decided to kill
their masters. And when that day came, the horror of war
was unleashed upon all twelve of the Colonies of Man. For
ten long and bloody years, humanity fought — not just for
freedom, but for survival. The Twelve Colonies, facing a
common, implacable foe, at last came together and joined as*

one. Many fought, and many died, in the effort to destroy the mechanized race that humanity itself had conceived and brought into being.

There would be no victory. But through valiant fighting, and with the mobilization of every available resource throughout the human sphere, the Cylons were gradually driven from the immediate part of space occupied by humanity. In the end, an armistice was declared. Humanity would live in peace, while the Cylons left to find another world to call their own. Live and let live was the philosophy . . . if 'live' was a term that could be applied to the existence of the robots. No one knew the location of the Cylon world. But to maintain the peace, a remote space station was built in the dark emptiness between the stars, to be a place where Cylon and human would meet and maintain diplomatic relations.

Once a year, every year, the Colonials sent an officer for the scheduled meeting. After the first year, the Cylons sent no one. No one had seen or heard from the Cylons in over forty years.

That was about to change.

PART ONE

IT BEGINS

CHAPTER

I

ARMISTICE STATION

The diplomatic spaceship emerged from its Jump with a momentary flash of light. Its prior inertia carried it like a boat on a river toward its destination. The only propulsion required was braking thrust.

The spidery space station hung silent in the darkness, billions of miles from the nearest inhabited world. A row of navigational marker lights winked along its vertical spine, barely illuminating its outline. The approaching spaceship, an ungainly white transport, pierced the darkness with tiny flares of its maneuvering jets as it slowed. Nearing the docking section, it rotated and pitched upward to align itself with the station. Practice made the intricate ballet of the docking maneuver seem casual; the pilots had performed it so many times it was an automatic movement, like a hand slipping into a glove.

The thrusters brought the ship to a halt a hundred meters from the station. A telescoping passageway emerged from the side of the station's docking port and stretched out, crossing the gap with a single gliding movement. It drew up into place against the ship's airlock, and with a series of thunks, the mag-locks made it fast.

Another scheduled meeting was about to begin. In theory.

The intercom crackled to life, and the pilot's voice filled the departure lock. '*Colonel Wakefield, we are docked. You may enter Armistice Station at your discretion. If you need anything, we'll be here. I hope you don't get too lonely over there.*'

The colonel pressed the TALK button on the intercom. 'Don't worry about me, Captain. I'm used to it by now. I'll be back soon enough, no doubt with nothing to show for it.' With the sigh of someone who had done this job many times already, he drew himself up straight and stepped to the airlock hatch. The latch mechanism stuck for a moment, then swung open, revealing the interior of the passageway. Picking up his briefcase, the colonel stepped across the threshold and began the long, deliberate walk down the passageway and into the station's interior.

There was an unavoidable grimness to the job, but he vowed not to give in to a sense of futility. If the Cylons did not show up – and he fully expected that they would not – he would not let that reflect on his own performance.

His footsteps echoed in the silence of the station as he left the passageway and airlock and passed through the long corridor leading to the meeting chamber. He shivered a little, and wrinkled his nose at the musty smell of the place. There was dust in the air – the filters must be in need of replacement – and a patina of grime everywhere. The maintenance robots must be breaking down, he thought. They were Cylon-built machines, of course – humans no longer had robots – but really, the wonder was that they still functioned at all. He doubted they'd been serviced since the station was built. What did that say about the endurance of the Cylon technology? The thought caused him a little shudder, which he did not allow to the surface.

Only once a year was there any official activity in the station. And that activity consisted of the colonel arriving, waiting three days for his Cylon counterpart to show up, and then leaving. Not once in the last thirty-nine years had a Cylon representative appeared, to meet with him or with any other member of the Colonial delegation. The colonel often wondered why they bothered. But he knew the reason: Even if the Cylons did not honor their commitment to the armistice terms, at least the Colonials were keeping up their end of the agreement. And how else could they maintain vigilance, since they did not even know in what direction to look for the Cylon world, or even if it really existed?

The colonel came to the massive closed doors of the meeting chamber and pulled them open. The sound reverberated in the room as the doors slammed closed behind him. He strode forward, heels clicking on the broad-tiled deck. The chamber was itself practically a hallway – long, widening slightly toward the center, with outward-canted walls and steel support beams arcing low across the room in closely spaced rows. It was a spare space, devoid of decoration or color, lit along the edges of the floor and by widely spaced ceiling lights. Its very shape seemed to suggest the meeting of adversaries: long, to permit ample time to view the approaching opposite, and barren, as if to deny any possibility of emotion or warmth.

A narrow table stretched most of the way across the center of the room, a single chair on either side. The

Colonial flag hung at rest on its pole at the left end of the table; there was no flag for the Cylons. The colonel sat down in the chair and snapped open his briefcase. With efficient care, he removed two framed photos from the briefcase – one of his son, and one of his wife – and placed them at his left hand on the table. He gazed at them for a moment, allowing himself the reminder of home, of what he was here to protect – before firmly assuming again an attitude of detachment. Then he took out a sheaf of papers and began leafing through them: briefing documents on the Cylons, as they had last been seen, forty years ago. He knew the documents by heart, but he reviewed them nevertheless, with the steady weariness of someone who has done the same thing over and over, year after year, for a very long time.

Nothing had changed, he thought, except him. A year older, a year closer to retirement, a year wearier of this charade. The Cylons would never come. For all he knew, for all *anyone* knew, they were extinct. Maybe they had turned on each other and annihilated their entire mechanical civilization. Wouldn't that be justice. Or maybe they had set off across the galaxy in search of new realms to conquer. But how would the Colonials ever know? When the robots departed the star system forty years ago, they hadn't left a forwarding address.

The colonel sighed and closed his eyes, resting his head against the seat back. It was silent here, but he was used to the silence. It was restful, in a way. Later, when the wait got to be too long, he would catch up on some reading. Or return to the transport ship for rest and relaxation. But for now, he would just sit here as a representative of his worlds, and soak in the solitude.

It wasn't long before he caught himself nodding off,

and he drew himself up with a deep breath. It wouldn't do to nap. He was on watch – even if he was here as a diplomat, and even if he passed the three days alone.

He glanced at the photos of his wife and son, and then looked over the Cylon briefing sheets once more. After a few minutes more, he closed his eyes again.

He jerked awake. Maybe he *was* getting old. It used to be he could stay alert on marathon watches with the best of them. He blinked and stretched his mouth in a yawn, shifted uncomfortably in the chair. Gradually, he closed his eyes once more. And began to dream of a place, more than a light-year behind him, where the sun streamed down onto a beach on Caprica, where he and his wife, both younger then, had played with their two-year-old son. That had been a happier time, perhaps the happiest of his life. That was before the stresses of parenthood, and those of the military and diplomatic life, had combined to take their toll.

He loved his wife and his son, of course. But still, there were times in his dreams when . . .

Boom.

The colonel started awake again. *What was that?*

He jerked up straight. The doors in front of him, at the Cylon end of the hall, were swinging open, splitting to reveal a blaze of light. Sweet Lords of Kobol. It couldn't be . . .

The sounds of footsteps were soft, but unmistakably metal on tile. Two huge chrome robots marched in through the open doors, then stepped to either side as guards. *Cylon Centurions. Modified, but clearly recognizable.* The colonel blinked, every sense afire now. The robots raised their arms, which appeared to end with the barrels of built-in weapons; the weapons folded back suddenly, revealing long, talonlike fingers that flipped forward to form something like hands.

The colonel stared at them, pulling momentarily at his collar before catching himself. The robots stood utterly impassive. Each had a single crimson eye that slid back and forth across the angular brow, scanning, scanning.

Something else was coming; the colonel could hear the footsteps. Another robot, he assumed. The two standing guard did not move an inch. The colonel licked his lips nervously, waiting.

A shadow moved in the light, a figure coming toward him. Walking. Emerging from the light . . .

It was a blonde woman, dressed in a crimson jacket and skirt, and elegant boots that came nearly to her knees. She was stunningly beautiful. She walked toward him with a precise, confident stride, one foot in front of the other. The closer she came, the more unnervingly beautiful she looked. She exuded sensuality. Her hair fell in loose waves and curls to her shoulders; her figure was riveting, her eyes sharp and probing. He drew a hoarse breath, only half-believing what he was seeing. But what he was thinking was, *A hostage of some kind. They're releasing a hostage.*

But why? Why would they do that? And why now?

The woman walked directly to the table, then came around the end, without a word. She leaned against the edge of the table, directly in front of him. *Can't get much more direct than that.* She might as well have been in his lap. His heart began pounding.

On her face was a hint of a smile, rather pensive. She cocked her head and listened, or perhaps was waiting for the colonel to say something. She leaned forward, bringing her face close to his. And she spoke the first words the colonel had heard since leaving his ship. In a low, sultry voice, she asked, 'Are you alive?'

The words went through him like electricity. He stammered, trying to reply, and finally managed, 'Yes.'

One hand on his shoulder now, she leaned closer still. He could feel her breath, warm and sweet on his face. *So beautiful, so . . .* Before he could complete the thought, she said, just a little more forcefully, 'Prove it.' And then, in an exquisite torture of slow motion, she moved her hand to the back of his neck, drew him to her and kissed him.

Kissed him. But why?

His mind went utterly blank, then returned with an awareness only of this moment. There was a power in this kiss, almost a supernatural power, that made other thoughts and cares flee. Her lips were afire with passion; they worked to discover the exact shape of *his* lips. Her breath was hot on him now. Lust, awakened from a deep slumber, began to flare to life in him. He returned the kiss now, answering passion with passion. Her grip tightened on the back of his neck. All thought of his mission fled, all thought of his wife . . .

In the deep, deep darkness surrounding the station and its docked spacecraft, another ship was moving. It was immense, and shaped something like two sea stars joined face to face, kissing, their arms twisted at odd angles. It was, unmistakably, a Cylon base star. Beside it, the Colonial ship and the station looked like tiny plastic toys. It was now moving away from the station, gaining a little distance – but not too much – before a single white point of light streaked out from somewhere within it, and began to turn in a graceful curve around the extensions of the base star's arms. Then the light whipped back inward, toward the little space station.

As it struck the station, there was a blinding flash . . .

The colonel felt the deck shudder beneath him, as the kisses came more and more urgently. It was almost as though she were trying to draw something out of him, some passion no human had ever touched before. *Something terrible was happening* – of that he was certain – but his mind was too fogged by her raw, commanding sexuality to focus and comprehend. And not just her sexuality, but a feeling that she was touching him in some inexplicably deep way, drawing from him emotions he could never express. Another shudder shook the room harder than before, and he tried to break from her kiss. For a fraction of an instant she smiled, a bit sadly and sweetly perhaps, and with a probing gaze, murmured, 'It has begun.'

He struggled to pull free, but there was an inhuman strength in the hand pulling him back toward her lips. Her mouth met his again as the papers on the table began to flutter and fly away. As she breathed in his mouth, he felt all the air rushing from the chamber. If he did not break free and get to a safe place, *he would die.*

The third and final shudder jarred his senses, but only for an instant – before he, the woman, and the entire space station exploded in a ball of fire and hull-metal shrapnel.

In the silence of deep space, there was no sound of the explosion. No human still living was close enough to see the flash of the fireball. And no warning signal was ever sent.

Its single, simple mission concluded, the Cylon ship quickly moved away and vanished back into the darkness of the interstellar void.

CHAPTER
2

Thump, thump, thump, thump . . . The rhythm of the running footsteps echoed in the spaceship's passageway, a high, trapezoidal corridor lit by regularly spaced, vertical blue-white light tubes along the slanted support beams. The passageway was spotlessly clean, but well worn with use, and now, as always, full of people.

Kara Thrace rounded a corner, jogged past a handful of crewmen coming the other way. Kara was an athletic, short-haired blonde woman in her late twenties, and a fighter pilot. She bore down on a knot of tourists gathered in the passageway ahead. She was already breathing hard, but that didn't stop her from yelling, 'Make a hole!'

That produced some startled looks from the visitors and their guide. They hastily backed to either side of the corridor and made a hole. Kara plunged through their midst and never looked back, though she shuddered a little at the tour guide's voice, telling the people about the history of the *Galactica*, the sole remaining battlestar from the era of the Cylon War. 'Originally twelve battlestars,' he said in a perfect museum guide's tone of voice, 'each representing one of Kobol's twelve colonies . . . *Galactica* represented Caprica . . .' Frak, Kara thought as she left the tourists behind. Wait until the ship *is* a museum, will you . . .

Such thoughts were very much in Commander William Adama's mind as he walked the ship's corridors. He had a speech to give, and he still hadn't quite worked out what he wanted to say. The *Galactica*'s stocky, craggy-faced commanding officer didn't much like giving speeches under any circumstances – throughout his long years in the service, he'd managed to avoid that duty whenever possible – and he certainly didn't like to dwell on the reasons for this particular speech. Nevertheless, it had to be done, and there was no getting around the fact that as *Galactica*'s final master, he was the one who had to do it.

Glancing down at the paper in his hand as he walked, he tried once more, in his deep, husky voice. 'Though the Cylon War is long over, let's not forget the reasons why—'

A voice from behind him interrupted. 'Commander Adama, if I may!' It was Captain Kelly, the Landing Signal Officer.

This was the third time he'd been interrupted before getting through the opening paragraph of his speech, but Adama didn't really mind. He glanced back as Kelly caught up with him. 'Captain?'

Kelly appeared to feel awkward now that he had his commander's ear. 'Well, sir, I . . . just want to say what a pleasure it's been . . . serving with you, under your command, sir.'

'Kelly.' Touched, Adama turned to shake the officer's hand. 'It's been my honor. Good luck in your next assignment.' Kelly was only the latest of many members of the crew to approach him with such sentiments today. Adama felt touched by all of them.

'Thank you, sir.' For a moment, Kelly looked as if he might have something more to say, but finally he just nodded and turned down a side corridor.

Adama kept walking, trying to remember the opening line of his speech without looking down. Murmuring, he began, 'The Cylon War is long over. Yet we must not forget . . .'

Jogging footsteps behind him, coming alongside. 'Morning, sir!' called a familiar voice.

'Good morning, Starbuck,' he answered, without looking up. 'What do you hear?'

'Nothing but the rain,' answered Kara Thrace, keeping pace beside him.

'Then grab your gun and bring in the cat,' Adama said, completing the ritual exchange he and Kara had shared for as long as she'd been a pilot on his ship.

Kara grinned and pointed a finger at him. 'Boom boom boom,' she said, and accelerated ahead to finish her morning jog. Adama watched her with a smile as she disappeared around the bend. There went one of his top pilots, and one of the biggest hell-raisers on his ship. Practically a daughter to him. He shook his head and went back to rehearsing his speech.

This time he made it to the fourth sentence before he looked up to see a trio of enlisted crewmembers from the hangar deck, a woman and two men muttering to each other with some urgency. Adama just caught the words '. . . wrapped that yesterday,' and some under-the-breath curses, as Specialists Socinus and Prosna passed something behind their backs, while trying to look innocent.

'Too late,' Adama said. 'What's up?' He wasn't worried; every commander should have such a reliable crew.

The three crewmembers saluted. Socinus made the quickest recovery. 'Nothing, sir, just another leak in that frakkin' window.' The young man hesitated. 'Pardon me, sir.'

Prosna, hands still behind his back, added, 'This is supposed to be a battlestar, not a museum. Sorry to say so, sir.'

'I couldn't agree more,' Adama said. 'Be careful out there, all right?' Letting them keep their secret, he turned back toward his destination. As he neared the Combat Information Center, he tried one last time to rehearse his speech, but it was no use. Once he stepped into the CIC, there was no such thing as a private moment.

The CIC, located deep in the belly of the massive ship, was the battlestar's nerve center. It was the center of both flight and combat operations – a huge, dimly lit room filled with consoles and overhead monitors, work counters and not enough seats to go around. During normal operations, there could easily be thirty or forty crewmembers moving about here; today, there were maybe a dozen. You could feel the coming decommissioning hanging in the air; it made Adama sad, but also proud to be here at the end.

Greeted by the Officer of the Watch, Lieutenant Gaeta, Adama kept walking – casting a casual but perceptive eye over the various workstations as Gaeta briefed him from the stack of papers in his hands, printouts of the day's comm traffic. This was the only battlestar in the fleet that still kept everything on paper, and that was exactly the way he wanted it. 'Anything interesting?' Adama asked, looking up to scan the overhead monitors.

Gaeta was young, efficient, and usually a good judge of what Adama was likely to consider interesting. Adama was going to miss him. 'Mostly just housekeeping,' Gaeta said. 'Though there is one sort of odd message we were copied on.' He handed Adama the printouts. 'It's the one from

Fleet Headquarters. The courier officer's overdue coming back from Armistice Station, and they're asking for a status report on all FTL-capable ships, just in case they need somebody to jump out there today and see if his ship is having mechanical problems.'

Adama chuckled as he flipped through the printouts. 'I think we're a little busy today. Wouldn't you say so, Lieutenant?'

The watch officer grinned. 'Yes, sir.'

'I'm glad we agree,' Adama said wryly. He handed the stack of printouts back to Gaeta and prepared to walk on.

Before he could take another step, though, Gaeta continued, 'May I take this opportunity to say what a pleasure and honor it's been to serve under you these past three years?' He gestured awkwardly, pushing the edges of the paper pile together.

'It's my honor, Lieutenant Gaeta,' Adama replied, saluting. Lords of Kobol, was everyone on the ship going to say that to him today? Perhaps he had better get used to it.

Turning, he glanced back at the piece of paper he'd been carrying for the last hour. To himself, he repeated softly, 'The Cylon War is long over . . .'

For Aaron Doral, the day had been a nonstop series of encounters with the news media and other VIPs newly arrived aboard *Galactica* – all of them here for the decommissioning ceremony scheduled for tomorrow. For today, his role was to explain and extol. His role was to interest the press and to lay the groundwork for the tour guides who would indeed be giving this spiel once the old crate was *officially* what it had been in reality for years now – a museum piece. But making the old seem fresh, and the ugly beautiful, was what Aaron Doral was good at. Aaron Doral was thirty-two, nattily dressed in a blue civilian suit, and a fast talker. Aaron Doral was a public relations man.

As he strode through the ship's passageways, leading a cohort of media reporters and others lucky enough to have wangled passes, he spoke energetically about what the ship had meant to the Colonies through the years, and why she was the way she was. Doral was a hard man to impress, but even he felt twinges of pride in this ship that had served for nearly half a century, at one time the flagship of the fleet, and now the oldest of all the battlestars. Also, a flying anachronism . . .

Doral gestured as he led the latest group through the public portion of the ship. 'You'll see things here that might look odd, even antiquated, to modern eyes,' he said, turning to face the knot of people following him. 'You'll see phones with cords, all kinds of manual valves in the most awkward places, computers that barely deserve the name.'

After confirming that people were nodding in acknowledgment, he continued, 'It was all designed to operate against an enemy who could infiltrate and disrupt even the most basic computer systems. *Galactica* is a reminder of a time when we were so frightened of our enemies that we looked backward to our past for protection. Backward to simpler computers, and away from the networking of the day, networking that at the time made us so terribly vulnerable to the Cylon threat. Of course' – he paused to gesture toward the CIC, which they would *not* be walking through – 'modern battlestars resemble *Galactica* in only the most superficial ways.'

Doral paused to say hello to an older gentleman with thinning gray hair – Colonel Tigh, the ship's Executive

Officer – but he got only a pained scowl in return as Tigh stalked past. Good God, the man looked hungover. Lucky *he* wasn't going to be serving on board much longer. One thing Doral knew was that he wasn't going to say anything about that to his audience. No, smile and show respect to the old fossil, that was the way to keep this audience pleased with their tour.

'Next,' he said, looking back over his shoulder again, 'we're going to walk down the port side of the ship to get a view of the real meat and potatoes of a battlestar – the hangar deck, where her real fighting force, the Vipers and Raptors, are serviced and kept ready for action at a moment's notice . . .'

The hangar deck was precisely where Commander Adama was headed at this moment, having completed his round of the CIC. The crew chief had asked him to come down to see something special.

Adama stepped down off the ladder onto the hangar deck, to be greeted by Chief Petty Officer Galen Tyrol. The chief was obviously working to keep a sober face as he called all hands on deck to attention. Adama saluted and as quickly put the scattered crew members back at ease. 'Morning, Chief. How are you, today?'

Tyrol, a seasoned leader of the hangar maintenance crews and one of the most respected noncommissioned officers on the entire ship, wore an uncommon expression of eagerness and maybe a bit of nervousness. 'Thank you for coming down, sir. We've been looking forward to showing you this.'

'Well, so have I, Chief. Whatever it is,' Adama said. He kept a dry expression on his face, but his curiosity was definitely piqued.

'If you'll just follow me, sir.' Tyrol led him around an array of machinery and spacecraft with maintenance panels propped open. A small crowd of enlisted deck hands accreted behind them as they proceeded. Tyrol brought Adama to a craft covered from nose to tail with a black tarp. It was clearly a Viper, the lines of the space fighter unmistakable under the covering. 'What's this, Chief?'

A grin twitched at the corner of Tyrol's mouth as he stood in front of the craft, waiting for the rest of the crew to crowd around. He seemed about to speak, then simply gestured to several of the deck hands, who hurried forward and swept the tarp smoothly off the concealed craft.

Adama stared. It was an old-style Viper, a fighter from the days of the Cylon war. 'Mark Two,' he said, in genuine wonder. 'I haven't seen one of these in about twenty years.'

'If the commander will take a closer look . . .'

Adama shot Tyrol a puzzled glance and stepped closer. Then he saw it – the name, stenciled on the hull, just below the lip of the cockpit canopy:

LT. WILLIAM ADAMA
'HUSKER'

He laughed. So that's what they'd been up to, painting his name and his old call sign on the vintage war-bird. But Tyrol was still talking:

'. . . at the tail number, Nebula Seven-Two-Four-Two Constellation.'

Adama's mouth dropped open, as he read the registration markings on the Viper's tail. *N7242C.* They hadn't just painted his name on any old warbird. '*Oh my God. Where did you find her?*'

Tyrol was openly grinning now. 'Rusting out in a salvage yard on Sagitarron. We had hopes the commander would allow her to participate in the decommissioning ceremony.'

Adama turned in disbelief. 'She'll fly?'

'Oh, yes, sir. We've restored the engines, patched the guidance system, replaced much of the flight controls . . .'

Adama hardly knew whether to laugh or cry. 'You guys are amazing.' He reached out to touch the hull of the craft. Viper N7242C. How many times had he flown this fighter, forty years ago? How many times had it survived Cylon attack to bring him safely back to the flight deck? *My God*, he thought.

'. . . she's fueled, armed, ready for launch, sir.'

Laughing quietly, Adama ran his hands over the aft engine cowling.

'Commander—'

He turned back. 'What? More?' Tyrol handed him a flat package wrapped in brown paper. Adama chuckled. 'Somebody's bucking for a promotion around here.'

Tyrol grinned and glanced at the deck crewman standing beside him. 'I believe that would be Prosna, sir. He found this in the Fleet Archives. He was doing some research for the museum.' Prosna lifted his chin slightly, but did not crack a smile.

It felt like a plaque of some kind. Adama tore the paper open and lifted out a picture framed in dark, heavy hardwood, square with all four corners cut off. It was a photo of himself as a young fighter pilot, standing in front of this same Viper, with two boys. *Sweet Lords of Kobol.* Zak and Lee must have been about seven or eight at the time. They were beaming with pride as they stood with their father and his Viper. Adama felt his mask of command begin to fail as a host of unexpected emotions welled up in him. *They look so happy.* A lump formed in his throat as he fought to keep his composure, to hold back the tears that were welling in his eyes. 'Thank you,' he said, looking up before he could crack, looking all around him to include the entire assembled crew. 'Thank you all.'

'You're welcome, sir,' said Tyrol. And as Adama stood, continuing to stare silently at the photo in his hands, Tyrol quietly dismissed the crew.

Adama stood motionless, lost in the past, lost in the photo, for a very long time.

CHAPTER

3

GALACTICA, OFFICERS' WARDROOM

The triad game was already well underway when Colonel Saul Tigh entered the officers' wardroom and headed shakily for the coffee table. He helped himself to a coffee cup, but did not fill it with coffee. From his pocket, he produced a small metal flask. He unscrewed the top and carefully poured a generous shot of whiskey into the coffee cup. If anyone noticed, nobody said anything. Colonel Tigh, the Executive Officer of the ship, was off duty. If he wanted to have a drink or two, there was nobody *here* who could tell him no. And it sure helped steady his nerves, and take the edge off that headache that pounded insistently at the back of his skull.

Besides, maybe it would help him shake things up a little here. These people were having too damn much fun.

Tigh pulled out the last remaining chair at the card table and sat down across the table from Lieutenant Kara Thrace – Starbuck, to the flight group. 'Uh-oh,' she muttered, without looking up. Whether she was talking about his arrival or the cards she was holding, he couldn't tell for sure. He'd find out; an opportunity to taunt Kara Thrace was something he could never resist.

'I'm in,' said Tigh, and waited while Thrace dealt him a hand of cards.

'Here we go.' That was from Helo, on his immediate left. Helo was the flight officer for the Raptor pilot sitting to *his* immediate left – Sharon Valerii, better known as Boomer.

Lieutenant Thrace's short blonde hair came just over her ears and eyebrows. She cultivated a tough-guy look, and was cockily smoking a cigar. She aimed it at Helo and said, 'If you're gonna play with the big dogs—' She pointed to the table. Helo dropped his chips onto the pile.

'No fair,' complained Boomer, squinting at her cards. Not such a good hand, maybe.

Colonel Tigh tuned out the banter while he examined his cards. Finally he looked up, as Thrace said with a laugh, 'Ohhh, Helo – when are you gonna *learn*? First you're flying with crooks, and then – *ow!*' – Boomer had just smacked her on the arm – 'and then you're bettin' against Starbuck!'

Tigh let out a snort. '*Star*buck. Now there's a call sign. *Starbuck*' – he gave a string of chicken sounds – '*buck-buck-buck-buck-buck!* Where'd you get that nickname, anyway? Was that *before* you were thrown in the brig as a cadet for drunk and disorderly, or *after*?' He glanced over his cards, not meeting Thrace's eyes.

Unperturbed, Thrace leaned back and blew a stream of smoke from her cigar. 'After,' she said smugly.

'After,' he echoed, searching for a snappy comeback but not finding one. 'That's right it was . . . after.'

'I'm in.' Helo tossed in some more chips. 'Bet's to you, XO.'

Brought back to the game by the sound of the chips, Tigh muttered, 'I'm in,' and followed Helo's chips with a few of his own.

Lieutenant Thrace had never dropped her gaze from him. 'How's the wife?' she asked, in slow, measured tones.

He stiffened, words lodging in his throat. God, no wonder he hated her. Anger, and the whiskey, made his skin burn – but he was damned if he was going to rise to the bait. Around him, the other players continued their banter, oblivious to the power struggle that had just begun. He barely heard them . . .

'. . . *that pyramid game on Geminon?*'

Arrogant bitch. Yeah, his wife was probably banging some other man right now. Wherever she was.

'*What were you doing on . . . ?*'

He hadn't spoken to her in the last month, and had no reason to think he'd speak to her in the next.

'. . . *girl there I know.*'

'*What girl don't you . . . ?*'

'The wife is just fine,' Tigh said evenly.

Lieutenant Thrace grinned and sipped from her mug. 'Talk to her lately?'

Tigh knitted his brow and scowled at his cards, pretending he hadn't heard. He raised his coffee cup to his lips, with an effort mastering the slight trembling in his hand. The whiskey burned as he swallowed.

Lieutenant Thrace had turned back to the game. 'All right. Thirty for me' – she threw in more chips – 'and it looks like I'll have to bring this *lovely* little game to a close, because' – she slapped her cards down onto the table – '*full colors! Ha-hah!*' Grinning like a kid with candy, she began raking the pile of chips toward her.

Tigh felt the fury rising in his chest. Thrace was doing a little dance in her seat now, singing and crowing. There were no words to express his disgust at her smug superiority. No words, but . . .

With a roar, he stood up and shoved the table over onto

her. Chips and cards flew across the room. Thrace looked startled for an instant, then lunged. Her fist landed on his chin before he could react, and he fell backwards over his chair, crashing to the floor. Stunned, and more than a little dizzy, he fought his way back to his feet, fighting off the helping hands of nearby crewmen. Thrace had been pulled back by Boomer and Helo, but she was struggling to break free. 'I'm fine – I'm fine,' she snapped. After a moment, they let her go. She pushed her hair calmly back out of her face, then lunged for him again. Helo grabbed her, and this time pushed her well clear of Tigh.

The colonel gathered himself, summoning all of his faculties to speak clearly through the alcohol haze. At last he had her where he wanted her. He pointed a finger at Thrace, a deliberate calm tightly wrapped around the steel anger in his voice, controlling the quaver that threatened to betray his real condition. 'You have finally gone too far. And now you're done.'

She sneered.

'Lieutenant – consider yourself under arrest, pending charges. Report to the brig.'

Thrace never dropped the sneer, but she did give him the satisfaction of looking surprised. She bent down, picked up her fallen cigar. Obviously making a deliberate effort to look unperturbed, she glanced around the room with a slight smile. 'Gentlemen,' she said and, jamming the cigar between her teeth, turned and swaggered from the room.

Tigh watched with scarcely contained fury. This time he had her. This time he would break her for good.

The photographers would be arriving soon, and Commander Adama had to get ready. He pulled a clean dress uniform jacket out of his closet. 'Are you really gonna press charges against Kara?' he asked, turning to look at Colonel Tigh.

Tigh was sunk into an easy chair in Adama's stateroom. He looked anything but at ease. 'For striking a superior officer? You're damn right I am.' Tigh pushed himself up and walked across the room to Adama's desk.

Adama grunted and refrained from saying a few words that came to mind. 'I heard you started the day off pretty early.' He was increasingly worried about Tigh's drinking problem. If they weren't both so close to retirement, he would be forced to do something about it. Saul had always been a drinker, but until the last few months, he had managed to not let it get in the way of his duties. Of course, until the last few months, his wife Ellen had been a lot more discreet about her infidelities.

Tigh picked up the framed photo that Adama had received from the hangar crew earlier in the day. 'I wasn't on duty,' he said with quiet defensiveness. He studied the picture as he carried it back to the easy chair. 'Now, where did you get this?' he asked in amazement.

'Tyrol's deck gang scrounged it up.' Adama still found it hard to believe. He sat on the edge of his bunk and began taking off his boots. 'I couldn't talk you out of it, could I?'

Tigh gave one of those silent snorts that Adama could have heard in the next room. 'Not a chance. She's insubordinate, undisciplined—'

Adama interrupted. 'She's probably one of the best fighter pilots I've ever seen in my life. She's better than I am. Twice as good as you.'

'Like hell,' Tigh growled. He tapped the photo. 'How long ago was this?'

Adama shrugged, wiped his face and neck with a towel.

26

'Must've been about twenty, twenty-five years ago. I don't know.' He put the towel down. 'Listen. I'm not going to defend what she did. Especially the crack about your marital problems. But you *did* kick over the table first.'

'I did not . . .' Tigh stopped suddenly and paused in thought. 'Unless I did.'

Adama just looked at his old friend for a moment, thinking of the long years they'd been together – of all the bar fights, all the Cylon fights, all the battles with military bureaucracy. Tigh had always been the one with the incendiary temper, and Adama the one to intervene with a cooler head. 'You did. What do you say you drop the formal charges and just let her cool her heels in the brig until we're home.'

Tigh sat silent for a beat or two, then – by way of conceding – said, 'You always did have a soft spot for her. Damned if I can see why.'

'Yeah, I guess I'm just a crazy old man,' Adama said with a soft smile.

'Yeah,' said Tigh. Beneath the gruffness of his words, Adama knew, was the unspoken trust between men who had been together through war and peace, honor and shame. 'You sure as hell are. Just like me. No wonder they're about to put us both out to pasture.'

Adama laughed. 'A couple of old warhorses, eh?'

Tigh grunted. 'More like a couple of old mules, if you ask me.'

CHAPTER
4

CAPRICA MEDICAL CENTER, CAPRICA CITY

Caprica City, capital of the Caprica Colony, largest city on the planet Caprica, was a modern metropolis. Traffic flowed nonstop through the air, along the ground, under the ground, and on the water offshore. Its skyscrapers and towers jutted into a blue sky. It was the epitome of hope, prosperity, and human achievement. The sight of the skyline was enough to make the heart soar.

All of this was visible right outside the window of the waiting room. Sitting silently in a leather armchair facing an unoccupied desk was an attractive forty-eight-year-old woman named Laura Roslin. She had a soft-featured, oval face and dark, shoulder-length hair. She wore a conservatively cut dress of a light periwinkle blue. Her gaze, deep and intelligent, was frightened. Though her eyes were apparently focused outside the long bay window, Laura Roslin saw none of the majesty of the great city. All she saw were the pale yellow saffron blossoms just outside the glass. *So lovely. So fragile.* Her thoughts were in turmoil. *When is he going to bring me those results?*

As if in response to her thoughts, the door behind her closed with a reverberating thud. She closed her eyes and listened to the doctor's footsteps as he crossed the long room toward the desk where Laura sat. *Who in the world got the idea that a doctor's office should be in a room the size of a small gymnasium? Could it possibly be more impersonal?*

The doctor came around the desk, glanced into the file folder in his hand, then closed it before speaking. His expression was sober, and she already knew what he was going to say. 'I'm afraid the tests are positive,' he said quietly. 'The mass is malignant. We'll do all we can, of course. But I have to be honest – it's advanced well beyond the point that we can have much hope . . .'

White noise filled Laura's mind as she looked at him, nodded, looked away, tried to hurl her thoughts as far away as humanly possible. *Get away, get away from here . . .*

'I'll contact the specialists at the Caprica Institute—'

She couldn't stand to listen anymore. Laura forced herself up out of the chair, forced a pained smile. 'Thank you, Doctor. If you'll excuse me, I have a flight to catch.'

'Dr Roslin, please call me as soon as possible. Any further delay will just . . .'

She barely heard him, as she hurried across that long floor toward the exit.

COLONIAL TRANSPORT 798

Buckled in, waiting, thinking, waiting. Staring out the window at the sunlight burning on the launch tarmac. She really had had a flight to catch. Off planet, to meet a warship. If only she could fly away from reality. *Dear Gods. Why? Why me? Why cancer?*

There was movement beside her, and she looked up to see a slender young man dressed in a jacket and tie, with a large briefcase, standing nervously in the aisle beside her. She tried to smile, but didn't feel as if she'd succeeded. 'Yes?'

'Secretary Roslin?' He paused. 'I'm Billy Keikeya.' Another pause. 'Your new assistant.'

'Ah.' That took a moment to process. Yes, the human resources people had promised her a new assistant in time for the trip. She hadn't thought she'd be meeting him for the first time on the transport, though. 'Well, then, hello. Have a seat.' She rose to let him past to the window seat, and extended a hand. He shook hands and sat down in one slightly awkward motion. He was a good-looking boy, with curly brown hair and an alert demeanor. But he couldn't be a day over twenty, and he was probably overwhelmed to be making a trip like this on his first day on the job.

As Laura settled herself back in her seat, Billy bent forward and extracted a thick three-ring binder from his briefcase. 'Sandra at the Education Ministry main office sent this briefing book to give you.'

'Thank you,' she whispered, resting it in her lap without looking at it. She looked back out the window, past Billy, eyes blurring. She was barely aware of the captain asking all passengers and flight attendants to fasten their seat belts: '*We are preparing for departure to Galactica, with an expected flight time of five and a half hours . . .*'

As the transport lifted from the launch pad and roared skyward, she rested her head against the cushioned seat back and shut her eyes tight.

'Uh – Dr Roslin?'

She blinked, realized they'd been talking and she hadn't

heard a word he'd said. 'What? Oh – I'm sorry. What were you saying?'

Billy looked a little puzzled at her lack of attention, but he said nothing about it. Instead he continued, 'I also sent the president a copy of your speech for *Galactica*'s retirement. Hopefully he'll have chance to review it. But . . . there is a thirty-minute time delay between the *Galactica* and—'

'Excuse me,' Laura said abruptly. She jumped up from her seat and hurried up the aisle, leaving a startled Billy behind her. *Too much. Too much.* She ran into the lavatory and shut the door behind her. In privacy at last, she leaned back against the door and breathed. Just breathed, and stared up into nothing. Fear and despair rose in her like poison in her bloodstream, threatening to choke her. She gasped, fought for air, each breath feeling as if it would be her last. She desperately wanted to cry, to flood the room with tears of grief and anger; but just as urgently, she fought against it, fought against giving this thing even that much of a victory. *How dare you invade my body, how dare you!*

With a muffled gasp of anguish, she pulled open the front of her jacket, exposed the white blouse that crisscrossed over her breasts. She thrust her right hand under her jacket, covering her left breast, covering the lump that was growing, the traitorous part of her that was devouring her body, devouring her life.

Damn damn damn damn damn . . .

CHAPTER
5

RIVERWALK MARKET, CAPRICA CITY

Clear breezy day, bright sunshine in a blue sky. Crowds of people milled about in the outdoor marketplace, enjoying the warmth of the perfect spring afternoon. One person felt differently about it, however – though you wouldn't have known from the way she looked around the crowd, tossing her shoulder-length, bleach-blonde hair with the movement of her head, or from the look of the bright hazel eyes taking in everything around her. Most people, male or female, would have called her stunningly beautiful. She wouldn't have disagreed, but she might have called it part of her job description: form follows function.

She walked casually and with no particular destination for the moment – but with a curious air of purpose, as though she did not yet know what she was here to do, but knew that it would be revealed to her when the time came. And that time, she had a feeling, would be soon. She brushed her fingertips along the blossoms of a lilacan bush, and gazed over the reflecting pool that formed a lovely interruption in the lines of the marketplace.

Something lay ahead for her; she sensed it. Her gaze wandered over the pedestrians moving about, and fell on a very small child in a stroller. *How darling.* She felt drawn to it immediately. She stepped closer and gazed down on the helpless thing. The sight stirred something in her heart, and it must have showed on her face, because the child's mother, standing just a few feet away, noticed and stepped closer with a tentative smile, taking the handle of the stroller instinctively, protectively.

'How small they are,' murmured the blonde woman, more to herself than to the mother.

'I know. But they grow up so fast,' the mother replied, casting her own loving gaze down on her child.

The two shared a beaming moment together, and then the woman gestured. 'May I?'

There was a moment of hesitation, and then: 'Sure.' It was the kind of 'sure' that guaranteed that the mother would be watching every move the woman made. As she should. The blonde woman might have been unmarried herself, but she absolutely approved of protective parenting – even if, in the end, parents had to die to make room for the children.

The mother scooped her child gently out of the stroller, cradling it for a moment before carefully placing it in the arms of the blonde woman. Such a small bundle.

'So light.' The baby give a plaintive squeak, and she calmed it with a light touch, stroking its cheek. 'So fragile. Shh-shh-shhhhh . . .' She soothed it again. 'You're not going to have to cry much longer,' she whispered.

The mother, nervous again, reached out. 'We really should be going.' Nearby, a man was looking over the heads of the intervening people, trying to wave her over. The father, no doubt. The woman smiled and passed the child back to its mother, who cradled it reassuringly, and then returned it to the stroller.

The woman leaned forward, to take one more look.

33

'It's amazing how the neck can support that much weight,' she said, marveling.

'Yes—' the mother started to say, but was interrupted by her husband calling, 'Centura! Honey!' She looked away to catch her husband's eye and wave. 'Come on!'

'Okay!' called the mother. 'Give me a moment.'

The interruption was quite enough time for the blonde woman to reach down one last time into the stroller, to slip her hand beneath the baby's neck, and to make one quick, silent movement. *You won't have to suffer any longer.*

She straightened and smiled sweetly, sadly at the infant. Then, not meeting the mother's suddenly worried expression, she turned and walked quickly away. She could feel the tension behind her, the inexplicable fear, as she put distance between herself and the mother and child. *No more suffering. Not for you.*

As the mother's scream of horror rent the afternoon peace, the blonde woman did not look back. Her brow was furrowed, though, and her heart was filled with a mixture of sadness and regret, but above all a certainty of the rightness of what she had just done.

I have spared you, little child.

CHAPTER
6

NEAR CAPRICA CITY
HOME OF GAIUS BALTAR, PH.D.

Overlooking the calm waters of King's Bay Inlet, not far from Caprica City, the residence of Gaius Baltar was a model of elegance and simplicity. Its clean, modern lines harmonized beautifully with the shoreline and the breathtaking expanse of the inlet waters. Inside, the clean design continued. The rooms were spacious and light, decorated with an impeccably tasteful eye for detail.

In the living room, Gaius Baltar himself was seated in a comfortable leather-upholstered chair, pensively sipping a glass of Olympia spring water, while an attractive TV anchor introduced the interview segment in which he was about to take part. Kellan Brody's face could be seen in the right-hand half of the TV screen that dominated the far wall of the living room; his own image was in the left-hand side. Dr Baltar was apparently lost in his thoughts, paying little attention to the TV, while she completed her introduction:

'*For those of you just joining us from the Pyramid Game on Geminon, welcome to The Spotlight – our weekly interview program devoted to people making news on Caprica. Today, we're talking with Doctor Gaius Baltar. Doctor*

Baltar has been the winner of three Magnate Awards over the course of his career. He is a media cult figure and a personal friend of President Adar's. He is currently working as a top consultant for the Ministry of Defense on computer issues. But he's perhaps best known for his controversial views on advancing computer technology. Doctor Baltar – again, welcome.'

Baltar nodded with suave grace. He was a trim, narrow-faced man with dark, collar-length hair combed straight back from his forehead. His relaxed posture and body language spoke of one who was used to the spotlight and to attention from admiring fans. He spoke effortlessly. 'Thank you, Kellan. And firstly may I say' – he smiled with just the right amount of debonair charm for the camera – 'how lovely you're looking. And secondly, what an absolute pleasure it is to be on the show.'

'Well, we're delighted to have you with us.' Ms Brody seemed to blush ever so slightly. 'Could you summarize your views for our audience?'

'Yes. I'd be happy to. My position is very simple. The ban on research into artificial intelligence is, as we all know, a holdover from the Cylon wars. Quite frankly, I find this to be an outmoded concept. It serves no useful purpose except to impede our efforts . . .'

As Doctor Baltar spoke, the front door of the house opened quietly, as a tall, slender, stunningly beautiful woman with shoulder-length blonde hair stepped into the house. Her name was Natasi, and she was expected. She was dressed in a sheer blouse and skirt combination that kept no secrets about the jet black lingerie she was wearing beneath. She closed the door silently, so as not to disturb the interview, and approached Baltar slowly from the side living-room entrance. A mischievously seductive smile flickered across her lips as she watched him finish the interview. She settled into a chair just out of range of the camera pickup, but in perfect view of Dr Baltar, and she crossed her legs provocatively.

She appeared to enjoy watching him squirm as he tried to keep his mind on the interviewer's questions. What was he saying? That it was only the irrational fears of those who could not put the past behind them that was keeping mankind from moving forward with the development of intensely interesting and useful technologies. Just because robotic inventions of a superficially similar nature had once gone awry didn't mean that humankind should forever be fearful. So much would be lost . . .

Baltar breathed a heartfelt sigh of relief as the interview ended, and his visage disappeared from the TV monitor. It had been an easy enough interview . . . until Natasi showed up and distracted him. 'You!' he said, in a tone that he hoped sounded more amused than reproving. He really was quite eager to see her. Especially dressed the way she was.

'Me?' she asked coquettishly. She uncrossed her legs in a way that spiked his blood pressure instantly. 'What have *I* done?'

'As if you don't know,' he said, his voice cracking a little. 'Would you like a drink?'

She shook her head. 'I don't need one. Come here, Gaius. I want to see something.'

'Mm?' he asked, standing up unsteadily.

'You heard me.'

'Yes, I did. Now, what did you want to see?' He smiled with anticipation as she leaned forward at his approach.

She tipped her head back to look up at him, as her

hands found him and began fondling him. 'I wanted to see how glad you were to see me,' she whispered.

'Very glad to see you,' he sighed, shutting his eyes with pleasure. He slipped his fingers into her hair and bent to kiss her. 'My Natasi, are you feeling particularly animalistic today?' he asked huskily.

By way of answering, she rose suddenly from the chair and pressed him backward, until she had driven him up against the nearby wall. She kissed him hungrily, and began pulling at his clothing. Soon she had him bare-chested, and her own blouse was on the floor. Her mouth eagerly sought his, and they stumbled into the bedroom, groping each other and kissing. 'Mm, d'you miss me?' she murmured breathlessly.

He struggled to catch his own breath, not wanting to miss a single kiss. 'How can you tell?'

A tiny laugh came from her throat as she placed her hands behind his neck and pulled him to her. 'Mmm, your body misses me,' she whispered, kissing him furiously, 'but what about your heart? Your soul?'

'Yeah,' he breathed. 'Those too.' He could not move his hands over her fast enough.

She rose on her tiptoes so that he could kiss her neck. She purred with pleasure. 'Do you love me, Gaius?' she asked, without interrupting the passionate kissing.

'Uh – *what?*' His heart fluttered; he wasn't sure he had heard her right.

She stopped what she was doing and cradled his face with both hands. 'Do . . . you . . . love me?' Her gaze penetrated his, penetrated the haze of his lust.

This time his heart didn't flutter; it froze in paralysis and even fear. *Do you love me?* Those were the words they'd never asked or given. This wasn't about love, this was about raw animal attraction, about kindred spirits in carnal lust. For a long moment, he didn't know what to say. Finally, because her eyes seemed starving for an answer, he murmured, 'Are you *serious?*'

She held his gaze just a moment longer, then suddenly grinned. He joined her in a quiet laugh, and they began kissing again. 'You had me . . . worried, there,' he managed, so relieved he couldn't even speak. She didn't answer, but kissed him more feverishly than ever.

Without warning, she pushed him backward onto the bed, practically threw him. Stunned – he never knew she had that kind of strength – he lay helpless as she grabbed the waistband of his leisure pants, and ripped them off with a powerful jerk. He was beyond stunned; he was at her mercy. With another murmur of pleasure, she hiked up her skirt and swiftly mounted him. He gasped with ecstasy . . .

Natasi rocked back and forth on the writhing figure of Dr Baltar. She peeled the rest of her own clothes off, panting with uncontrolled passion. 'I'm hot, Gaius,' she moaned. 'I'm . . . *so hot.*'

As their lovemaking mounted toward a climax, the wall behind her was warmed slightly by a peculiar, nearly invisible light. The doctor never saw it – and wouldn't have, even if he had been less distracted. The light was mostly infrared, with just a hint of gamma radiation. If his eyes *could* have seen it, they would have seen the glow of fiery embers, the glow of heating coils. It was a soft glow, but growing in intensity, growing with the woman's sexual fervor. Indeed, it came from, and illuminated, the spine of the gorgeous, naked being who was rocking and bobbing as she made love to Gaius Baltar.

CHAPTER
7

GALACTICA, EN ROUTE TO CAPRICA

The immense, lozenge-shaped battlestar grew to resemble
a fortress wall in front of the dome of stars, as the fighter-
craft arrowed in smoothly on its landing approach. The
pilot, Captain Lee Adama, was on a 'high downwind
approach' – named for a purely imaginary wind that the
battlestar flew into like a seagoing aircraft carrier turning
into the wind so that its planes could land. And indeed,
the battlestar was very much like an aircraft carrier in
space. In normal operations, it carried as many as fifty
fighter, recon, and other spacecraft to support its mission;
Galactica carried fewer now. Lee rolled his craft to permit a clear view out the canopy as he glided past the
great ship's nose, and then her upper left flank. It was
standard practice to make a visual inspection of the ship
on approach, but also good sense: If you'd rather not fly
into something, make sure you can see it.

For Lee Adama, it was a view of a ship he had not seen
in a long time. *Galactica*'s basic shape was pretty simple, a
sort of boxy whale shape – but its surface was convoluted
with ridges and canyons and a huge landing pod on either
side. Some of its hull plating appeared pretty battered, and
the ship as a whole looked scoured and worn with age, as

he knew it would. *Galactica* was long past ready for retirement.

The voice in his helmet was clear and matter-of-fact: '*Viper Four-Five-Zero, this is* Galactica, *approach port landing bay, hands-on, speed one-zero-five, checkers red, call the ball.*'

Lee thumbed the mic switch. '*Galactica*, this is Viper Four-Five-Zero. Check that. Did you say hands-on approach?'

'*Viper Four-Five-Zero, that's affirmative. Hands-on approach.*'

'Copy, *Galactica.*' That seemed a bit unusual. The last time he'd served on a battlestar, manual approaches were made only for training purposes or if there was a problem. Of course, that had been *Atlantia*, the newest battlestar in the fleet, not the oldest. 'Port landing bay, hands-on approach, speed one-zero-five,' he repeated back, as he applied braking thrust and began the flip-over-and-thrust-downward base-leg maneuver that would bring him to the level of the aft landing-bay door. As he rotated and pitched over again to face forward relative to the ship, the landing bay came into view, and along with it the landing guidance lights. The lights traced a welcoming line into the bay. 'I have the ball.' He applied thrust, to accelerate to final approach speed.

If he hadn't had other things on his mind, he might have enjoyed the hands-on approach. It was what flying was all about: man and machine, spinning and dancing through space. Right now, though, he was tired and preoccupied. He brought the Viper into the long, cavernous landing bay with practiced ease, slowing as he approached the red-checkered landing pad. He made the final maneuver, turning to use his thrust for braking, and popping side thrusters to line up on the pad. He felt the thump of contact, and killed the power.

'*Skids down, mag-locks secured.*'

That was the LSO, the Landing Signal Officer, announcing the arrival – not so much for his benefit as for the deck crew's. The elevator pad he'd landed on was already lowering him into the hangar deck below. He could feel the Lorey-field gravity pulling him down into his seat.

'*On behalf of* Galactica, *I'd like to welcome you on board, Apollo. It's an honor to have you with us.*'

Lee made a quick acknowledgment as he went quickly through the post-landing checklist. Confirm main thrust off, fuel flow off, maneuvering thrusters off, transponder off . . .

Minutes later, a tractor was towing him from the elevator pad into the brightly lit main hangar area. He pulled off his spacesuit gloves, pressed the time-of-arrival button on the flight computer on his wrist, and took a moment to draw a deep breath. The flight was over; now the ordeal would begin.

The canopy lifted, and a deckhand reached in to help loosen his spacesuit helmet and lift it away. Lee took half a moment to gather himself and unbuckle his harness, then he climbed out of the cockpit and down the steps that the deck crew had pushed up. Other hands were already at work servicing his craft. And standing in front of him, dressed in the orange-and-black jumpsuit of the hangar crew, was a serious-looking young man, hand to his forehead in salute. 'Good morning, sir. Chief Tyrol. I'll be your crew chief while you're aboard.'

'Morning, Chief. Captain Lee Adama.' He tried to make it sound polite, but he knew that his lack of enthusiasm probably showed.

Tyrol was undeterred. 'It's a real pleasure to' – Lee was already walking away, ducking past the other Vipers, but Tyrol hurried to keep up – 'meet you, sir.' Lee didn't answer. 'I'm sure you've heard this before, but I'm a great admirer of your father's. The service is going to miss him when he retires.'

There it was. It hadn't taken two minutes from his arrival. He tried to keep his true feelings in check. 'Well, I'm sure someone will.' Quick change of subject. 'Is your auto-landing system down? I was hands-on for the whole approach.'

Tyrol look puzzled and a little taken aback. 'It's all hands-on here, Captain. There are no auto-landing systems on the *Galactica*.' He paused, then added pointedly, '*Commander* . . . Adama's . . . orders.'

Lee hesitated. What *could* he say? It was explain everything, or nothing. Finally, he simply said, 'Is that right?' and walked away across the expansive hangar deck, leaving the crew chief standing perplexed behind him.

'*Attention in the port hangar bay. Raptor touching down. Clear. The checker is red.*'

The craft coming in behind the Viper – one of *Galactica*'s own – wasn't doing so well in the final positioning and flare for landing. Crew Chief Tyrol watched on a monitor, wincing, as the LSO rasped out instructions to the pilot to watch her drift and cut her approach speed. The craft was rocking back and forth on the roll axis, and more alarmingly, skidding first to one side and then the other as it approached the assigned landing point. Finally it slammed onto the landing pad with a jolt that Tyrol could feel all the way down on the hangar deck. '*Frak*,' he muttered, and strode out to await the Raptor's crew as the elevator brought it down into the hangar.

Where the Viper looked like a flying stinger, the Raptor seemed more like a hunched-over beetle – not unbeautiful to anyone who loved flying machines, but definitely ungainly. The Raptor was a multipurpose tactical-strike/combat-coordination craft, an important part of *Galactica*'s flying arsenal. It was also, at the moment, in the hands of the youngest rookie pilot in *Galactica*'s squadron. Tyrol met the Raptor as it was being towed into its parking space, and hopped onto the side-flare of the hull that served as an entry platform, without waiting for the craft to come to a halt. He was met in the hatch-by the pilot, a hassled-looking Sharon Valerii, known in the cockpit as Boomer. She was a strikingly attractive, petite brunette with Oriental features. Right now, she looked ready to kill someone.

He wasn't about to cut her any slack. 'Nice landing, Lieutenant. I think they heard that one all the way up on the bridge.'

Boomer glared at him and retorted in a rapid-fire stream. 'Yeah, I'm gonna catch hell from the LSO. But it wasn't entirely my fault, Chief. The primary gimbal's acting up again.'

Tyrol rolled his eyes, following her down off the Raptor to the hangar deck. 'Oh, it's the gimbal's fault.'

Exasperated, Boomer turned to her copilot and electronics officer, who was just emerging from the Raptor, clipboard in hand. 'Helo, am I lying?'

Helo worked a wad of gum around in his mouth. 'Gimbal looked bad to me.'

Tyrol blew up. 'I've pulled that gimbal three times and stripped it twice. The gimbal's not the problem. *Sir*.' He stalked away from the craft, followed briskly by Boomer.

'You're not listening to me, Chief.'

'Lieutenant, I listen very closely to what each and every one of my pilots has to say.' *Even the rookies*, he thought but did not say aloud. He turned back to look at the rookie pilot, who happened also to be his superior officer.

Boomer had calmed slightly, but remained adamant. 'You're not the one out there trying to bring in *fifty tons of Raptor* onto a moving hangar deck – with a bad gimbal.'

Tyrol yanked open the swinging steel door to the tool room and yelled back at her as she followed him into the cramped, walk-in storage closet. 'I've got ten years' experience—'

'Here we go!' she cried, slamming the bulkhead door shut behind her.

'—of breaking down and stripping every component of every system that's—'

Boomer chanted the rest of his tirade right along with him.

'—ever been installed in every spacecraft on my hangar deck!' As they berated each other, he was loosening and removing his tool belt – and she was yanking loose the hardware that secured her flight-suit.

He whirled around, dropping the act. Grabbing her by the front of her flight-suit, he pulled it apart from the neck down to the waist, and with her help, peeled it roughly off her shoulders and arms. Underneath, she was wearing a plain brown tank top. As he pulled her toward him, she grabbed his chin with one hand, pinching his cheeks together. 'The gimbal – is – faulty,' she growled into his face.

'Shut up, sir,' he muttered, and pulled her into an urgent kissing embrace. She clutched him just as urgently. They kissed like forbidden lovers, tearing at each others' clothes as if they couldn't get enough, fast enough. There was, in fact, no telling how long they had, or when they'd get another chance – or whether they'd be caught this time, or the next. Neither of them spoke, not now, at least not in words . . .

Outside, on the hangar floor, deck crewman Jane Cally paused in what she was doing, which was helping her crewmate Leonard Prosna into a spacesuit for a maintenance job. 'Hold it,' she said, trying to get him to stand still for a moment. Then, louder, 'Hold up!' Prosna looked puzzled, but she wasn't speaking to him, she was yelling to Brad Socinus, who was heading for the Tool Room with a heavy toolkit in his arms.

'What?' Socinus asked. 'Oh, don't tell me.'

'Yeah, the groping light is on in there.'

'Oh, frak me,' Socinus said, looking for a place to set down the crate.

'Just put it over there,' Cally said, pointing to a work bench that had a small, bare patch on top.

Socinus groaned and set the load down. 'This is getting out of control, you know. Has the chief lost his mind?'

'Hey,' said Cally, getting back to adjusting Prosna's spacesuit, 'it's none of our damn business, is it?'

Prosna finally snorted. 'It's our frakking business if he gets busted for banging his superior officer. They'll *both* get busted. You think that won't affect us?'

Cally started to reply, but finally shrugged it off with a shake of her head. They all knew Tyrol's affair with Boomer was highly illegal, and a mighty dangerous game. So far, they were all looking the other way, out of loyalty to Galen Tyrol. But how long could they protect him? How long before someone less forgiving – someone like the XO, say – found out what was going on? Maybe they were just hoping that the ship would be retired before it happened.

'Let's just hope they don't get caught,' Cally said at last, having no other answer.

'Fat frakking chance,' was all Socinus had to say.

The Squadron Ready Room was nearly filled with pilots when the CAG, Jackson Spencer, started the briefing. The Commander Air Group was the chief pilot for all the squadrons on the ship, and the one who was charged with seeing that all flying squadrons faithfully executed the orders of the ship's master, Commander Adama. It was the CAG who set both the tone and the rules, and if any of his pilots busted either, it was his job to bust them. That rarely happened with a crew as well trained as this one, though. Mostly his job was to see that the flying went smoothly, and safely.

The CAG began the briefing with a review of the mission immediately before them: 'Today's the main event. We have a formation demonstration – flyby maneuvers in conjunction with the decommissioning ceremony. I've got a few changes to the flight plan. Lieutenant Thrace is being replaced in the slot by Lieutenant Anders.' There was no need to say why; everyone knew that Kara Thrace, Starbuck, was in the brig. 'Also, we have Captain Lee Adama joining us, and he's going to be flying lead during the flyby, so . . . please, welcome the captain!'

That brought some applause, many turned heads, and a number of calls of welcome, as all the other pilots in the room craned their necks to see the flyer they knew by reputation, and to greet the man they knew to be their commander's son. Lee himself shifted in his seat, and forced an uncomfortable smile.

The CAG continued. 'Now, thanks to Chief Tyrol and his deck gang, Captain, you're going to have the honor of flying the actual Viper that your father flew once, forty years ago.' The CAG paused for a reaction from Lee.

Momentarily unable to speak, Lee fiddled with his pen for a few seconds. Finally, he said awkwardly, 'Great. That's um . . . that's . . . quite an honor.'

Around him, silent puzzlement registered at his apparent lack of enthusiasm; one or two of the pilots snorted softly. *Let them,* Lee thought. *They don't know him the way I do.* The CAG's face darkened almost imperceptibly as he responded, 'Yes, it is, Captain. And personally I can't think of a better way to send this ship into retirement.'

And personally you can't think of a reason why they would invite a jerk like me to a ceremony honoring my father, right? Well, I could name a lot of better ways to retire this old hulk. And the man you all look up to so much.

Lee managed another smile, and a nod.

The CAG moved on to the down-and-dirty details of the maneuvers they would be flying later that day.

It was a day that, for Lee, could not end soon enough.

CHAPTER
8

CAPRICA CITY, GOVERNMENT CENTER PLAZA

Coming down the steps from the Defense Ministry, her arm draped over Baltar's shoulder, Natasi listened tolerantly as Gaius went on about the success of his latest project, the Central Navigation Program currently being deployed and tested in the Colonial fleet. Really – she loved him, and could barely keep her hands off him, but when he got going on his accomplishments, there was no shutting him off.

'It may interest you to know,' he was saying, tightening his arm around her waist, 'that the final results are in on the CNP project. It's working at close to ninety-five percent efficiency throughout the fleet.' She half expected him to stop and take a bow, but instead he continued without a beat, 'Hold your applause, please.'

'No applause for me?' she asked, her head turned away from him. *My, aren't you satisfied?* 'I doubt you would ever have completed the project without me.' She finally looked at him.

Gaius casually drew a mouthful of smoke from his cigar. 'Yes, well, you . . . *helped* a bit . . .'

'I *rewrote* half your algorithms.'

'All right, you were extremely helpful.' He peered at her

through his dark glasses. 'But let's not forget, you got something out of it. All that poking around inside the Defense mainframe should give you a huge advantage bidding for the contract next year.'

She turned to face him. 'You know that's not really why I did it.'

He paused and looked away. 'No, you did it because you love me.'

She drew him back and allowed just a flicker of a smile on her lips. 'That, and God wanted me to help you.'

A pained expression crossed his face, and he pulled off his dark glasses. 'Right, he spoke to you, did he? You had a chat?' Now, instead of pained, he looked supercilious.

Deliberately and tolerantly, she said, 'He didn't speak to me in a literal voice. And you don't have to mock my faith.'

'I'm sorry,' Gaius said. 'I'm just not very religious.'

To say the least. 'Does it bother you that I am?'

He sighed, obviously groping for words. He put his arm back around her waist, and began walking again. 'It puzzles me that an intelligent, attractive woman such as yourself should be taken in by mysticism and superstition.' His voice suddenly turned lecherous. 'But I'm willing to overlook it, on account of your other attributes.'

She laughed, and turned to stop him with a hand to his chest. 'I have to go. I'm meeting someone.'

'Really? Who is he? I'm insanely jealous.'

She leaned into him with a chuckle. 'I doubt that.'

Gaius looked slightly disconcerted. He put a fingertip to her nose. 'So touchy today.' Almost imperceptibly gathering his ego, he continued, 'Well, as a matter of fact, I'm meeting someone, too – business. A new project at Defense I might do. So, uh' – he kissed her on the cheek –

'you'll call me later. Right?' Without waiting for an answer, he sauntered away.

She watched him go, then turned to be on with her business. She stopped before she'd taken more than a step. Her entire mood and outlook changed as she greeted her colleague. 'It's about time,' she said. 'I wondered when you'd get here.'

Her contact nodded. 'It is indeed. The time has almost come.'

She drew a breath and sighed. *So soon. The work is nearly finished.* 'All right, then. I'd like to be with him.'

The other nodded again. 'Of course. There is much for him to do yet. And one way or another, you will always be with him.'

CHAPTER
9

GALACTICA, PORT AND STARBOARD LANDING BAYS

The giant warship *Galactica* boasted two complete landing systems – essentially, parallel runways enclosed in enormous tubes, one on either flank of the great spaceship. On the right, or starboard, side, the huge landing bay had already been turned into a huge museum hall. Twenty-odd older-model Vipers of various vintages had been brought in, and were in the process of being converted to display units. Various historical exhibits were being prepared, including actual Cylon Centurions, warrior robots captured during the Cylon War forty years ago. A scale model depicted the most dreaded of all war machines, the Cylon base star – the enemy's counterpart to the Colonial battlestar, but much larger, and in nearly every way more powerful. The work on preparing the exhibits proceeded quietly, steadily, and for the most part, outside the day-to-day awareness of the *Galactica* crew. It was far enough along, though, to make quite an impression on visitors for the dedication ceremony.

On the opposite side of the ship, the port landing bay was still very much in use. In fact, it was busier than usual, what with the arriving vessels and the fact that it was now doing the work of two bays. The large passenger transport coming in just now looked like a toy boat as it settled to a stop in the long cavern of the landing bay. It was carrying the chief VIP for the dedication ceremonies, the Secretary of Education for the Twelve Colonies.

'*Colonial Transport Seven-Niner-Eight heavy, welcome to* Galactica. *Please stand by, and keep your passengers seated, while we bring you down into the hangar deck.*'

'Galactica, *Colonial Seven-Niner-Eight heavy, roger.*'

It took a little longer to get the large transport squared away than it did a small Viper, but eventually its doors opened, and people started streaming out. They were escorted across the hangar floor by the deckhands, and shown the way to the ladders that would take them down to E Deck, where their guides awaited them.

Billy Keikeya was first down the ladder, but the well-groomed man in civilian dress who waited to greet them called first to Laura Roslin as she was still negotiating the ladder. 'Secretary Roslin?'

'Yes.' The secretary stepped off the ladder and turned.

After greeting her, the man finally spoke to Billy. 'Mister Krekare?'

'Keikeya,' Billy corrected him.

'Oh – sorry. My name's Aaron Doral.' Shaking hands with both of them, Mr Doral spoke quickly as he continued, 'I'm from Public Relations. I'd like to welcome you aboard *Galactica*.'

'Thank you,' Laura said.

'If you'll follow me, I'll show you to your quarters.'

They set off through the corridors, and Billy was almost at once overwhelmed by the new sights and the bustle of activity, with ship's crew members striding purposefully through a bewildering series of intersecting corridors. The whole look of the place was surprisingly clunky and old fashioned compared to the transport he'd just come in on – or to just about anything on Caprica. The passageways were blocked off at regular intervals by bulkheads and huge metal hatches with rims, or coamings, that one had to step over to get from compartment to compartment. Storage lockers lined the walls everywhere, filling just about every nook and cranny. If he hadn't known better, he would have thought he was on a submarine.

Overhead speakers kept coming alive for announcements. At one point, the announcement was to welcome the Secretary of Education to the *Galactica*. Billy was tired, but intrigued. He paused at one intersection to look around. His eye was caught by an attractive, copper-complexioned crewwoman with long dark hair in a pony-tail, and he turned to watch her pass. It was only when she turned to look back at *him* with a sharp, captivating gaze that he realized he was staring. He returned to his senses with a start, and hurried after the Secretary and Mr Doral.

The only problem was, they were out of sight. He whirled this way and that, trying to figure out which way they might have gone. Too many choices. 'Madame Secretary?' he called. Taking a guess, he chose a passageway branching off the right, followed it a short distance, then halted, suddenly uncertain. He started down another, turned a corner, and realized he was now completely lost. Sweating, feeling like a dunce, he tried a different direction. *Great. If they didn't already think you were too young for the job, this'll clinch it.* 'Madame Secretary!'

He moved more quickly, down a hallway that at least seemed large enough to be a main corridor. There was an announcement tone overhead, and the intercom voice, saying, '*Attention all hands. There is an EVA in progress outside the hull. Do not radiate any electrical . . .*'

Billy found himself in front of a large hatch. Well,

maybe they'd gone this way, and that was why they couldn't hear his calls. Taking a breath, he pulled it open. To his complete embarrassment, he found himself standing in the doorway to a large bathroom, in which about a dozen men – and women – were in various stages of undress while showering or washing at sinks.

The nearest woman, dressed only in a black bra and the bottom half of a jumpsuit, glared up from the wash basin and said, 'In . . . or out!'

'Excuse me?' He realized, dizzily, that this was the same dark-complexioned woman he had seen just a few minutes ago in the corridor.

'Get in or get out. Shut the hatch,' she said, continuing to scrub at her face with a washcloth.

'Oh – sorry!' he said, reaching to pull the hatch closed behind him.

The woman looked up at him with tolerant exasperation. She had gorgeous eyes. 'Where are you trying to be?'

He struggled to find his voice. 'Uh – visitors' quarters.' He winced, stepping aside for more people coming into the room. 'I'm a visitor.'

That brought a giggle from the woman, who glanced at her nearest neighbor. 'Huh! Never would have guessed!'

Billy's face burned with embarrassment. Two women entered behind him and went into toilet stalls.

'Never been in a unisex head before?' the woman asked.

'Uh – no, not really.'

She nodded. 'Well, there's not much privacy on a warship. So the first rule is, don't get your panties in a bunch at being seen. Second rule is, *don't stare.*'

Which, he realized with a lurch, was exactly what he'd been doing. Again. 'Um – sorry.' He looked quickly away from her.

'C'mon,' she said, zipping up her jumpsuit. 'Let's get

you home.' She grabbed his elbow and propelled him out the door. As she led him down the passageway, she glanced at him with a grin. 'What's your name?'

He swallowed, trying not to be dazzled by her smile. She had a great smile. 'Billy.' *And I'm not really a complete dolt, I just look like one right now.*

'Hi, Billy. I'm Petty Officer Dualla, Crew Specialist.'

'Hi – Petty, uh—'

Her grin widened. 'How about just Dualla. Better yet, call me D.'

'Hi, D.,' he said, blushing, but feeling much better already. He had a feeling he'd just made his first friend on *Galactica*.

'The answer's no,' Commander Adama said, walking with Laura Roslin and Aaron Doral through the D-Deck passageway. They had met in the corridor and Adama had turned aside from his immediate destination to walk with them for a few minutes. Unfortunately, Laura had brought up what apparently was a very touchy subject.

'It's a *visitor's guide*,' she said, amazed that a pleasant so-good-to-meet-you conversation had turned so tense, so quickly. 'It tells people where things like the restrooms are. Or what the lunch special is in the cafeteria. Or how to buy a *Galactica* T-shirt. *Galactica is* going to be a museum, after all.'

Adama shook his head. 'What you're talking about is an integrated computer network, and I will not have it on this ship.'

Laura stared straight ahead as they walked, and tried not to sound derisive. 'I heard you're one of those people. You're actually afraid of computers.'

'No, there are many computers on this ship. But they're not networked.' Adama stopped and faced her.

Laura tried to maintain a polite smile, but it was difficult in the face of such obstinacy. 'A computer network would simply make it faster and easier for teachers to be able to teach—'

He interrupted impatiently. 'Let me explain something to you. Many good men and women lost their lives aboard this ship during the Cylon war, because someone wanted a faster computer to make their lives easier – but you know what happened. The Cylons took control of every computer network in the Twelve Colonies.' He was starting to lecture now. 'I'm sorry that I'm inconveniencing you or the teachers, but I *will not* allow a networked computerized system to be placed upon this ship while I'm in command. Is that clear?'

Stunned by the sudden display of authoritarianism, Laura managed a tight, indignant smile as she said, 'Yes, *sir.*'

Adama nodded. 'Thank you.' And with that, he excused himself and strode away.

Laura glanced at Doral, who was obviously feeling a little flustered at the abruptness with which feelings had gotten out of hand. Well, she didn't have time to worry about the PR guy's feelings now. Nor Billy's, she thought as she saw him come around the corner with an attractive female crewmember. 'Where you been?' she murmured, not really caring.

'Uh – I got lost, but – D., here, helped me out,' Billy said, gesturing awkwardly. D. smiled briefly and walked on.

'Fine. Good.' Laura raised her chin and said to Doral, 'Would you be so good as to show us to our quarters now?'

*

The brig was a small compartment, which always surprised Kara Thrace when she thought about it. She guessed there weren't that many frak-offs like herself getting themselves locked up for stupid reasons. That was why there was just one guard, who had nothing to do but sign in visitors and let the food come through at mealtime. The place was grungy as hell, too. The walls were lined with ugly, composite *pegboard*, probably to absorb the sounds of screams – of boredom. The whole place, including the bars on her cell, needed a good paint job, and the mattress on the bunk smelled pretty ripe. It definitely wasn't the cleanest compartment on the ship – which she particularly noticed when she got down on the metal floor to do push-ups. Which was precisely what she was doing, trying to stay in some semblance of shape, when she heard a voice from the past. *Oh frak, not now.*

'This seems familiar,' said Captain Lee Adama, gripping the bars and looking in on her.

Kara got to her feet, allowing a guarded smile. She felt a rush of complicated emotions at the sight of the man. She didn't know *what* to feel. Here was the handsome, chiseled-featured, cocksure, all-star pilot who would have been her brother-in-law, if it were not for . . . *Let's not go there now, shall we?* There was something about him that always got her going. It was probably a good thing they didn't see each other often.

Sighing, resting her hands on her hips, she approached the bars. 'Captain Adama, sir,' she said finally. 'Sorry I wasn't there to greet you with the rest of the squadron.' A mischievous grin tried to find its way to her face, but she held it off. 'Did they kiss your ass to your satisfaction?'

Her poker face finally broke, and she felt as if they were picking up a conversation right where they had left it yesterday, instead of – who knew how long it had been.

Lee rewarded her gibe with a pained half-smile. He looked up at the ceiling. 'So . . . what's the charge this time?'

She laughed to herself and shook her head. 'Striking a superior asshole,' she said, grinning openly now.

'Ah!' He rocked back with a chuckle. 'I'll bet you've been waiting all day to say that one.'

She thought a moment, nodding. 'Most of the afternoon.' She laughed and drew closer, leaning on the bars. 'So, how long has it been?'

'Two years.'

'Two years!' She shook her head. 'We must be getting old. It seems like the funeral was just a couple of months ago.' Her voice started to crack, and she could feel herself starting to tear up.

Lee nodded, longer than necessary. He was obviously holding in his own emotions. 'Yah,' he said at last.

Pull it together now. She drew a breath. 'Your old man's doing fine. We don't talk about it much – maybe two, three times a year.' She peered at him, trying to gauge his reaction. Guarded, very guarded. Old Lee wasn't letting anything out. 'He still struggles with it, though.'

Lee looked away. 'I haven't seen him.'

Damn. I knew it. 'Why not?'

Long pause. No answer. She let out a sigh of exasperation.

'Kara. Don't even start.'

'How long are you going to do this?' Exasperation giving way to annoyance.

He pulled back uncomfortably. 'I'm not doing anything.'

Oh frak. How long is this going to go on? 'He lost his son, Lee.'

'And who's responsible for that?'

Kara winced in pain at the memories *that* brought up. *Let's not go there, either.* She shook her head in disbelief. 'Same old Lee.' She tried to find words. 'You haven't changed, either.'

He flared with anger. 'Zak was my brother.'

'And what was he to *me*? Nothing?' *Only the man I was going to marry.*

'That's not what I meant, and you know what—'

'You know what, you should go,' she interrupted. She thought a moment longer. 'I'm getting an urge to hit another superior asshole.'

Lee looked startled, but only momentarily. He nodded, and almost smiled. She'd gotten under his skin, at least temporarily. He looked as if he was trying to think of something to say. But then he simply turned and did as she'd asked. She watched in silence, alone behind the bars, as he left the compartment. And she sat on the bunk, in silence, and thought about all the things that had gone before. Things she could never forget – but didn't really want to remember.

The funeral. And before that, the smoke, the wreckage of the Viper . . .

The death. Of the man . . . and of her hopes for the future.

CHAPTER
10

THE HOUSE OF GAIUS BALTAR, SOUTH OF CAPRICA CITY

In the still of the early morning, the one known as Natasi sat in a chair by the window, with the sun and the water at her back. She noticed neither the water nor the sun. She saw only the bed on the other side of the room. 'Gaius,' she said softly.

Across the bedroom, there was no response.

'*Gaius.*'

This time she got a reaction. Gaius Baltar's head appeared from under the comforter. A moment later, the head of a very beautiful, and very naked, brunette appeared. The brunette, seeing Natasi in the shadows, hastily yanked the covers up to her neck. Gaius simply looked flustered and embarrassed. 'Wh-what are you doing here?' he asked.

The brunette was more direct. 'Who the hell *are* you?'

Natasi allowed no emotion to show. 'Get out,' she said.

'Gaius, who *is* this woman?'

Stammering, he managed, 'She's just a friend.' And immediately realized that *that* was the wrong thing to say. 'Well – more than a friend – when I say friend, what I—'

'*Get — out.*' Natasi raised her voice only a little, but it was enough to cause the other woman to rethink whatever might have been on the tip of her tongue. She turned to Gaius for support. *Spineless*. He gestured helplessly.

With a sigh of disgust, the woman rolled out of bed. 'This is *just . . . great.*' She gathered up her clothes and stalked from the room.

'Bye,' Gaius called after, in a little boy's voice. A moment later, there was the sound of the front door shutting.

Gaius turned slowly and looked at Natasi guiltily, shamefacedly. He made another helpless gesture. He'd been caught red-handed, and he clearly felt — for the moment — bad about it. Natasi could see the wheels turning in his head. He was obviously trying to decide on a strategy, and his decision was to plead for mercy. 'Look, it's me. It's *me*, all right?' He rolled out of bed on the other side. 'It's totally me. I — I screwed up.' He pulled on a pair of loose-fitting sweatpants and stood up. 'I *am* screwed up. Always have been.' He shrugged on a robe. His gaze became very thoughtful, as though he were peering deep into his own soul. 'It's a flaw in my character that I have — I've always hated, and I've tried to overcome—'

'Spare me your feigned self-awareness and remorse,' she said sharply. *You're such a child, Gaius. Is that why I love you?* 'I came here because I have something to tell you.'

For a moment, he looked startled, then relieved. Then scared. 'Oh.' He sat back on the edge of the bed, his voice very small. 'Okay.'

Natasi gazed at him pensively for a few long moments. Then she stood and turned to the window, staring out at the daylight creeping over the sound, illuminating the tops of the trees. 'Gaius,' she said without looking at him. 'I'd like you to consider something.'

'What's that?' he asked.

'I'd like you to consider the relationship of a child to its parent.' She turned back to him.

Gaius rolled his eyes with a sarcastic laugh. 'Philosophy – at five in the morning?'

She said nothing. She simply looked at him.

'Which is *fine*,' he said hastily. 'Great. Fine. Absolutely.'

She continued, very quietly and seriously. 'Children are born to replace their parents. That is God's plan.' She waited a moment to see if he would react, or make some crack about God and his plans. *No? Good.* 'God plans the death of a child's parents, the very act of death itself, to be a critical part of a child's development into adulthood.'

Gaius was looking very nervous now. He reacted, as always, with a bad attempt at humor. 'Nothing worse than parents who hang around too long,' he said, clapping his hands together. 'Mine certainly did.'

Again, she said nothing. But her gaze was withering.

'Sorry,' he murmured.

She would keep trying. 'God wants children to grow and develop on their own. He wants them to reach their fullest potential. And so . . . it is . . . that all parents *must die*.' She paused to let that sink in. 'But parents who stand in the way of God's plan, parents who defy his will . . .' She paused again and gave him half a smile. 'They don't just die. They must be struck down.'

That hit a nerve, and he jumped up, twitching. 'Where the hell are you going with this? Natasi, what are you talking about?'

Her smile was full now. 'The world is changing, Gaius. The world is changing . . .'

CHAPTER

II

GALACTICA, OFFICERS' WARDROOM

The wardroom was crowded with photographers and people with microphones, and the PR flack Aaron Doral, who was in charge of keeping order. Commander William Adama, stiff and uncomfortable in his full-dress uniform, waited in the shadows in the back of the room, glancing around, trying not to think about a lot of things. This room was usually used for briefings and planning sessions – not photo ops. The walls of the wardroom were lined with pictures, plaques, flags, and other mementoes of *Galactica*'s long service to the Twelve Colonies. Several of the photos included Adama himself.

Usually the commander derived a feeling of family from looking at those pictures – the family of his brothers and sisters in uniform, those he had served under and over and with, those who had moved on to other lives, those who had stayed, those who had died. Right now, he didn't get much of that feeling. Because right now, a member of his real family was approaching, and he didn't get much of a feeling of family out of that, either.

At the other end of the room, Doral suddenly called out to the photographers to spread apart, and make room for the approaching officer, also in full-dress uniform. 'Captain – thank you. Aaron Doral.' There was some awkward shaking of hands, before Doral turned and pointed in the direction of Commander Adama. 'If you'd like to stand up there, we'll get a few shots of you and the commander. Thanks.'

Lee Adama stoically stepped past the photographers and into the center of the room, and Commander Adama stepped forward to join him. 'Captain,' he said, without making eye contact. Lee said nothing.

Doral came forward, effusive. 'Great! Okay, gentlemen, could you maybe stand a little closer?' Disguising his emotions with full military bearing, Adama edged sideways toward Lee. 'Fantastic. Commander, could you put your arm around your son?' Without a word, Adama encircled Lee with his arm, barely resting his hand on Lee's far shoulder. The photographers jockeyed for position. The camera lights flashed. The happy family reunion was captured for broadcast to the public. 'Great! Perfect. Thank you very much,' said Doral, cutting it short as quickly as he could. 'See you both at the ceremony.'

With that, Adama's arm came down, the tableau dissolved, and the photographers crowded through the door on their way out. Commander Adama turned away from his son and walked over to the refreshment counter.

He was aware of Lee reacting with a cynical, near-silent laugh at his abrupt move away, and of Lee then starting out the door after the photographers. Before his son could make it past the threshold, Adama turned to him and said, 'Do you want some . . . coffee? We make a really awful cup of coffee here.'

Lee stopped. 'No, sir,' he answered. 'Thank you, sir.' He had stopped, but clearly had not committed to staying for conversation.

Adama's gut was knotted like a waterlogged rope. He fiddled with the glasses and water pitcher as he said, 'Why don't you . . . sit down.'

Lee repeated his half-laugh, the bitter expression still on his face. He turned back into the room, gazing around at the long tables with empty chairs. It was a place for military talk, business, planning, he seemed to be thinking – not *this*. He remained standing, only half facing his father.

'Congratulations on making captain,' Adama said, pouring himself a glass of water. 'Sorry I wasn't there.'

'Thank you, *sir*,' Lee said stiffly.

'How's your mother?'

'Getting married.'

Adama absorbed that for a moment, let the inevitable pain wash over him and fade away. Finally he nodded, raising his glass of water and turning it in his hand – his back still turned to his son. 'Good for her,' he said, sincerely. 'We spoke about a year ago, had a real heart to heart. It was good.' He drank half the glass of water, a little too quickly.

Lee's words came even more quickly. 'I'm glad to hear that, sir, will that be all?'

His defenses finally broke, for a moment – but he still couldn't turn toward his son. 'Why don't you talk to me, Lee?'

'Wh—' Lee began to laugh openly. 'Well, what do you want to talk about?'

'About *anything*. You've been here for an hour.'

'Well, I don't have anything to say.' He began walking toward Adama, but his posture was anything but conciliatory. 'My orders said to report here for the ceremony. So, I'm here.' He produced a pained smile that was bursting with anger. 'And I'm going to participate in the ceremony. But there wasn't anything in my orders about having heart-to-heart chats with the old man.'

Adama tried to conceal his wince of anguish. 'Accidents *happen* . . . in the service,' he said quietly, looking up at the wall. And there it was, the inescapable memory: the ruin of the Viper, the flag-draped coffin, the utterly distraught Kara grieving for her lost fiancé. Adama and the boys' mother – already divorced – grieving separately for their dead son. And Lee, not grieving so much as bitterly angry. And he'd been angry ever since.

'Dad. Listen, I—'

'You know, all the things that you talked about, the last time we were together—' *The things that practically killed me, then and now . . .*

'I really don't want to—'

'—at the funeral—' *Words that still echo like gunshots.*

'I *really* don't want to do this.'

'—they still ring in my ears, after two years.'

'*Good!*' Lee barked, fire flashing in his eyes. He hesitated, gathered himself a little. His face was still drawn taut as he said, 'Good, because . . . because you know what? They were meant to.'

Adama allowed no reaction to surface. He couldn't; the pain ran way too deep. 'Zak had a choice, you both did.' He raised his chin and scowled at the wall.

Lee snorted, gesturing angrily. 'A man isn't a man . . . until he wears the wings of a Viper pilot. Doesn't that sound at all familiar to you?'

Stung to the quick, but unwilling to show it, Adama raised his glass and answered stoically, 'That's not fair, son.' He took another sip of water.

'No, it's not fair.' Lee stood close now, making his points like rapier stabs. 'Because one of us wasn't cut out to wear the uniform.'

'He earned his wings just like we all did.'

'*One* of us wasn't cut out to be a pilot. *One* of us wouldn't have even gotten into *flight school* if his *old man*, his daddy, hadn't pulled the strings!'

'That's an exaggeration,' Adama replied. 'I did nothing for him that I wouldn't have done for anyone else.' *Did I? Lords of Kobol, did I?*

Lee appeared dumbstruck. He struggled to find words. 'You're not even listening to me! Why can't you get this through your head? Zak *did not belong* in that plane!' Gesturing futilely, Lee paused for breath. 'He shouldn't have been there. He was only doing it for you.' Lee collected himself and delivered his words coolly, with a tiny, deadly smile. 'Face it. You killed him.'

The words hit Adama with the force of a physical blow. He grimaced very slightly, but refused to allow the pain to show on his face. *Did I? No, damn it, I didn't. But if that's how you really feel, there's nothing more to be said, is there?* Without turning to face Lee, the commander dismissed him in his gravelly voice: 'That'll be all, Captain.'

Lee stood for about ten seconds, stunned by the dismissal, struggling with his own pain, perhaps trying to think of something more to say. Perhaps wishing he could take it back. Adama remained unmoved. Lee finally turned and strode from the room. Adama stood silent for a long time after that, head bowed in grief and pain, and in regret for all the words. He had never felt quite so . . . old . . . as he did now. Old, and used, and wondering how his life had gone so terribly wrong.

CHAPTER
12

MASTER BEDROOM OF GAIUS BALTAR

Baltar sat rigidly in his upholstered reading chair and tried to keep his thoughts on a rational, safe, analytical level. Which was very hard to do, given what he had just been told. 'So . . . now you're telling me . . . now you're telling me you're a machine.'

Natasi sat in his recliner, a few arm-lengths away, her bare legs outstretched on the raised foot of the chair. She crossed her legs, and he could not help but follow the movement with his eyes. 'I'm a woman,' she said.

'You're a machine.' He let out a frustrated breath. 'You're a synthetic woman. A robot.' He let out another breath, which sounded like a laugh but was a cry of pain. *I've been sleeping with a robot. A Cylon. No, that is not possible.*

She calmly answered, 'I've said it three times now.'

His answer was anything but calm. 'Well, forgive me, I'm having the tiniest bit of trouble believing that, especially since the last time anyone saw the Cylons they looked like walking chrome toasters.'

'Those models are still around,' she said dismissively. 'They have their uses.'

He looked away, looked back. 'Prove it,' he said. 'If you're a Cylon, prove it to me right now.'

'I don't have to. You know I'm telling the truth.'

Do I know that? I know nothing of the kind! Flustered, Baltar struggled to bring himself back to the analytical state of mind that he prided himself on being able to achieve. He failed. But he argued nonetheless. 'You see – stating something as the truth does not make it so, because the truth is, I don't believe anything you're saying—'

She leaned forward. 'You believe me because deep down you've always known there was something different about me, something that didn't quite add up in the usual way.' A coy grin played at the corners of her mouth. 'And you *believe* me, because it *flatters your ego* to believe that alone among all the billions of people of the Twelve Colonies, *you* were chosen for my mission.'

That sent a shock through his system. 'Your mission? What mission?'

'You knew I wanted access to the Defense mainframe.'

His heart nearly stopped. '*Def* . . . wait a minute. The *Defense mainframe?*' A terrible ringing was starting in his ears. He could hardly think, and could not breathe. 'What exactly are you saying?'

'Come on, Gaius.' Her delight in her accomplishment spread across her face. 'The communications frequencies, deployment schedules, unlimited access to every database . . .'

The ringing was growing louder. 'Stop it!' Baltar shouted. 'Stop it right now!'

She smiled seductively. 'You never really believed I worked for some mysterious "company," either – but you didn't really care.'

'No! That's not—'

'All that really mattered was that only *you* could give

me that kind of access. You were special, you *knew* you were. And powerful . . .'

'*Oh my God!*' Baltar jumped to his feet and walked slowly away from her, as he absorbed the full enormity of what he had done. He turned and spoke as forcefully as he could. 'I had *nothing* to do with this! You *know* I had nothing to do with this!'

Natasi got up, shaking her head with a smile. 'You have an amazing capacity for self-deception. How do you *do* that?' She walked toward him, and she had never looked so sexy – or so frightening.

Baltar could feel panic rising like bile in his throat. 'How many people know about me? About me – specifically? That I'm involved?'

'And even now,' she said, touching his chest seductively, her voice low and sultry, 'as the fate of your entire *world* hangs in the balance, all you can think about is how this affects *you*.'

'Do you have any idea what they'll do to me, if they find out?' he cried.

'They'd probably charge you with treason.'

'Treason is punishable by the death penalty.' His voice was shaking now, and he could feel himself sweating. 'This is unbelievable.' He crossed the room and snatched up his phone.

'What are you doing?'

'Phoning my attorney.'

'That won't be necessary.'

'He'll know what to do. He'll sort this out. He's the best in the business.' He finished punching in the number and pressed the phone to his ear.

'It won't be necessary, because in a few hours, nobody will be left to charge you with anything.'

Baltar froze, and slowly lowered the phone from his ear. 'What . . . exactly . . . are you saying?'

She gazed at him evenly, unsympathetically. 'Humanity's children . . . are returning home.' She paused a beat to let that sink in. 'Today.'

Baltar stared at her uncomprehendingly, unbelieving, unwilling to believe. He turned to look out the window toward the seaward end of the sound, northwest toward Caprica City. At that precise moment, a burst of blinding white light expanded on the horizon. A light as bright as the sun, but rising to a full brightness, and then fading away.

CHAPTER
13

GALACTICA, STARBOARD LANDING BAY
DECOMMISSIONING CEREMONY

The ceremony was proceeding pretty much as these things always did, with too many minor speakers, each one followed by polite applause. The priest, a dark-skinned middle-aged woman named Elosha, was by far the most interesting to Laura Roslin. But though Elosha spoke eloquently of the service *Galactica* and her crew had given, both in war and in peace, she received polite applause just like the minor dignitaries before her. Just as Laura herself had, when she'd presented her own speech as Secretary of Education, as the one who ultimately would oversee the conversion of this magnificent ship into a vessel of history, a tool for education.

The master of ceremonies, Aaron Doral, following Elosha onto the podium, moved the ceremony briskly along.

'Thank you so much for those words of inspiration. And now it's my great honor to present to you a cere-monial, precision-formation flyby of the very last squad-ron of *Galactica* fighter pilots, led by none other than Captain Lee Adama.'

This could not help but be a crowd pleaser. The aft end

of the landing bay had been outfitted with an enormous video projection screen, giving a marvelous illusion of being an open window into space. The landing bay could not, of course, actually be *open* to space; that would make it a little hard for the audience to breathe. But gazing at the lifelike image of the approaching squadron of Vipers, one could easily forget that.

For a few moments, the squadron hardly seemed to be moving. That illusion vanished as they drew closer at high speed. The squadron team zoomed toward the ship in an arrowhead formation, eight Vipers swooping up from below to pass directly before the onlookers, and then splitting apart to fly off in four different directions. Then came the leader, spiraling up, piloted by the younger Adama, the one known as Apollo. Laura watched with heartfelt admiration and amazement as the pilots showed off their training – flying in perfect, tight formation, rejoining and breaking apart, again and again. It was a demonstration as old as aviation itself – daredevil flying joined with the artistic flak of a great dance performance. In space, it was even harder than in the air. Each of those maneuvers required each pilot to time perfectly a complex sequence of thrusting and turning, and braking and thrusting again – all carefully choreographed to look nearly effortless.

In the final maneuver, it indeed looked effortless, as all but one of the squadron came together just shy of the aft end of the landing bay, then split off in a star-burst formation. And spinning up through the center of them came Apollo, roaring directly over the landing bay, so that in the screen he seemed to fly nearly straight into the crowd, and right over their heads. Indeed, Laura and just about everyone else ducked involuntarily, and turned to watch on another screen as he disappeared up and out.

The crowd – even members of the ship's crew who were here for the ceremony – erupted in spontaneous applause.

As the Vipers regrouped and circled away, Aaron Doral once more took the podium. It was time to bring on the next speaker. This was the headliner, the person they'd all been waiting to hear from. As applause for the flying team slowly died down, Doral said, 'And now, it is my great pleasure to introduce the last commander of the battlestar *Galactica*, a man who served on this ship as a young pilot during the years of the Cylon War, and later came back to command her through years of peace – Commander William Adama.' With a gesture, he invited the commander to rise from where he sat among the gathered officers at the front, and to take the podium.

Laura, sitting just on the other side of the podium, was struck once more by Commander Adama's rough-hewn good looks, rock-solid demeanor, and obvious intelligence. Despite their earlier encounter, Laura was eager to hear what the commander would have to say. He mounted the stage slowly and deliberately, and took a few moments, standing there before the assembly, as though reflecting on what he wanted to say. And then he began, in that deep, attention-commanding voice:

'The Cylon war is long over.' He looked out, as though to meet the gaze of everyone in the crowd, one by one. 'Yet we must not forget the reasons why so many sacrificed so much in the cause of freedom.' Pause to let that sink in. 'The cost of wearing the uniform . . . can be high.' And when he paused this time, it was for a long moment that stretched into several moments, while some in the crowd stirred restlessly, wondering if he'd lost his place in the script, or forgotten what he intended to say. Laura sensed that that was not the case, though, and waited with growing anticipation to see what this stubborn, unconventional man would say next.

Adama finally, slowly, removed his eyeglasses and looked out over the gathered assembly. 'Sometimes it's too high.' Even from where Laura sat, she could see the pain behind his eyes. What was he thinking of, his crewmates who had died in the war? His son, who died in a tragic peacetime accident? Adama continued, 'You know, when we fought the Cylons, we did it to save ourselves from extinction. But we never answered the question, *Why?* Why are we as a people worth saving? We still commit murder because of greed, spite, jealousy. And we still visit all of our sins upon our children.'

As Adama spoke, Laura could see members of the audience shifting a little with discomfort. She was surprised to discover how much she was moved by the questions Adama was raising. She could not have known it, but out in space, circling in a patrol pattern around *Galactica*, the Viper pilots were listening on the wireless, and one in particular, the one called Apollo, was also surprised by the commander's words. And even in the brig, Kara Thrace listened, wondering. And in the CIC, the officers on watch. And throughout the ship, everywhere crewmembers had a moment to pause in what they were doing and listen.

'We refuse to accept the responsibility for anything that we've done. As we did with the Cylons – when we decided to play God. Create life. And that life turned against us. We comforted ourselves in the knowledge that it really wasn't our fault. Not *really*.' He drew a breath. 'Well, you cannot play God and then wash your hands of the things that you've created. Sooner or later the day comes when you can't hide from the things that you've done anymore.'

Commander Adama looked out over the audience, as

though trying to decide what to say next. Finally, probably to everyone's surprise, and maybe even his own, he simply turned and stepped down from the podium, and walked back to his seat.

Laura watched him pass, and as Doral got up to go make his closing remarks, Laura began to clap her hands. She wasn't sure exactly what had just happened there, but she knew that the commander had dared to speak a truth that most would rather have left unspoken. For a moment, the only sound was her hands clapping, and then the others took up the applause. By the time Adama reached his seat, it was strong and steady.

Colonel Saul Tigh was one of those who had sat in stunned silence as his friend Bill Adama spoke. What the frak *was* Bill driving at? Tigh had known him for what – better than forty years? He never known Bill to stir needlessly at a hornet's nest, unless it was some bureaucracy that needed a kick in the ass. But this – they were supposed to be having a polite retirement exercise. They were turning the ship over to become a museum, not running for public office. As the commander sat down beside him again, Tigh leaned and muttered, under the sound of the applause, 'You are one *surprising* sonofabitch.'

In response, Adama just turned his head and looked at him – with his familiar steady gaze, and almost, but not quite, with a smile.

GALACTICA DEPARTURE PATTERN

The colonial transport accelerated smoothly out of the launch tube of *Galactica*, and proceeded at a stately pace away from the warship. A lone Viper came up alongside, then moved into position just ahead of the transport. The wireless call went from the fighter craft to the cockpit of the transport: *'Colonial Heavy Seven-Niner-Eight, this is Viper Seven-Two-Four-Two. My call sign is Apollo, and I'll be your escort back to Caprica.'*

Inside the old Viper's cockpit – his father's old Viper – Lee Adama was filled with mixed emotions as he flew away from *Galactica*. Relief, sadness, anger. Regret over some of the things that had been said, or not said . . . and some genuine astonishment over his father's words in that address to the VIPs. Some of the things the old man had said actually sounded thoughtful. That part about accepting responsibility . . .

Lee shook off the thought. *Don't get maudlin. And don't give him credit for things he wasn't really saying.*

The transport pilot answered, *'Copy, Viper Seven-Two-Four-Two. Glad to have you with us.'*

Another call came a moment later, this one from the squadron circling *Galactica* in formation, and visible to Lee at about ten o'clock high. *'Viper Seven-Two-Four-Two, Raptor Three-One-Two. This is Boomer. Just wanted to say it was an honor to fly with you, Apollo.'*

'The honor's mine, Boomer,' Lee said in acknowledgment. For all that they'd had a rocky start, he and the *Galactica* pilots had flown well together. They'd earned his respect, and he hoped he'd earned theirs. 'Where are you heading after Caprica?' How was it he had never asked that? Too busy thinking about other things, probably.

'Right on to Picon after refueling,' Boomer said. *'Squadron's being reassigned there temporarily – then they'll be splitting us up. We plan on having a frakking good party before we go our separate ways, though. Are you sure you can't join us?'*

'Wish I could,' Lee said. 'I've been playing hooky with you kids for too long already, I'm afraid. Hoist a glass for me, though, will you?'

'*Roger to that. Have a safe trip, Apollo.*' As they signed off, the squadron formation changed course like a flock of birds, away from *Galactica* and in the direction of Caprica. The last of *Galactica*'s active fighters; all the others were now part of the museum.

Apollo lifted a hand to them in silent salute.

In the cabin of the transport, a weary Laura Roslin was collapsed in her seat, eyes closed. A tired but still energized Billy sat beside her in the window seat. From a speaker overhead, a voice came from the cockpit: '*Ladies and gentlemen, we are now en route back to Caprica. If you look out the starboard window, you might be able to see one of Galactica's old Mark Two Vipers, which is escorting us. That's the same Viper once flown by Commander William Adama, during the days of the Cylon War . . .*'

Laura smiled faintly, remembering the precision flying demonstration the Viper pilots had staged for them just a short time ago. She felt vaguely comforted to know that one of those pilots would be flying alongside them as they returned home. She felt even more comforted to know that the pilot was Commander Adama's son, Apollo.

CHAPTER
14

HOUSE OF GAIUS BALTAR

Baltar sat frozen, haunted, sweating, watching the newscasts on the video screens. He had seen numerous flashes outside on the horizon, but somehow those hadn't seemed as real to him as the newscasts. Surely, he had thought, the newscasts would tell the truth. Would somehow *dispel* this awful truth. But they hadn't. It was real.

On the left half of the screen, Kellan Brody, the newscaster who had interviewed him just two days ago, was barely managing to keep up a brave front. '. . . *Trying to piece together unconfirmed reports of nuclear attack. We don't have any further information yet. No actual enemy has been sighted . . .*'

On the right screen, a man was broadcasting frantically from the street. '*Official confirmation that the spaceports have been hit. No spacecraft left that can leave Caprica. Our best advice is to stay inside – or if you must leave, head out into the country . . .*'

Kellan Brody: '*Officials are saying that there doesn't seem any doubt—*' She turned suddenly, terrified by something she'd just seen or felt – and the screen went white with static.

The man on the right screen flinched at a dazzling flash

from off-camera – then hunched against a sudden gale-force wind that blew debris sideways past him. An instant later, that screen went white, too.

Gaius Baltar bowed his head. 'What have I done?' he whispered. He looked up again at the blank screens. *What have I done?* He sat, shaking, for a few moments, tears welling in his already reddened eyes. *What . . . have . . . I . . . done?*

Finally he stood up, the feeling of finality washing over him. 'There's no way out,' he whispered.

Natasi walked to him from behind. 'I know.' She moved to place her hands comfortingly on his shoulders.

He wrenched away from her. 'Sure you know! That's *your doing*, isn't it?' He strode away, furious, despairing. Then something occurred to him. 'Wait. Wait, there has to be another way out of here. *Wait!* You must have an escape plan, right? You're not about to be destroyed by your own bombs, are you? *How are you leaving?*'

At that instant, a blinding flash came through the windows, from somewhere over the water. He cried out in pain and bent double, covering his eyes. Behind him, Natasi continued to talk calmly. 'Gaius – I can't die. When this body is destroyed, my memory – my con-sciousness – will be transmitted to a new one. I'll just wake up somewhere else in an identical body.' She was touching him now, caressing his neck and cheek, in a way that ordinarily would have been comforting. It made him nearly insane.

Fighting back tears, horrified at the thought he was about to voice, he said, 'You mean there's more out there like you?'

She faced him closely, and said very matter-of-factly, 'There are twelve human-type models. I'm Model Number Six. There are many like me.'

This was too much to bear. He began sobbing. 'I don't want to die. I don't want to—'

'*Get down.*' Interposing herself between him and the window, she shoved him to the floor – an instant before an enormous wall of wind and water rose up and smashed through the side of the house, destroying it like a plaything.

Baltar knew only a moment of pain and terror as he was hurled across the room by the force of the blast. Then he knew only darkness.

CAPRICA ORBIT

High over Caprica they circled, the Cylon raiders, lobbing nuclear warheads down onto the planet. From a distance, there was a certain kind of surreal beauty to the rain of death; from a distance, no one could hear the screams, no one could feel the pain or know the fear or quail in the face of certain death. Unless it was the Cylons themselves. Could they? That was a question no human could answer. And the Cylons weren't speaking to humanity. The Cylons were eradicating humanity.

From space you couldn't even hear the booms, or feel the rush and suck of wind, the blaze of hard radiation. It was just a silent display of *flash* . . . *flash* . . . *flash* . . . Even the flashes were somewhat concealed, half hidden from view by the thick cloud cover. But there was no mistaking them, either, if you happened to be in orbit around the planet, as many spacecraft were. Caprica was dotted with flashes deep in the cloud cover, and as the mushroom clouds grew and spread, the cloud cover thickened until from orbit it looked like a continuous murk surrounding the world.

For human spacecraft in orbit, or nearing the planet, the prognosis was no better than it was for Caprica itself. The raiders that were not busy lobbing bombs were just as busy hunting and killing humanity's spacecraft. It was no match: Few of the spacecraft were armed in any way, and even those that had weapons were hopelessly, hopelessly outmatched. It was over quickly for most of them. For those that somehow escaped notice, the reprieve seemed too good to be true, and for most of them it was. Most of the reprieves ended all too soon, with sudden detection, and a fiery death.

Meanwhile it seemed that the planet could hardly sustain any further punishment. *Flash . . . flash . . . flash.*

And still it continued.

PART TWO

ARMAGEDDON

CHAPTER
15

GALACTICA, CABIN OF COMMANDER ADAMA

It had been a very long day, full of speeches and strong emotion. Adama was sitting at his desk in his under-shirt, taking a few minutes to unwind with a good book before turning in for the night. It was a history book, *A Time of Changes: Five Colonial Presidents Before the War*, an old favorite about a series of influential leaders of Caprica in the years leading up to the Cylon War. He was really just leafing through it, recalling passages he had read many times before. The ceremony today, and the thought he had put into his speech (such as it was in the end – his own critique was that he had sounded disjointed and inconclusive), had put him in a mind to peruse stories of a time when things were very similar to today, and at the same time very different.

The comm set buzzed twice. A metallic voice, distorted by the tiny speaker in the ceiling, said: '*CIC to commanding officer.*'

Reluctantly, he set the book down and reached across to the wall for the phone. He pulled the bulky handset on its cord back to where he was sitting. His voice sounded tired and gravelly. 'Go ahead.'

The voice in the phone was Gaeta's. '*I'm sorry to disturb*

you, sir, but we had a Priority One Alert message from Fleet Headquarters. It was . . . transmitted in the clear.'

Now that was odd. 'In the clear?' Adama pulled off his reading glasses. Priority One, not encrypted? Damned odd. 'What does it say?'

Gaeta sounded as if he were having to work hard to keep his voice steady, also odd. *'Attention, all Colonial units. Cylon . . . attack . . . underway. This is no drill.'*

In that instant, Adama felt as if he had entered another world, another dimension. It felt too unreal to respond to, or even entertain as possible. The moment seemed to stretch like a rubber band – and then suddenly it snapped, and he was back in the present. He fought to find his voice, as the full realization of what Gaeta was saying penetrated. 'I'll be right there,' he said at last, and hung up the phone.

For a moment, he could not rise. *Cylon attack. War. After all these years. So much bloodshed. And now, again . . . with us again . . .*

In his own cabin, Colonel Tigh was reclining on his bed, in a melancholy frame of mind. Mellow, though – he had several shots of good whiskey under his belt. His left hand held a photograph of his wife, Ellen, a beautiful picture from a time when they'd been happy, when *she'd* been happy, when she hadn't been off frakking around with every man who caught her eye. In his right hand, Tigh held a lit cigar. Slowly, methodically, he brought the fiery tip of the cigar into contact with the back of the photograph, right about where her face was. And slowly, satisfyingly, it was burning through the face of the photo – right through the image of her eye, in fact. *Dear Gods, this feels good, you miserable bitch . . .*

At that moment, the ship-wide alert buzzer began sounding. Tigh looked around in alarm. *What the hell . . . ?*

In the hangar, Cally and Prosna had been vacuuming and swabbing the deck. In the maintenance shed, Tyrol was looking over some disassembled Viper parts. The buzzer sounded, and everyone looked up in puzzlement. The attention-tone was followed by Gaeta's voice from the CIC: '*Action stations. Action stations. Set Condition One throughout the ship. This is not a drill.*' There was no one on the hangar deck who was not astounded to hear those words. People everywhere scrambled to get rid of what they were doing and race to their stations. '*Repeat: Action stations. Action stations. Set Condition One throughout the ship. This is not a drill.*'

'Not a drill!' shouted Prosna, hurrying to put down the mops and pails he was carrying. 'He can't be serious.'

'Sounds like it to me,' Cally said, racing with him.

'What are we gonna shoot with? The ship's got no ammunition.' They hurried into the utility room to get rid of the cleaning gear.

Outside, Tyrol was pulling himself together and starting to do the same with his people. 'All right, people, let's go! Let's get this hangar bay ready for possible incoming!' All over the hangar deck, and throughout the ship, people were now running with real purpose. A genuine Condition One alert should have been impossible; the ship had just been officially retired. Be that as it may, the crew were moving fast, following old routines. What else *could* they do?

*

89

In the CIC, Adama stood at the situation table, studying the comm printouts. Tigh came striding in, calling, 'What've we got? Shipping accident?' No one answered him, though a lot of people were talking.

Adama handed him the top printout without saying a word. He was sternly silent, his mind wheeling to take in all the information he had seen, and to pull together a plan. It made no sense; all of this was supposed to have been behind him. But it wasn't, and now he had to put everything else out of his mind and think what to do. As Tigh read the report, Gaeta hurried to the commander with an update. 'Condition One is set. All decks report ready for action, sir.'

'Very well,' Adama said, and looked back down at the printouts.

Beside him, Tigh looked up, incredulous. 'This is a joke! The fleet's playing a joke on you. It's a retirement prank!' When Adama didn't respond, he pleaded, 'Come on!'

With the announcement phone in his hand, Adama finally looked at him. 'I don't think so.' Tigh looked bewildered. His jacket was open, and it was clear he'd been drinking.

Adama raised the heavy microphone in his hand and keyed the attention-tone. He spoke clearly, but in a modulated voice as he addressed the entire ship. 'This is the commander. Moments ago, this ship received word that a Cylon attack against our home worlds was underway.'

He paused to let that sink in, then continued grimly, 'We do not know the size or the disposition or the strength of the enemy forces. But all indications point to a massive assault against the Colonial defenses. Admiral Nagala has taken personal command of the fleet, aboard the battlestar *Atlantia*, following the complete destruction of Picon Fleet Headquarters in the first wave of the attacks. How – *why* – doesn't really matter now. What does matter is that, as of this moment, *we are at war.*'

Again he paused, and was well aware of the sober, frightened expressions on the faces of the crewmembers in the CIC, which he knew reflected reactions throughout the snip. He continued in measured tones. 'You've trained for this. You're ready for this. Stand to your duties. Trust your shipmates. And we'll all get through this. Further updates as we get them.' He looked around the CIC, meeting the eyes of everyone nearby, wishing he could meet the eyes of every crewmember on the ship. They were all young, and with the exception of Tigh, none of them had ever been in combat before. 'Thank you.' He released the PUSH-TO-TALK button and hung up the handset.

Speaking to the crewmembers at nearby workstations, he began issuing orders. 'Tactical – begin a plot of all military units in the solar system, friendly or otherwise.' As Gaeta acknowledged, Adama turned to Tigh. 'XO!'

'Sir.'

Adama lowered his voice, as Tigh stepped to his side. 'If we're going to be in a shooting war, we need something to shoot *with*.' His gaze met Tigh's.

Looking stricken, as if he still couldn't believe they were once again at war, Tigh said, 'I'll start checking the munitions depots.' He hurried away.

Adama swung around again. 'D.' Petty Officer Dualla was already looking at him. 'Send a signal to our fighter squadron. I want positions and tactical status immediately.'

'Yes sir,' said Dualla.

'And get Kara Thrace out of the brig.'

Following Commander Adama's announcement, Chief

Tyrol faced a circle of deckhands who all looked as if they'd been punched in the stomach. *We are at war.* The fear was etched in their faces; he felt it himself. Not a one of them had ever been in battle before, including Tyrol himself. No matter, he knew his responsibility: He had to be strong so that they could be strong. As he spoke, he turned in place to face the circle. 'All right, people – this is what we do.' Keep turning. Meet their fears head-on. 'We're the best. So let's get the old girl ready to roll – and *kick some Cylon ass!*' He smacked his hands together. '*Come on! Let's go! Move!*'

As the deck crew broke to their duties, preparing for the return of their squadron, Tyrol put his hands on his hips and muttered under his breath, 'This had better be for real.'

CHAPTER
16

GALACTICA'S LAST ATTACK SQUADRON
TWO HOURS FROM CAPRICA

Sharon Valerii – Boomer – was in the right seat in the cockpit of the Raptor when the signal from *Galactica* came in. Helo, in the left seat, was spelling her at the controls. The Raptor, while somewhat slower and less maneuverable than the Vipers, was a more complex ship. It had room to carry a small complement of commandoes, and it was crammed with surveillance and intelligence-gathering equipment. The instrument panel in front of the pilot was easily twice the size of the panel in a Viper. In a space battle, the Raptor would be the one standing off at a distance, tracking the enemy and sending directions to the fast fighters. But in a landing operation, it could be in the vanguard, carrying soldiers to the front line.

This was a low-key flight, ferrying the squadron of Vipers and the Raptor itself to their next assignment. For most in the squadron, it was a bittersweet departure. Sharon didn't know anyone who didn't have pangs about leaving *Galactica* and the command of William 'Husker' Adama; but for most, there was also the challenge of the next assignment to look forward to. Many felt that they'd been in the public-relations business for too long.

Galactica herself, as the oldest battlestar in the fleet, had been performing mostly ceremonial duties for years now. For Sharon, though, the departure was all bitter, no sweet. She'd barely had time for a proper good-bye with Galen Tyrol. She didn't know when she'd see him again, or whether there was any possibility of maintaining their relationship.

It was possible, she supposed, that it could be a blessing in disguise. Sooner or later, their affair on *Galactica* was bound to blow up in their faces, and at least now they would no longer be engaged in an illicit affair, *Lieutenant* Sharon Valerii with her subordinate officer, *Chief* Tyrol. And they wouldn't be asking the whole deck crew to cover for them.

Frakking small consolation.

The wireless buzzed. It was Dualla, on *Galactica*. They'd spoken three or four times since the squadron had departed. This was no doubt just another check-in. 'Raptor Three-One-Two,' Sharon answered. 'What's up, D.?'

'*Boomer, we're recalling you! There's been a massive Cylon attack throughout the system – all Colonies under attack, including Caprica! Repeat, we're recalling your squadron. Please acknowledge.*'

Sharon exchanged horrified glances with Helo, in the left seat. She had to work very hard to keep her voice from quavering. '*Galactica*, Raptor Three-One-Two, roger. What are our instructions?'

'*Raptor Three-One-Two, report your current position and tactical status. Scan your area for Cylons and estimate your time back to* Galactica.'

Helo was already out of his seat, climbing back to the instrumentation section. 'I'm on it, Boomer, just give me a minute. Better put your helmet on.'

Sharon managed to secure her helmet on her neck collar, but she was otherwise nearly frozen with panic. She was not just a rookie, she was the youngest pilot in the whole *Galactica* detachment. And because her Raptor was the Command and Communication center for the squadron, *she* had taken the call, and *she* had to pass the news on to the rest. Swallowing, she called the CAG, Jackson Spencer, lead pilot for the squadron.

'*I heard it, Boomer. Send* Galactica *all the data you can, and plot us a course back. Squadron, prepare for immediate course change.*'

Searching for Cylons was one thing. But they were far enough from *Galactica* that it was going to be hard to return with the fuel they had. Reversing course in space was a *very* fuel-intensive thing to do. 'Helo!' she yelled. 'What have you got?'

'Holy frak, Sharon—'

Before Helo could continue, the CAG broke in again. '*Disregard previous orders. Boomer, inform* Galactica *we've detected a formation of Cylon fighters directly ahead. And I intend to attack.*' Pause. '*Boomer, do you copy?*'

Sharon saw the Cylon formation on her own dradis screen. The ghostly contacts had appeared out of nowhere. 'Copy that,' she managed to reply to the CAG. *Holy frak, is right.*

Helo was leaning over her shoulder, apparently sensing her alarm. 'Ease up there, Boomer,' he said calmly. 'Take a deep breath.' She gulped and nodded, and slowly relaxed her white-knuckle grip on the control stick. He patted her on the shoulder, through her thick spacesuit, and headed back to his instruments as she made the call to *Galactica*.

'Stand by,' she said to Dualla, after giving the preliminary information. 'Helo?'

Back at the instrument panel, Helo was scanning the

area. '*I show ten – no, no, make that five Cylon raiders on course three-two-four mark one-one-zero, speed seven-point-one. Time to intercept . . .*' There was a long hesitation. '*Seven minutes.*'

'*You don't sound too sure.*' That was the CAG.

Sharon could see most of what Helo was coming up with on her own dradis display, though she couldn't enhance the image the way he could. She answered for him, 'There's a lot of jamming going on out there. The Cylons are using a lot of sensor decoys. We're sorting through them, but—'

'*Understood,*' said the CAG. '*Just take your time. Guide us in. We'll do the rest.*'

'Yes sir.' *Just do it one step at a time,* Sharon thought, swallowing bile. *One step at a time . . . into your first taste of combat. Don't be scared . . .*

GALACTICA, COMBAT INFORMATION CENTER

In the CIC, Gaeta was using colored grease pencils to mark out the tactical situation on a large light table, using readings from their own dradis, as well as information received from *Atlantia*. A series of lines traced the positions and courses of a number of Colonial forces, relative to the closest worlds. 'So that would put our squadron about here,' he said, marking a spot in blue between *Galactica* and Caprica. 'Now, it looks like the main fight is shaping up over here, near Virgon's orbit. Even at top speed, they're still over an hour away.'

Adama frowned over the display. 'Plot a course along this axis' – he traced a finger over the table – 'and keep Virgon between us and the battle. We might be able to get pretty close before the Cylons are even aware—'

As Gaeta acknowledged, Adama looked up and saw Dualla returning to the CIC, with Kara Thrace right behind her. Tigh was following Kara's appearance with a frown. She tossed him a mocking half-salute, then presented herself soberly to Adama. 'Commander?' This time her salute was thoroughly professional. 'Ready for duty, sir.'

'Good.' His voice was terse and grim; he didn't have time to think about the nonsense between her and Tigh.

Kara waited a heartbeat for Adama to say something more, then blurted, 'Where the hell did the Cylons come from?'

Adama looked up. 'All we know for sure is that they achieved complete surprise. We've taken heavy losses. We lost thirty battlestars in the opening attack.' He said it matter-of-factly, but just voicing the numbers made his heart heavy.

Kara didn't flinch, at least not outwardly. But her voice conveyed disbelief. 'That's a quarter of the fleet.'

'I need pilots, and I need fighters.' He stared hard at the plotting table, trying to see a way out of the seemingly hopeless situation.

'Pilots you got. I just passed twenty of them, climbing the walls down in the ready room. But fighters—' She shook her head. The last active wing had left yesterday for Caprica and Picon. There were just a few Vipers, undergoing maintenance, last she'd heard.

Adama turned to meet her gaze squarely. 'I seem to remember an entire squadron of fighters down in the starboard hangar deck yesterday.'

For an instant, Kara's face was filled with incredulity – *a squadron of obsolete, worn out, deactivated Vipers?* – and then the incredulity gave way to resolve, as she realized the same thing he had. Those retired Vipers were their only hope. 'Yes *sir*' she said, saluting smartly – and spun away and left the CIC at a dead run.

The starboard hangar deck had truly been turned into a museum, and had the subdued lighting of a museum gallery, with soft-focus beams aimed at the Vipers on display. Kara had a momentary feeling of invading the peace of the place, as she, the other pilots, and the hangar crew dashed onto the floor and began pulling down the velvet-rope guardrails around the meticulously placed Vipers. Then someone turned on the bright overhead floodlights, and the feeling vanished. Suddenly they were liberating fighting ships, ships needed on the front lines. Museum signs and placards soon littered the floor, torn in haste from the craft.

Everyone seemed to know instinctively what to do. The pilots started making walk-around inspections of the fighters, while the deckhands made quick checks under access panels, removed wheel chocks, and began moving tow-tractors into position. Kara strode alongside the nearest Viper with Chief Tyrol and squinted through the cockpit canopy. 'Are you sure they'll fly?' she asked doubtfully.

Tyrol paced energetically, swinging his arms as he surveyed the collection of fighters. 'Well, the reactor cores are all pulled, of course – but they're stored hot, and they'll pop right back in. Then all we have to do is recalibrate, restore the hydraulics and batteries, refuel, load the ordnance, and you're ready to go.'

Kara looked back at him, biting her lip. 'I thought all the ordnance was taken off back at Rhapsody Station, everything but what the CAG's squadron took with them.'

Tyrol looked pained. 'Yeah, most of it's gone. In fact,

the only reason we have any at all is that Caprica Base wanted us to offload some there.'

'So, we've got—'

'We've got about enough to load up your cannons. Not a hell of a lot more.'

Kara took a deep breath. 'Okay.'

'The biggest problem is getting these things over to the port launch bay.'

Kara looked sharply at Tyrol. 'Why can't we use the starboard launch?'

'It's a gift shop now.'

'*Frak me.*'

'All right, let's go!' Tyrol called out. 'Everybody pick a bird, we're going to the port launch bay! Get the tows on the ones closest to the service passage, and let's get 'em moving! Reactor crew, get back to port-side and start breaking the reactor cores out of storage! Let's go, we need to get these birds flying!'

The first Vipers were already in motion, on their way to the port hangar.

Things were for the moment quiet in the CIC, as everyone did their jobs and prayed for better news. Still no word on a place to find ammunition. A course had been plotted that would take them to the biggest fight, but right now they had nothing to fight with even if they got there. The commander was very quiet, waiting for developments, especially word from the hangar deck – and word from the CAG's squadron.

Petty Officer Dualla was scowling over the latest incoming comm printouts when Lieutenant Gaeta peered over her shoulder. 'What's the latest, D.?'

She felt a knot in her stomach as she said, 'A lot of

confusion. I'm not getting much solid information from the fleet, but I keep seeing these weird reports about equipment malfunctions.'

'Why's that weird?' Gaeta asked.

Dualla shook her head. 'It's the *number* of malfunctions. It's happening all through the fleet. One report said an entire *battlestar* lost power just before it came into contact with the enemy. They said it was like someone just turned off a switch.'

Gaeta frowned at her. 'And?'

'Apparently that was the last message from her, on an emergency transmitter.' Her voice faltered. 'Before she was destroyed.'

Gaeta didn't answer, but his face was grave as he turned to report to the commander.

CHAPTER

17

GALACTICA VIPER SQUADRON, NEAR CAPRICA

The CAG's squadron was rapidly approaching the reported position of the Cylon formation. Its numbers and configuration seemed to be changing every time they took a new dradis reading; the electronic interference was infuriating. At the surveillance panel behind Boomer, Helo was giving minute-to-minute updates on the long-range situation. 'We're down to *two* confirmed Cylons now. Approaching visual range on their formation.'

The CAG, leading the Viper formation, called back, his voice distorted by interference on the wireless, '*Okay, Boomer, we'll take it from here. You back way off.*'

'Roger that,' Sharon replied – and hit the maneuvering thrusters, lifting the Raptor out of the Viper formation, then allowing it to fall back behind their advance. She had her fingers crossed, and she was scared to death. She knew they all must be. Even the CAG, all toughness and confidence, was flying into his first kill-or-be-killed combat mission. He never let it show, but he knew his limitations; they all did. And Sharon . . . *Stop it. Stop thinking about it. Do your job, just do your job and don't let anyone down, all right?*

'All right, boys and girls,' the CAG was saying. '*Break*

101

into attack formation. There might be only two of them out there, but I want you to stick with your wingman and do not get overconfident.'

The Vipers were nearly out of visual range, ahead of the Raptor. Boomer followed their progress by their wireless chatter, and by the little blips on the dradis screen, brightening as the little hoop-shaped lines of the scanner beam rotated past them. Still only two . . .

'Anybody know what these things look like?' someone asked. Scott, Boomer thought.

He was answered by a female voice. Erin. *'The pictures I've seen of old Cylon fighters, they looked like a big flying wing.'*

A third voice: *'Those pictures are forty years old. How do we know what they look like now?'*

'Just shoot at whatever you see,' answered Erin, with a laugh that was maybe a little too carefree to be real.

'Okay, keep the chatter down,' the CAG interjected.

'Boomer,' said Helo, behind her.

Sharon looked again at her dradis screen. The number of Cylons approaching the Vipers was multiplying rapidly. *Oh frak.* 'CAG, Boomer. We've got a lot more contacts coming up. We've got a couple of squadrons, at least.' She was trying to count them, but the display kept changing too rapidly. 'Look sharp, you guys . . .'

In the dark of space, where nothing lived, the Cylons came in search of prey. They were silver, sleek, and powerful, with gull wings that swept sharply forward and inward at the tips, like great claws. The machine intelligence that drove them was relentless and implacable. They feared nothing; they would stop at nothing; there was nothing they would not destroy, if it bore the scent of humanity.

The nose of each raider was a shrouded metal head. In another time and place, it might have been taken for the helmeted head of a warrior, a visored knight on his way to a joust. But as it drew close to its quarry, the visor opened, and where there might have been eyes there was only a single red glowing spot, and it swept back and forth, back and forth, as it sought to identify its targets.

And then its deadliest weapon of all was unsheathed, as its silent and invisible electromagnetic talons stretched out to find its enemy's pitiful computer networks, and turn them off. Like flipping a switch . . .

Jackson Spencer, the CAG, felt a satisfying rush of adrenaline as he caught first sight of the enemy, emerging from the glare of the sun, dead ahead. He heard the warning from Boomer, but they were committed. 'All Vipers, weapons free. Let's go get 'em.'

Together, in perfect formation, the twenty Vipers fired their main burners and accelerated toward the enemy. So far, he still saw only two Cylons on his small dradis screen. As they drew closer, he could just make out their shape. They looked almost batlike, with hooked wings. It was impossible to tell what their weaponry was, or what method of attack . . .

What the frak—?

Spencer glanced down at his instruments. Every single display was flickering and distorting. An instant later, they went dark. He had no instrumentation.

And . . . he had no power, of any sort. Thrusters were gone, lights were gone, ventilation was shut off. Complete systems failure. The Viper was suddenly drifting, turning, all attitude control gone. Spencer blanched, feeling more helpless than he'd ever felt in his life. There was no way he could lead the squadron. He quickly keyed his mic. 'I've lost power! Jolly! Jolly, take over! Jolly, can you read me?' He turned his head to the right, trying to visually keep his bearings with the rest of the squadron.

His heart sank. All of the Vipers were dark, drifting. They'd *all* lost power. A couple were pitching slowly end over end. He looked to his left, just as one of the other Vipers careened toward him and slammed into the side of his ship, then bounced away. Shaken, he started running through his emergency checklist, but there was nothing he could do; he was dead in space, helpless. And so was his entire squadron . . .

Boomer gazed at her dradis screen with growing fear. *What's happening to them? Why are they drifting like that?*

Helo leaned over her shoulder. 'What're they *doing*?'

'I don't know. They're just going straight in,' Sharon replied, struggling to keep her voice steady.

'The comm chatter's gone. They're not talking anymore.'

Sharon keyed her mic. 'CAG – Boomer.' Shut her eyes for an instant. 'CAG – Boomer. Do you read?' She glanced back at Helo, her fear now turned into full-blown horror.

The Vipers tumbled, coasting straight into the jaws of the enemy. Spencer had tried everything. He kept trying, snapping switches, struggling to get some spark of life out of his ship. Main power was dead. Auxiliary power . . . he couldn't tell, because all the meters were dead. He continued calling on the wireless: 'Boomer

– CAG. If you can hear me – they must have done something to our computer systems. Some sort of electronic jamming. I've never seen anything like it.'

He fell silent, as the two Cylon raiders swooped down on them, like sharks out of the depths of the ocean. There was a bloodred light sweeping from each of them. The Cylons arced past, as though inspecting the squadron, giving him a surprisingly clear view of them. As they circled back, CAG thumbed his mic again. 'There's no cockpits! There's nobody flying these things!'

An instant later, he saw the contrails of missiles erupt from the Cylons, like streamers in a fireworks display. At least two dozen missiles had launched at once, and they were streaking in perfect arcs toward the Viper squadron. 'Oh my God.' Words failed him utterly as he watched helplessly, adrift, as the crisscrossing streamers flawlessly targeted every Viper in his squadron.

He saw three of his fighters explode in balls of fire in the instant before his own missile found him. And then his world ended abruptly in a flash of fire and death.

Sharon was paralyzed with horror at the sight of every single Viper flaring on her screen with the telltale signature of exploding metal, then vanishing. It was unbelievable. The entire squadron, utterly destroyed.

Except for them, in their Raptor.

And the dradis contacts of the Cylons were now changing course, turning toward them.

'Boomer, get us out of here!' Helo shouted, heading back for his console.

'Right!' she cried, bringing the Raptor quickly about and opening the throttle to the redline. The Raptor sprang away from the scene of the disaster, with the Cylons in pursuit.

Behind them, the debris of the Viper squadron swirled like flotsam left in the wake of a typhoon.

CHAPTER
18

COLONIAL HEAVY 798, NEARING CAPRICA

Laura Roslin was barely able to stand in the tiny shipboard lavatory. She hunched over the washbasin, pressing a damp cloth to her face, fighting to stop the tears. *Damn you, body. Damn you, cancer. How dare you do this to me! How dare you make me so weak!* She shuddered uncontrollably, as the feelings of sickness and helplessness overwhelmed her. Finally she hauled in a ragged breath, willing herself to regain control. She dried her face, then straightened up and breathed deliberately in and out until she had reestablished a façade of calm. Opening the lavatory door, she stepped back out into the cabin of the transport.

The pilot was speaking to the passengers. Everyone looked grave. *Something bad is happening. What?* She pushed forward to her seat, trying to hear what the pilot was saying.

Unfortunately, he was just concluding, 'Once again, we are processing the information we have been given. And I urge you all to try to stay calm. As we get more information, I will pass it along to you. Thank you for your patience.'

Laura settled into her seat beside Billy. She let her

bewilderment surface to her face. Billy looked scared. 'What's going on?'

'I'm not sure,' he said.

'But *something* is happening that's not good, am I right?'

'Yeah. Some kind of civil defense emergency on Caprica. That's all he could tell us,' Billy said.

Laura nodded and sat back. She was not reassured.

The cockpit of the transport looked, at first glance, pretty much like the cockpit of any large airliner, with perhaps a couple dozen additional instruments dedicated to orbital position and navigation, environmental controls, Lorey-field gravity, reactor status, and the like. The pilot, Captain Russo, returned to his seat, confirmed to his copilot that he was taking the controls back, and keyed the wireless mic. 'Any luck over there, Captain?' he asked, peering out his left window to catch a glimpse of the Viper Mark II. He was hoping their escort, Captain Adama, might have more information. Russo and his copilot had not much more information than he had given the passengers, with one exception: Fearing panic, they had not told the passengers that among the confused messages they had heard was one, completely unconfirmed, containing the words 'Cylon attack.'

Apollo's voice was scratchy coming from the speakers. '*No, just picking up a lot of confusing chatter.*'

'Well,' said Captain Russo, 'to be honest with you, I'm glad you're sticking around. Makes us all feel better just seeing you out there.'

'*Well, don't get too comfortable,*' Apollo answered. '*This junker I'm in was meant for show, not combat. If we run into a problem, I'll do what I can to protect you. But at the first sign of trouble, you pour on the speed and you run.'*

'Don't you worry about that,' said the pilot. 'I've got my hand on the throttle. It hasn't left since I got the first message.' He drew a deep breath. 'Colonial Heavy Seven-Niner-Eight . . . out.'

Two Cylon raiders, one fleeing Raptor. Silent as space.

And in the silent darkness, a missile sprang from each of the raiders, trailing white contrails. They arced with flawless guidance toward the Raptor, as the Cylons pitched up and away.

In the Raptor's cockpit, Boomer and Helo were working frantically. *'Two missiles now!'* Helo called from the situation console.

'Jam their warheads,' Boomer cried desperately.

'I'm trying! I can't find the frequency. *Drop a swallow!'*

Boomer worked silently. 'I've got two left.' She dropped one of the two remaining decoys, which spun downward out of the belly of the Raptor as she fired thrusters to lift in the other direction. The missiles took the bait and veered toward the decoy. Or one did; it intercepted the decoy in a heartbeat and exploded. The other changed course and resumed its pursuit of the Raptor. 'Damn it! *C'mon!'* Sharon breathed, working the controls feverishly.

'Aw, *frak!'* shouted Helo.

'What?'

'Check the screen ahead!'

She did, and winced. A swarm of Cylons had appeared in front of them. 'I guess we found the main fight.' No time to worry about that right now, though. They had a missile on their tail. She gave sharp thrust to the left and down, trying to evade it.

An alarm starting beeping. Behind her, Helo snapped, '*Missile lock!*'

Sharon shook her head. 'We've got one left.' She released the last swallow.

It spun away, and miraculously, the Cylon missile pitched over to follow it. The two zigzagged for a moment, perilously close to the Raptor, and the missile hit the decoy. It blew in cascading explosions. Sharon's heart leapt in triumph – and an instant later a cloud of shrapnel from the explosion hit the Raptor with a series of sickening thumps. Sparks and bits of molten metal flew through the cockpit. Alarms went off all over her board. She heard Helo howl in pain. *Frak it frak it frak it!* She tried to assess the damage quickly for critical failures, and keep flying the craft at the same time.

'We're hit!'

'*Oh, really!*' Helo gasped.

She finally managed a look over her shoulder, and saw Helo bent over at his seat, jamming an emergency patch over a hole in the floor. Blood was spurting from his thigh. *Oh frakking Kobol!* She had to keep flying, but a moment later she managed to turn again. 'Helo – hey! Are you *okay*?'

'*Aahh.* Present.' He had one hand on his thigh, trying to stop the bleeding, and the other on the deck, struggling to position the patch to stop the venting of air from the cabin.

The cabin's leaking, his suit's punctured, he's wounded . . . Keep flying the ship! 'Stay with me!' she shouted over her shoulder.

Ferociously, she focused on the board in front of her. 'Okay,' she breathed. 'We have a fuel leak! We need to put down to repair it! The nearest world is Caprica.'

'A lot of company between us and there.'

'Yeah,' she said, and glanced back. He was sitting upright, putting pressure on his thigh. *Good. Good.* She couldn't help him, except by getting them down. If he could just tend to his own wound a little longer . . .

But all those Cylons out there, between them and Caprica! How, could she possibly get past them, especially in their crippled condition? She bit her lip, thinking. Then she had it. She aimed the ship carefully, hit full throttle for a few seconds, and cut the engines. Then she reached over to the fuel valve and shut off the flow from the tank, to stop the loss of the precious Tylium. Finally, she killed power to lights, gravity, and everything else that might be detected from the outside. The cockpit went dark, except for starlight coming in through the windows.

Helo looked up in the gloom. 'So we're coasting?'

She answered anxiously. 'Best way to avoid attracting attention. No power signature. Go in a straight line.' As she talked, Helo had his hands clamped to his thigh, gritting his teeth against the pain. 'Unless somebody actually gets close enough to see us, we'll look like a chunk of debris on the sensors.' She stopped her machine-gun-like delivery for a moment to assess the readings on her instruments. 'I think we have enough inertia to make it to Caprica's ionosphere. Then we power up, and find a place to land.'

'Nice,' Helo panted. 'Nice thinking there.'

Sharon checked their course one more time, then unbuckled to float back to help Helo, grabbing the first-aid kit on her way. 'Frak, Helo, you're hurt bad,' she said, bracing herself against a panel so she could tend to his wound.

For a second, he looked as if he was going to make light of it – but as soon as she touched his leg, he gasped in agony. A piece of shrapnel, probably molten metal from the hull, had gone straight through his thigh. It must have missed the arteries, though, because the bleeding was slowing down. She had to cut the leg of his spacesuit, praying the cabin pressure would hold. Then she was able to get closure-patches on the wound and start wrapping cloth tape around it. 'Hold still,' she said, grabbing a hypodermic. Before he could say a word, she'd stuck him full of antibiotic and painkiller.

He sat back, breathing hard, as she handed the tape to him. 'I have to check our position,' she said. Then with as much of a smile as she could manage, she added, 'Stick with me, partner. We've got to get through this together.' She caught his hand and held it tightly until he nodded. 'Good.' Because Helo wasn't just her partner, he was her best friend in the world – Tyrol excepted, of course. She'd be devastated if anything happened to him. 'Good,' she repeated, then turned and floated back to her pilot's seat.

Caprica was drawing visibly closer, and she was starting to be able to pick out something of the situation there. The world was slowly being swallowed up by murky clouds, and here and there lighting up with flashes of light under the clouds. *Lords of Kobol, what's happening?* she thought. And then she realized: All those flashes were nukes going off on the surface of Caprica. The planet was being destroyed.

'Helo,' she said shakily. *Don't tell him how bad it is, not yet.* 'We're getting close to the atmosphere. I'm going to set up for entry. I think—' She checked her instruments again before continuing. 'I think we can make it close to Caprica City. The city itself may be under attack, so I'm going to aim for the area just to the south.'

'Okay with me,' he said. 'Just so you do the flying.' He barked a laugh to mask his pain.

'I will,' Sharon said. *I will.*

And with that, she powered up the systems and began steering the Raptor toward a smoking, high-speed entry into Caprica's atmosphere.

CHAPTER
19

GALACTICA, COMBAT INFORMATION CENTER

The assembled personnel in the CIC stood silent and grave as Commander Adama, bulky microphone in his hand, addressed the ship. Adama's voice echoed through the corridors. 'Preliminary reports indicate that a thermonuclear device in the fifty-megaton range was detonated over Caprica City thirty minutes ago.'

Though Adama could not see it from where he stood, all through the ship, shock waves reverberated among the crewmembers who had not previously heard the news. The Viper mechanics one by one stopped their work, reactors half-installed, their hands and their bodies seemingly drained of life. *Caprica City, nuked* . . . Caprica City was the ship's home port, and to many of the crew, it was the city they called home. Many of them had family, friends, and other loved ones in Caprica City and the surrounding region. *Caprica City* . . . It was too shocking to grasp, that this city, their home planet, was being destroyed by the Cylon attack.

Adama continued. 'Nuclear detonations are also being reported on the planets of Aerilon, Picon, Sagittaron, and Geminon. No report on casualties. But obviously, they will be high. Very high.'

On the hangar deck, holding a piece of test equipment in her hands, test equipment that right now felt meaningless, Specialist Cally asked without looking at anyone, 'How many people in Caprica City alone?'

Kara Thrace answered, her voice barely audible, 'Seven million.'

Seven million. How many were already dead?

Standing almost like a statue in the CIC, Adama continued, with barely suppressed emotion, 'Mourn the dead later. Right now, the best thing we can do is get this ship into the fight.' He paused for a very long beat. 'That is all.'

And on every deck of the ship, crewmembers who had halted their work slowly came to, picked up their tools again, and continued their preparations to do exactly what their commander had asked.

COLONIAL HEAVY 798, COCKPIT

It seemed like a very long way, as Laura Roslin mounted the flight of steps – only about six steps in reality – that led to the cockpit door. She drew a breath and knocked. When the captain opened the door, she started; she was on edge, and she knew it wasn't going to get better soon. 'Excuse me,' she said to the captain, stepping past him into the cockpit. He was holding a printout in his hand, and his face was ashen. He backed away to let her into the cockpit.

Once Captain Russo had closed the door again, she faced him. She thought she knew what was on that printout. 'One of the passengers has a shortwave wireless,' she said softly. 'They . . . heard a report that Caprica's been nuked.'

The captain's face was immobile with shock; he seemed unable to answer.

'It has, hasn't it?' she asked, barely keeping her own expression together.

The captain finally managed to reply. 'Caprica and three other colonies.' He handed her the printout. His hand was shaking. Laura took the printout from him. With her other hand, she clasped his, and held it tightly. *Stop shaking. We have to be strong. If we're not, who will be?* She looked at the printout, and saw that it was exactly as she had thought and feared. She wept inwardly, but pushed the feeling away.

The captain turned from her, pulling his hand away. 'I guess I, uh' – he rubbed his chin nervously – 'should make an announcement or something.'

You're in no condition to be making an announcement, she thought. *The last thing they need is to see their pilot shaking, the same way they are.* 'I'll do it,' she said. 'I'm a member of the political cabinet. It's my responsibility.' She could see the relief on his face as he nodded. 'While I'm doing that, I would ask that you' – she had to think a moment, about what she should or could do – 'contact the Ministry of Civil Defense. See what we can do to *help.*' She made her voice sound deliberately upbeat on that last note. He accepted her offer with a desperate nod.

After reading over the printout one more time, Laura returned to the cabin and stood at the front, where she could address the passengers. She motioned to Billy to stand with her. She drew a breath, let it out slowly, drew another. Then she began speaking to the passengers, in a quiet but steady voice. 'The reports are confirmed. There has been a Cylon nuclear attack on at least four of our worlds – including the colonies Caprica . . . Picon . . . Aerilon . . . and Tauron.'

The passengers were immediately up out of their seats, all talking at once – asking for more information, demanding to be taken home, or simply crying out in fear. Laura gestured with both hands for people to quiet down. 'Please! Please stop. Please.' The cabin quieted, but only slightly. 'I'm trying to reach the government now to get more information. In the meantime, we should all be prepared for an extended stay aboard this ship. So, uh' – she was thinking rapidly now, on her feet – 'you, please, and you' – she turned, pointing to two of the flight attendants – 'take an inventory of the emergency supplies and rations.' Both flight attendants nodded and began moving to their jobs.

'Wait – wait a minute,' said one of the passengers. It was Aaron Doral, the public relations officer who had guided her around the *Galactica*. He looked distrustful and belligerent; with his PR demeanor completely gone, he seemed a different person. 'Who put you in charge?'

Laura was momentarily caught off guard by the challenge. Around her, the faces of many of the other passengers were filled with sudden uncertainty as to her authority. She thought of how to answer, and decided to approach it – and Doral – head on. Just like a teacher being challenged by a student in a classroom. Walking toward him, she said, 'Well, that's a good question. The answer is, no one.'

She pressed her lips together, holding the printout tightly in her hands. 'But . . . this is a government ship, and I am the senior government official, so that *puts* me in charge, so' – she raised a hand to gesture to him – 'why don't *you* help me out, and go down into the cargo area, and see about setting it up as a living space?' Before he could answer, she turned away from his scowl and said to the others, 'Everyone else, please – *please* – try and stay calm. Thank you.'

With that, she took Billy by the arm and pulled him aside. She handed him another piece of paper that the captain had given her. 'All right – this is the passenger manifest.' Billy took it from her, and he was nodding, but he looked very shaky. His hand, like the captain's, was trembling. She paused in her train of thought and looked at him closely, meeting his gaze. 'Are you all right?'

Billy straightened a little, and suddenly seemed energized. Too energized. '*Yeah.* Yeah.' He swallowed. 'My parents . . . moved to Picon two months ago . . . to be closer to my sisters, and their families, and their grandkids, and . . .'

Laura sighed deeply, but refused to let the pain onto her face. She gazed at Billy, letting him see her sympathy, but not weakness. At that moment, the captain appeared at the head of the aisle. 'Madame Secretary – we've got your comm link.' She nodded acknowledgment, but before turning away, put a steadying, motherly hand on Billy's arm. She made sure he registered the gesture, then hurried away to the cockpit.

Seated in the copilot's seat with a headset on, Laura tried to decipher what she was hearing over the wireless. It was Jack Nordstrom, an advisor in the president's office, with whom Laura had worked for years. It was clear from his voice that Jack was exhausted, distraught, and probably frantic with worry about everyone he cared about.

'*Thank God you're not here, Laura . . . thank God. It's complete chaos. Never seen anything like it.*'

'Jack! Where is the president?'

'*The dust in the air. People wandering the streets.*'

She spoke deliberately, insistently. 'Where . . . is . . . the president, Jack? Is he alive?'

'*I don't know. I think so. We hear all kinds of things.*'

Laura let her breath out in frustration. 'Have the Cylons made any demands? Do we know what they want?'

'*No. No contact. I'm pretty sure about that.*'

Insane. It was just insane. She struggled to ask this next question. 'Has anyone discussed' – she paused and shook her head, then pushed on – 'has anyone discussed the possibility of surrender? Has it been considered?'

Jack answered immediately. '*After Picon was nuked, and three other planets, the president offered a complete, unconditional surrender. The Cylons didn't even respond!*'

Before Laura could think of an answer to that, she turned her head at a flash of rocket thruster, and out the cockpit window beyond Captain Russo, saw the Viper blast away at a sharp angle. The captain was talking to someone on another frequency. 'Colonial Heavy Seven-Niner-Eight . . . where?' His hands worked at the nav and dradis screens as he listened. He looked scared. 'What should we do?' He found what he was looking for, and his finger tapped a fast-moving blip on the dradis screen. 'Uh . . . copy that.'

His gaze jerked to meet Laura's. His hand went to the throttle. 'The Cylons have found us. There's an inbound missile.'

Laura craned her neck this way and that, trying to spot the missile. 'Where the hell'd our escort go?' Together with the captain, she looked everywhere. 'Is that it? It's moving too fast.' *We don't stand a chance . . .*

Lee had the throttle of the old Viper pegged to the limit. How the frak did they ever win the first war, flying these crates? He was flying purely by the seat of his pants, trying to get in front of the missile. The projectile was *fast*, and it was flying a swerving, evasive course. And that was just what Lee was doing with the Viper, too.

The darkness of space might have seemed a good place to try playing chicken with a deadly missile. Except the missile wasn't after him, it was after the transport ship carrying a hundred or more people. Lee maneuvered smartly, pushing the aging fighter to its limits. He drew close, then swerved sharply into its path, and flew ahead of it, rolling and pitching, and finally breaking away from the course that was rapidly taking them both back toward the passenger ship. The missile followed him, locked on his engine heat. *Good. Good.* Lee maneuvered hard left, hard right, trying to keep it distracted. It was closing on him. *I think it's good.*

Close enough, and far enough from the transport. Lee gripped the stick tightly, and with a quick application of thrust, chopped the throttle and flipped the Viper one hundred eighty degrees around. Now he was flying backward in front of the missile, gazing straight down the barrel of its nose. It was arcing toward him, fast. He sighted, waited just the right amount of time, then opened fire with both rocket-cannons. A hail of glowing projectiles flew out from his Viper. A heartbeat later, the missile exploded.

He felt elation for one more heartbeat. And then the concussion from expanding gas and debris hit him. The Viper caught it squarely under the nose and flipped nose over tail, tumbling. The instruments flickered once, then went dark. Lee cursed, struggling to bring the Viper back under control. It was all he could do to get the tumble stopped, then slow his movement away from the transport. He was out of the fight. He had no more maneuvering capability.

Frak!

There did not seem to be any other Cylon missiles in the area, though, and he caught a glimpse of the transport, dwindling. It was safe, for the moment. He thumbed his mic. 'Krypter, Krypter, Krypter! This is Apollo to Colonial Seven-Niner-Eight. I'm declaring an emergency. My systems are offline. I need assistance.'

And then he could only wait.

CHAPTER
20

SOUTH OF CAPRICA CITY

Miraculously, part of the house was still standing. Even more miraculously, Gaius Baltar was still alive. Bruised, bleeding, he sat up coughing amidst the concrete debris and shattered glass. His ears were ringing, and his eyes were gritty with dust. *They nuked my house. I just survived a nuke.* It was unbelievable.

It was far from over, though. He could hear the sounds of distant explosions, and twice as he looked around he winced at a sudden flash of light. None as close as the burst that had destroyed his home. *Not that that one was really so close. It must have been thirty klicks away.* He suddenly remembered, with a shudder, the video images of Caprica City being bombed. How many people had died in the last hour? *How did I manage to survive? What did I do to deserve survival? Nothing . . .*

With that thought, he suddenly remembered Natasi, the way she had shoved him to the floor and thrown her body over his. He'd still been tossed across the room by the force of the blast. But without her actions, he wouldn't have survived. '*Natasi!*' he shouted, in a panic. He scrambled up to look for her. '*Natasi!*'

He did not have to look far. Her broken body lay where

it had been thrown against the far wall. Her neck was twisted at an unnatural angle, her body was bleeding where she had been hit by flying debris. He approached her slowly, somberly. 'Oh, Natasi,' he said, his voice breaking. He knelt beside her, and gently stroked her hair. 'What did you do? You saved me. You saved my life. Why did you do that?' For a moment, his rage of just a short time ago was forgotten. He lowered his head and shook with grief and terror. What had happened to his life? Why had the world so suddenly gone insane? Was it really all his fault?

Another nuke flashed behind him, making him flinch. It felt a little closer, close enough to shake the ground. He had to get out of here. No more time to mourn what he had lost – the *one* he had lost. And come to think of it, now that he was starting to emerge from the mental haze that had fallen over him, she was not just the one he had lost, *but the one who had brought this all upon them.* He began to feel the rage close in again. The rage and shame. He pushed himself away from her body in disgust, heaved himself up one more time, and looked around wildly, trying to make a plan. *Head for the hills*, he thought. That meant going south, and east.

Grabbing a jacket, he ran for the door – what was left of it. Halfway through the shattered opening, he suddenly turned back and rummaged through the debris in the remnant of his living room until he found what he was looking for: his leather briefcase, with summaries of all his recent work. All the classified information, the information he had given to Natasi. To the enemy. He didn't know what difference it made, but he wasn't going to leave it lying around the house, where anybody could find it. Where they could find it, and know what he had done.

With that tucked under his arm, he ran to his car. He

would drive until he could go no farther – which probably would not be very far. And then he would go on foot. And if necessary, he would crawl, to get away from this nightmare . . .

No one was going to criticize Sharon for her landing this time. It had been a bruising reentry, through Caprica's upper atmosphere. They'd broken out of the clouds not more than a few thousand feet above ground level. She'd steered clear of the obvious nuke attacks, while getting them reasonably close to Caprica City, in case there was some good they could do there. (Clearly out of the question now.)

She was searching the ground for a feasible landing spot. 'There!' she shouted to Helo – to keep him engaged and alert. 'I can put us down in those low hills. Hang on! Tighten your belt!'

Cautiously, she turned the fuel valve back on. She only needed power for a couple of minutes. 'Try not to leak too much,' she muttered to the ship. 'Just hold on.'

Skimming low over the hills, she picked out a spot and turned in to her final approach. Firing belly thrusters, she slowed, and lowered the Raptor to the ground. She killed the rockets and the craft thumped into the grass and skidded a little. Then it stopped dead on the top of a knoll. *Best damned landing I ever made in my life.*

She hoped she hadn't broken anything that would keep them from taking off again.

'I'm going outside to patch the fuel line,' she said, squeezing past Helo. 'How's the leg?'

'Good enough to come out there with you,' Helo said, wincing.

'No, stay here. I can handle it.'

He was already pushing himself up out of the seat. 'The hell . . . you say. We do . . . this together.'

Helo, in the end, wound up leaning against the side of the ship, wrapping his leg with more strips of cloth and adhesive, while Sharon crawled under the Raptor with a couple of toolkits to fix the fuel line. At least the bleeding had stopped. He wouldn't be good for running any marathons, but at least he could stand. He hoped Sharon could stop the fuel leak as effectively.

In the distance, mushroom clouds rose against the horizon. It was surrealistic – nuclear explosions reigning over this beautiful panorama of green hills and scattered trees. He saw another flash, another mushroom cloud. 'That's six!' he said in disbelief. What could the damn Cylons be hitting? What was left? He ducked his head down to look under the craft. 'How you coming on that fuel line?'

'Almost there,' Sharon said. 'We'll be airborne pretty soon. And get back in the fight.' She peeled the backing from a large patch and reached up into the engine compartment to wrap it around the ruptured pipe.

'Yeah. Back in the fight.' Helo limped forward, away from the ship. It hurt to walk, but he saw something coming over the hilltops, and he wasn't sure he was going to like it.

'Okay,' said Sharon, her voice muffled under the craft. 'That should do it.' His back was to her, but he could hear her close the access panel, and pull the toolkits out from under the Raptor.

'Sharon?' he said suddenly. 'Grab your sidearm.'

A moment later she was beside him, and they both had their weapons out – large-caliber, Previn automatics.

A sizable crowd of people was coming over the hilltop toward them. 'Helo?' Sharon asked uncertainly.

'Stand your ground.' Helo raised his handgun and leveled it with both hands. Sharon did likewise.

It looked like forty, fifty, maybe even a hundred people – all running for their lives over the hills. They were headed straight for the Raptor. Some carried suitcases, some books, some children. Some were falling down and getting up again. One was on crutches. Helo thought he knew what they all wanted. They all wanted to get off this planet before it was completely destroyed. They had just fled from Hell, and they wanted to live.

There was only one spacecraft in sight, and that was their Raptor. And they weren't here to carry passengers.

CHAPTER
21

COLONIAL HEAVY 798

Laura Roslin leaned over the pilot's seat and pointed out the cockpit window at the tiny, tumbling spacecraft. 'There he is. Can you maneuver over and bring him on board?'

Captain Russo and his copilot, Eduardo, to whom Laura had relinquished her seat, checked a few instruments. The pilot craned his neck to look back at her. 'We can. But it's risky. I do have to think of the safety of the rest of the people back there in the cabin.'

Laura put a hand on his shoulder. 'Captain, if it weren't for Captain Apollo out there, *none* of us would be alive right now. Bring him in. Please.'

The pilot nodded. 'Yes, ma'am.' He glanced at his copilot. 'Let's set up for a docking. If he can't maneuver, we'll just float the number two cargo bay right over him and bring him inside.'

'Let's just hope the Cylons don't come looking, while we're wallowing around doing that,' Eduardo muttered.

Laura closed her eyes, praying she wasn't dooming the transport in the effort to save Captain Adama. 'I have complete confidence in you,' she said at last. 'Now, while you're doing that, I have to see how our emergency planning is coming along.' Without waiting for an answer, she headed out the cockpit door to the passenger cabin.

At this point nothing in the Viper was working except the battery-powered emergency life-support and wireless – and at that, the wireless mostly just produced static. Lee Adama could only sit and wait. He would not have blamed the captain of the transport if he had hit full throttle and run for safety, just as Lee had told him to do. After all, he had a shipload of passengers who were his responsibility. In fact, that was probably what the captain *should* have done. But Lee was grateful, nevertheless, for the sight of the big ship maneuvering toward him, its cargo bay door open.

As the Viper continued its slow tumble, the transport rotated out of view. Lee turned his attention back to his lifeless panels. If he could just get attitude-control thrusters working again! He didn't want to be rescued just to crash on the inside of the ship's cargo bay! Well, he hadn't tried *everything* yet. There was still this manual control bypass down under the instrument panel. Maybe he could fire the individual thrusters using the hand valves . . .

Pop . . . BAM . . .

Whoa. He had just slowed his pitch-over tumble. Or had he? No, that was the wrong way. He groped around for the opposite lever and yanked it. *BAM . . . whoosh . . .*

By the gods, it was working. Good thing, too, he realized, as the transport came back into view, looming suddenly very large outside the cockpit. He was about to be swallowed up by that big, yawning cargo bay.

*

The Viper slammed and skidded onto the deck of the hold, as it came suddenly into the influence of the Lorey-field gravity. Somehow it slid to a full stop, just before smashing into a wall with a wingtip. Lee laughed to release the tension, as he waited for the cargo bay doors to close and the area to repressurize. It wasn't a *good* landing, for sure – but if he could walk away from it, then it was good enough. When he saw a couple of crewmembers from the transport running from a stairway toward him, he realized pressurization was complete, and he pushed the cockpit canopy open.

Loosening his helmet, he was happy to hand it to the first man to reach in. 'Welcome aboard, Captain Adama,' the crewman said.

'Thank you,' Lee said, climbing over the edge of the cockpit and carefully down the ladder that the crewman had propped against the side of the craft. He stepped away from the Viper and looked around at the cargo bay – surprisingly large, like the lower deck of a seagoing ferry, and mostly empty. Then he turned back to gaze at the battered antique Viper. *No more complaints from me. You got me here in one piece, and you took out that missile that would have been the end of all of us.* Taking a deep breath, Lee pulled off his gloves as the transport crewman helped loosen the collar ring of his spacesuit.

'Captain! Are you all right?' A vaguely familiar-looking man was running up to him.

'I'm fine.' Lee turned to inspect his craft more thoroughly. As he did so, he caught sight of some very large coils just ahead of his Viper in the cargo bay. He walked over to take a look at them.

'My name's Aaron Doral,' said the man, practically demanding attention. 'I met you before. Took some publicity photos with you and your father.'

Right – the publicity guy. Lee was more interested in these components.

'What *are* those things?' Doral asked, disconcerted by Lee's seeming inattention.

That was what Lee had been wondering, and he had just figured it out. 'Electric pulse generators, from the *Galactica*.'

'Really,' said Doral. 'That . . . that's interesting.' He became more sober and determined. 'Uh, Captain, I – I can't tell you how glad I am to see you!'

'Oh? Why's that?' asked Lee, finally turning to see what the man wanted.

Doral looked extremely agitated. 'Well, see, Captain – personally, I would feel a lot better if someone *qualified* were in charge around here.'

Lee looked at him in surprise. 'Is something wrong with your pilot?'

'No,' said Doral. 'It's just that he's not the one giving orders.'

Lee studied the man's face for a moment, then decided he'd better go see for himself what was going on. As he walked away, Doral followed closely behind. 'This is . . . uh, this is a bad situation, isn't it, sir?'

Now, that's stating the obvious, isn't it? 'Yes,' answered Lee. 'Yes, it is.'

He found the stairway and ran quickly up out of the cargo area. In the passenger cabin, he didn't have to look far to see who was apparently giving the orders. The Secretary of Education, Laura Roslin, was surrounded by a group of people, whom she was questioning closely. She was a middle-aged woman whom Lee had met before only briefly. An educator. Quietly intelligent, attractive, almost motherly. Probably not the leader type, he would have guessed. She had a thin blanket wrapped around her

130

shoulders, as though she were cold. But if that suggested any weakness, the impression was dispelled at once. 'What if we transferred the L containers from Bay Three to Bay Four?' she asked a man crouched beside her. 'Then we could use One, Two, and Three for passengers.'

Lee recognized the man she was talking to as the transport pilot, Captain Russo. 'Yeah,' Russo said, 'that's doable. It's a lot of heavy lifting without dock loaders, though.'

'A little hard work is just what the people need right now,' Laura said. She looked up and saw Lee, as he strode forward to shake the pilot's hand. 'Captain! Good to see you again.'

'Likewise,' Lee answered. To Russo, he said, 'Thanks for the lift.'

The pilot laughed. 'You should thank her,' he said, nodding in Roslin's direction. As Lee followed his glance, puzzled, the pilot slapped him on the arm and headed back to the cockpit.

Roslin had already returned her attention to the discussion with the young man who appeared to be her assistant. 'Start the cargo transfer and then prep Bay Three for survivors,' she said, with startling authority and efficiency.

'Yes, ma'am,' the young man said, and moved off to follow his instructions.

Lee was still trying to put all this together in his mind. 'I'm sorry. Survivors?'

Roslin looked back up at him and explained rapidly. 'As soon as the attack began, the government ordered a full stop on all civilian vessels. So now we've got hundreds of stranded ships in this solar system. Some are lost, some are damaged, some are losing power. We have enough space on *this* ship to accommodate up to five hundred people, and we're going to need every bit of it.' She stood up abruptly, as though intending to walk away.

Behind Lee, Aaron Doral was sputtering. 'But we don't even know what the tactical situation is out there.'

Roslin angled a glance at him and looked thoughtful. 'The tactical situation is that we are losing.' She swung her gaze around to look Lee straight in the eye. 'Right, Captain?'

Lee could hardly lie. As far as he had heard, they were losing *badly*. 'Right,' he answered, with a nod.

'So,' Roslin went on, without a trace of self-consciousness about giving orders, 'we pick up the people we can and try to find a safe haven to put down.' She walked toward the cockpit door, then turned. 'Captain, I'd like you to look over the navigational charts for a likely place to hide from the Cylons.' She nodded. 'That's all.' And she turned away.

Lee, stunned by her complete command of the situation, glanced at Doral, who was still standing nearby, fuming – no doubt waiting for Lee to take over. Lee had to work a bit to hide a smile. As he walked away, he said simply, 'The lady's in charge.'

An unhappy Aaron Doral glowered after him.

CHAPTER

22

THE HILLS, SOUTHEAST OF CAPRICA CITY

Helo aimed deliberately low and to one side and squeezed off a single round from his Previn automatic. The round exploded in the ground, throwing a cloud of dirt into the air between Helo and the advancing mob. The people fell back, but his action did nothing to calm them down. Now they were not just scared and desperate, they were angry.

He called out, 'That's as close as you get – okay? Let's just settle down here. Settle down, and no one gets hurt.' Even as he said it, his heart was going out to the people. Could he blame them? Wouldn't he be just as desperate to get off the planet?

Shouts of anger gave way to pleas. One man was waving a fistful of money. 'I have to get to the port! I'll give you fifty thousand cubits!'

'Sixty thousand!' a woman shouted.

'We're not taking money!' Helo shouted back. 'This isn't a rescue ship. This is a military vessel.' He leveled his weapon again as the crowd surged forward, pressing their case. Beside him, Sharon had her own gun aimed at the crowd, protecting him, and protecting the Raptor. 'We're not taking money!' he repeated.

Several of the people in the front of the crowd made as

though to charge. Sharon raised her gun and fired a warning burst into the air. The people fell back again in alarm. But voices soon rose again, one woman calling, 'But what about the children?'

That was too much. 'All right, all right!' Sharon yelled, her change of heart taking Helo by surprise. 'All right.' She caught her breath, but did not lower her weapon. 'Children first. *Children.*' She was suddenly flushed with an awareness that *she*, not that many years ago, had through good fortune alone escaped a cataclysm on her own homeworld of Troy. Why should she deny that same fortune to these children?

There was a stirring in the crowd, as parents pressed bags or keepsakes into the hands of their tearful children, and hustled them to the front of the crowd before they could protest or refuse. Sharon and Helo waved the children into the Raptor. Sharon silently counted them as they ducked through the entry hatch. When all the children were aboard, she turned back to the crowd, her face drawn and harried. 'All right – we can take three more people.'

An assortment of hands shot up, and people started calling out again. 'Why only three?' someone called.

'That's the maximum load if we're gonna break orbit,' Helo said, shouting over them.

The man who'd been about to charge a minute ago strode forward with gritted teeth and a clenched fist. 'Who chooses the three – you?'

'*No* one chooses!' Sharon called out. 'No one.' She hesitated. 'Lottery.' She glanced at Helo, and he nodded in appreciation at her quick thinking. 'Everyone gets a number. We put 'em in a box, pull out three. *That's it.* No arguing, no appeal.'

For a tense few moments, the crowd absorbed that.

Helo thought maybe they weren't absorbing it enough. 'I will shoot the first person who tries to board before then,' he said, waving his gun enough to make the point.

That quieted them down. Sharon cast him another glance. 'Helo, get out your flight manual and tear out the pages . . .'

CHAPTER
23

The race against time was heating up in the Viper maintenance area. The deck was littered with service racks and forklifts. Chief Tyrol was striding from one workstation to another, consulting, cajoling, and whipping his people into faster action. The good news was that they'd managed to plug reactors back into a dozen of the fighter craft – thanks to the modular swap-in, swap-out design of the systems. And they'd filled the fuel tanks with quantum-catalytic Tylium, so the reactors had something to burn. The bad news was that they were still frantically trying to *calibrate* the power plants so they could fly without blowing up, test the valves and hydraulics, check out the flight instruments, and load ammunition into the recoilless rocket cannons.

If he had to, Tyrol figured he could have six or eight of them flyable in a couple of hours, though how *well* they would fly was another question. Word from the CIC was that they could expect Cylon company any time now. Tyrol was wound about as tight as he had ever been in his life, determined to have these Vipers ready when the commander called for them.

And every once in a while, he spared a few moments

for worrying about Boomer and Helo, from whom nothing had been heard since their brief, truncated report that the entire Viper Mark VII squadron had been destroyed, leaving the Raptor alone and fleeing for its life.

COMBAT INFORMATION CENTER, NINETY MINUTES LATER

Commander William Adama stood silent and sober as the attention-tone preceded an announcement from Executive Officer Tigh, standing beside the dradis console officer. '*Attention. Inbound dradis contact, rated highly probable, enemy fighters. All hands stand by for battle maneuvers.*'

Adama turned his head to meet Tigh's gaze. 'What's the status of our Vipers? Can we launch?'

Tigh had a handset stretched on a long cord from another console, and he was talking into it. He looked up. 'Chief says we can launch six. He needs more time with the others.'

Six Vipers! To defend the ship? Adama drew a silent breath. It was the only defense they had. There was no ammunition on board for *Galactica*'s own guns. 'Launch Vipers,' he said grimly to Petty Officer Dualla, who was at her station with a headset on, watching closely for his orders.

'Vipers! Clear to launch,' Dualla said crisply.

Now they could only wait, and do their best to steer the ship away from trouble if anything got past the Vipers.

Behind a window overlooking the launch bay, Launch Officer Kelly ran quickly through the checklist. 'Choker, this is Shooter. I have control – stand by.' On the far side of the window, a Viper Mark IV was lined up in the launch tube, fuming and ready to go. The pilot, Choker, glanced at him and gave a thumbs-up inside his closed cockpit. In two other launch tubes, the identical ritual was playing out.

'Viper One-One-Zero-Four, clear forward.' Kelly verified that all systems were ready. 'Nav-con green . . . interval check . . . mag-cat ready—'

At those last words, a powerful piston slid forward and latched onto the Viper's undercarriage, ready to catapult the fighter to launch speed. At the same time, a great steel door in front of the Viper dropped down, exposing the launch tube to open space.

'—check door open . . . thrust positive, and . . . good luck.'

The launch officer pressed the button that fired the electromagnetic catapult. The Viper pilot was slammed back in his seat as the fighter rocketed down a long, triangular tube.

Outside *Galactica*, the Viper shot out of the launch port in the side of the ship, followed quickly by four more. They grouped up, waited a few moments for the sixth and last to appear, and when it didn't, they got their clearance and lit their thrusters and fired off on an intercept course with the incoming enemy.

In launch tube four, Kara 'Starbuck' Thrace sat sealed in her cockpit, steaming as she waited for the launch officer to complete the checklist. She heard '*Interval*' – and raised a thumbs-up, eyes straight forward – '*check*' – every fiber of her body focused on the battle she was about to join, as the launch officer went through the items: '—*thrusters positive . . . stand by.*' Kara winced. What this time?

Then she heard words she hated. '*Thrusters fluctuating. Abort takeoff.*'

Frak!

'*Galactica*, Viper Eight-Five-Four-Seven, throttle down to safe.' Making it sound like a curse, she powered the thrusters down.

'*Roger, Viper.*'

'*Frak* – get me out of here!' she shouted angrily.

Outside the launch tube, the crew was in frantic motion. 'Let's go, let's go!' Tyrol shouted. As soon as the exhaust cleared, the rear section of the launch tube opened, exposing the Viper, and the mechanical crews swarmed over her. 'Let's get her out of there. Cally! Prosna! Figure out what's goin' on!' The two specialists were already up on a service ladder, opening the engine compartment panels.

When the cockpit canopy lifted, Kara ripped her helmet off and glared furiously at Tyrol. 'Three frakkin' aborts, Chief?'

'We're on it, sir. It's the pressure-reg valve again.'

'We should pull it!' Cally called, leaning in to look at the valve.

'We can't,' Prosna said. 'We don't have a spare.'

Despite his words, Prosna and Cally quickly disconnected the valve and lifted it out. If they couldn't fix this thing in minutes, Starbuck was going to be out of the fight – and maybe they all would be . . .

As they worked, Starbuck could do nothing but listen to the wireless chatter coming in from the Vipers already out there. It didn't sound good.

'*Inbound enemy contact . . . bearing two-four-seven . . . range one-one-five . . . closing . . .*'

Kara couldn't take it anymore. 'Let's *go*!' she screamed at the deck crew.

Tyrol was caught up, as well. 'Come on, let's go, let's go!'

Cally, up on top of the engine pod, called down, 'We should just pull the valve and bypass the whole system.'

'We can't do that, the relay will blow,' Prosna said, struggling to loosen a connector.

'It'll hold! I'm telling you, I put that—'

'*Just pull the valve!*' Chief Tyrol roared.

Overhead, someone on the wireless was shouting, '*Wedlock, you and Keyhole, over the top . . .*' All those pilots out there were in combat for the first time in their lives. *They need me out there!*

In the engine compartment, several pairs of hands worked furiously to bypass the faulty valve, while Starbuck came closer and closer to blowing her stack.

In the CIC, Adama called out commands for the manoeuvering of the ship, as he kept his ears tuned to the reports coming in from the Vipers. '*Firing. Miss!*'

Adama winced. 'Bow up half. Forward left . . . one quarter.' He was watching the attitude readouts with one eye, and position reports of the Vipers and the Cylon raiders with the other. 'Stern right full.' The thruster controls, scattered from one end of the ship to the other, were all under manual control. 'Engines all ahead full!' He had chosen his direction. Now he was going to try to get *Galactica* out of harm's way, and let the Vipers do their jobs.

'*I can't, I can't get a lock! I can't get a lock!*'

'Ahead full, sir,' reported Colonel Tigh. 'Engines report full.'

Overhead, the wireless had more reports from the Viper squadron. '*Oh wait I've got it. Karen's got him, Karen's got him – no!*'

Adama turned away, grimacing, then looked back up.

'*I can't get a shot! I can't get a shot!*'

Adama fumed. Where was Starbuck? Why wasn't his best pilot out there?

'*They're comin' on. Vipers, stay in formation! I can't get a lock . . . ! Oh wait – I've got him. I've got him!*'

'*Come on!*' screamed Starbuck.

'Ready! Ready!' shouted Prosna, slamming the engine access port shut.

'Clear the tube, let's go!' shouted Tyrol. 'Get her in!'

Starbuck smacked her helmet back on over her head and secured it. The crew was lowering the cockpit canopy, while the chief hollered, 'Move – move!'

About one minute later, flying a Viper that had 'Raymond the Raygun' stenciled on its cockpit, Starbuck shot out of the side tube of *Galactica*, a tight grimace on her face. As soon as she was clear, she kicked in her thrusters and slammed herself into a sharp turn. She passed quickly alongside *Galactica*, then rocketed ahead, on her way to the battle.

She didn't have far to go. The sky ahead was criss-crossed by maneuvering Vipers . . . and by Cylons. It was her first look at a modern-day Cylon, and she hated them on sight. She had just enough time to think, *Damn, I've never done this before, either, never had something actually trying to kill me.* That thought vanished as she flew straight into the chaos of battle. Her gloved thumb was on the firing button on her stick, and as soon as she had a free-wheeling Cylon in her sights, she let loose with a volley. She missed. She looped around. These older Vipers were a little slower, and a little different handling in tight maneuvers, and their display screens were way more primitive. *That's all right, just focus on the other ships. A dogfight is the same, no matter what your instruments . . .*

Wheeling around, checking in with the rest of the squadron, Vipers flying every which way across her field of view, she found herself facing a Cylon raider, maybe the same one and maybe another. She got a good look at its red nose sensor, sweeping back and forth. And she got a look at something else, too, on her instruments.

'Oh, frak me!' The thing was beaming an energy pulse at her. She checked her instruments again, and reported back to *Galactica*, 'He's radiating some sort of weapon at me, but it doesn't seem to be having any effect.'

And that sudden steadiness on the part of the Cylon gave her the opening she needed. She let loose a burst from her machine cannon, and the tracers fled out before her – and the Cylon exploded in a fireball. Her heart leapt. Her first kill! *Galactica's* first kill.

'All Vipers! Systems are go!' she called with a grin. Everything was still fully operational on her fighter. Whatever weapon the Cylons had used against the others, it wasn't working now.

The dogfight heated up. The Viper pilots, emboldened, flew closer and tighter. And the Cylons, screaming among them, were no longer trying to shut them down, but were simply aiming to outfly and outshoot them. One got in a shot, and Kara saw a Viper disintegrate in a fireball. She couldn't tell who it was, and didn't have time to ask. 'Hold it together, guys!' she shouted.

She maneuvered hard and fast against the quick-reacting enemy. She didn't get another shot, but something got a shot on her – there was a slam on her tail, and alarms started beeping furiously as she tried to dampen the sudden oscillations in her flight path. 'I'm all right!' she shouted, trying to reassure the others, and maybe herself, too. It took a few seconds to get enough control back to reassure herself that she really *was* all right.

As she swung herself around, trying and failing to turn fast enough to shoot at a Cylon passing close by overhead, she nevertheless got a good look at its underside. The exposed rack of missiles she saw sent chills down her spine . . .

In the command center, Dualla turned and called a warning to the commander. 'Radiological alarm!' A beeper was sounding the same warning.

Beside Adama, Tigh stood close and said in a quiet, steely voice, 'He's got nukes.'

In quick succession, three missiles streaked away from the Cylon. Kara saw it and reacted in fury. '*Come on!*' she screamed, and came around faster and sharper than she'd ever managed in her life. She opened fire on the Cylon, and it exploded. But its missiles were in flight. Kara didn't even pause for breath, but continued her tight circle, following the arcs of the missiles.

It was impossible, nobody could shoot a missile out of flight with a cannon. But that didn't stop her from trying. She fired a continuous stream from her machine cannon, tiny rockets pouring out, a hail of fire chasing the missiles.

One exploded. She swerved ever so slightly, flying with deadly precision. A second missile exploded.

The third was too far away, and it was inbound at high speed toward *Galactica*. Another Viper streaked past going the other way; she nearly hit it with her cannon.

'*Galactica*, you've got an inbound nuke! All Vipers, *break break break!*'

There was nothing they could do for *Galactica* now except veer out of the way and try not to get caught in the explosion . . .

'Right bow, left stern – emergency full power! Main thrust emergency full!' Commander Adama snapped the commands, doing the only thing he could to try to evade the missile. As he watched the screen, he knew it wasn't enough. They were going to take a nuclear blast in the flank. Very softly he said to his old crewmate Tigh, 'Brace for impact, my friend.'

'I haven't heard that in a while,' Tigh replied grimly.

'Collision alarm!' Adama shouted. Klaxons started sounding throughout the ship. All any of them could do was brace, and pray.

The missile struck the ship on the port side, and its nuclear warhead lit up the sky.

CHAPTER
24

GALACTICA, BURNING

Starbuck winced in pain at the dazzling light from the nuclear explosion, but her Viper was far enough from *Galactica* to avoid sustaining further damage itself. She took a moment to regroup her thoughts, then made a fast scan to see if there were any more Cylons in the area. It seemed either she had destroyed the last one, or any others had left.

'Vipers, set up a patrol around the ship,' she ordered the surviving members of the squadron. 'I'm going in to inspect the damage.' She fired her thrusters and flew in toward the ship, passing the floating hulks of two dead Vipers on her way.

There was no time to mourn them now; *Galactica* was burning. Kara flew alongside the port flight pod, close and slow enough to get a good look. '*Galactica*, Starbuck. If you're reading me, the forward section of the port flight pod has sustained heavy damage.' It was a terrible sight, but it could have been a lot worse. She saw a lot of crumpled hull plating, and fire erupting from several compartments in the flight pod. Debris, smoke, and vapors were billowing into space. After a nuke, she was surprised the ship still *had* a port flight pod. '*Galactica*, you've got violent decompression all along the port flight pod. Do you read me? *Galactica?*'

There was no answer, but that could mean anything from an antenna being knocked out of alignment to the whole crew being dead. Kara kept a tight control on her thoughts and her flying, and kept circling the ship, reporting in the blind. It was all she could do.

GALACTICA, COMBAT INFORMATION CENTER

The CIC was damaged but mostly intact. Crewmembers were moving quickly, tending to the injured, hoisting fallen equipment off the floor, and trying to get meaningful information out of partially damaged consoles. Ship-to-ship transmission was out, though they could just make out Starbuck's scratchy reports. Adama was trusting to the remaining Vipers to protect the ship from outside dangers while they dealt with the emergencies on the inside.

Adama's neck was craned, as he squinted up through his glasses at one of the few working monitors, above the light table now being used for damage assessment. 'Radiation levels within norms. The hull plating kept out most of the hard stuff.' Beside him, Tigh was using a grease pencil to correlate damage reports on a large transparent schematic of the ship.

Gaeta called out more reports as they came in. 'Sir, port stern thrusters are locked open. All bow thrusters unresponsive. We're in an uncontrolled lateral counter-clockwise spin.'

'Send a DC party up to aux control,' Adama said, 'and have them cut all the fuel lines to the stern thruster.'

Tigh spoke as soon as he was finished. 'Okay, we have

got buckled supports all along the port flight pod, and chain reaction decompressions occurring everywhere forward of frame two' – he paused to check the printout in his hand – 'two-fifty.'

'That's a problem,' Adama said grimly. It was a massive understatement; if that went unchecked, they could lose all launch and recovery capability, at the very least.

'Kelly says he's got three uncontrolled fires. That's why he hasn't been able to stop the decompressions.'

Adama ran a finger along the diagram. 'If the decomps continue along this axis, they could collapse the port pod.' He looked up at Tigh, his face grave. 'Saul – take personal command of the DC units.'

'Me?' Tigh asked, his face registering sudden apprehension.

Gaeta interrupted at that moment with, 'Sir, the stern thruster's still locked open.' He gestured with a printout. 'We need you.'

And I need you, Saul. This is no time to frak around. Adama eyed his old friend, painfully aware of just how far he had fallen to the booze and self-pity. But he had to put his faith in the man now; he had no choice. In a low voice, he said, 'You're either the XO or you're not.'

At those words, Tigh stiffened, clearly struggling with his self-doubts. 'Yes, sir,' he said. Adama turned and strode away with Gaeta, leaving Tigh to make up his mind.

On the far side of the CIC, Chief Tyrol and Captain Kelly had arrived at a dead run from the hangar deck and were working furiously to coordinate the repair teams from the damage control station. Most of the remote videos were shorted out, but the alarm board was still functioning.

A wall schematic of the ship, it used rows of indicator lights to display which sections were affected by decompression and fire.

In the one functioning video display, they could see disaster unfolding on Port Deck D, Frame 32. The fire there was advancing rapidly, filling the compartment with smoke and toxic fumes. Something exploded with a bright flash, blowing out through the hull. Three more alarm lights lit up on the DC board. In the monitor, they could see that only two men in the crew of fifteen had breathing gear, and those two were frantically trying to herd the others out of the doomed compartment. One of the deck hands had grabbed a phone handset right next to the sending camera. He was choking in the smoke. '*Chief! We're losing pressure! The port pod – it's buckling! We need help!—*'

The screen went white, and static filled the voice line. Tyrol cursed, just as Colonel Tigh stepped into view behind him. 'Report,' demanded the XO.

'Another compartment losing pressure,' said Kelly. 'We just lost the monitor and comm.'

Tyrol pointed to a line of pressure-alarm lights on the DC board. 'There's structural buckling all along this line! *We've gotta get those fires out!*'

'I know! I know!' Kelly snapped.

The phone rang, and Tyrol picked it up, covering his other ear to hear.

Kelly continued, pointing for Tigh's benefit. 'Fire suppression's down. Water mains are down. We've got gravity fluctuations all through the compartments. We're trying to fight the fire with handheld gear, but—'

Tyrol interrupted, relaying another report. 'We've got another decompression on Deck D, close to the port pod!'

Kelly turned to Colonel Tigh. 'What are your orders, sir?' He waited for an answer. 'Sir?'

Tigh stood motionless, a hundred thoughts clamoring in his mind. Sweat broke out on his upper lip as he struggled to make a decision. He *knew* what needed to be done, but they'd never forgive him for it. He'd never forgive himself. He turned, without quite being aware of it, and across the CIC saw Bill Adama hunched over a table with Gaeta, planning whatever needed to be done to solve the thruster problem. Bill's voice, harsh and unyielding, echoed in Tigh's mind: *You're either the XO, or you're not.*

Beside him, Kelly stopped waiting for an order from Tigh, and leaned in to Chief Tyrol 'All right, listen,' he said quietly, 'I need you to take the rest of your DC teams down from the landing bay, to give them a hand . . .'

Tigh turned back to them, suddenly realizing what Kelly was proposing. 'There's no time! Seal off everything forward of Frame Thirty and start an emergency vent of all compartments.'

Tyrol lowered the phone in dismay. 'But wait, I've got over a hundred people trapped up behind Frame Thirty-Four!' He pointed to the display on the board. 'I just need a minute to get 'em out!'

'If we don't seal it off now, we're gonna lose a lot more than a hundred men,' snapped Colonel Tigh. 'Seal it off! Now!'

Tyrol exploded with anger. '*They just need a minute!*'

'*WE DON'T HAVE A MINUTE!*' Tigh bellowed. 'If the fire reaches the hangar pods, it'll ignite the fuel lines and we'll lose the ship! *Do it!*'

Nearly apoplectic with rage, Tyrol keyed the phone for an all-ship announcement. He clearly had to fight to get the words out. *'All hands. Seal off . . . all bulkheads twenty-five through forty. That's an order.'*

In the burning compartment, a deckhand with a respirator and an air tank on his back was shouting to the others, 'Get out of here now! *Go!* They're gonna vent the compartment! Let's go! We need everybody out!' As he yelled, he waved a chemical fire extinguisher, trying futilely to put out the closest flames. But flames were everywhere. Gravity was shifting, throwing everyone off balance. It was impossible, and getting worse by the second.

From the far end of the compartment came shouts and banging. 'The bulkheads are closed! *Let us out!*' Men were crowded up against the end bulkhead, where the smoke was thick but the flames had not yet reached. They were hammering on the locked bulkhead doors. *'Let us out!'*

But there was no escape.

Colonel Tigh inserted the key into the emergency vent switch and twisted it. He stepped back grimly to watch the board.

Deep in the ship, relays tripped and motors surged. Dozen of large air vents opened. On the outer hull, hatches blew open, releasing enormous gouts of fire and smoke from the flaming compartments. Along with the fire, dozens of dying crewmen hurtled out into space like so much debris, tumbling head over heels into space, before vanishing into the darkness. It was all over in a few moments. The flames went out as the last of the air vented from the savaged compartments.

At the damage control board Tigh, Tyrol, and Kelly

waited in stony silence until the board indicated all clear – fires out, temperatures dropping toward normal, pressure zero in the vented sections and holding steady in all others. Finally Kelly affirmed what they all saw: 'Venting complete. Fires are out.'

Tigh stared solemnly at the board, not meeting their eyes. He knew damn well what they were thinking. But he told them anyway: 'If they remembered their training, then they had their suits on and they were braced for possible vent action.'

Chief Tyrol, too, was staring at the board, a haunted expression on his face. 'There were a lot of rooks in there.'

'No one's a rook anymore,' said Tigh, and turned away to return to the CIC.

CHAPTER
25

SOUTH OF CAPRICA CITY, SOMEWHERE IN THE HILLS

Gaius Baltar fidgeted as he stood amid the crowd of people near the Raptor spacecraft. He couldn't believe he had gotten this far. He had driven only about four miles before the crush of people crowding the road, and the obstruction of abandoned vehicles, had made it impossible to drive any farther. He had abandoned his car, like many before him, and taken to the hills on foot.

He was several hours into his hike when someone shouted that they saw a Colonial spaceship coming down – landing in the hills to the southeast. Without hesitation, Baltar joined the breakaway mob that ran in that direction, hoping for rescue. Why else would anyone land a ship within a thousand miles of this madness, if not to look for survivors?

The discovery that it was a military craft, downed for emergency repairs, had been a blow to the crowd, and to Baltar himself. So much for his perfectly reasonable hope that someone had miraculously come down to give *him* a ride off the planet. But then, against all odds, the Raptor crew had agreed to a lottery, to take three adults plus some children to safety. Perhaps God – if there was such a being, and he laughed silently at the notion – wanted to help him to safety, after all.

Numbered pieces of paper had been distributed, and one person, a middle-aged woman, had been selected so far. Two more chances to go. Baltar bit his lip, sweating.

The female pilot reached into an open toolbox lying on the ground in the sun. The box was filled with torn pieces of paper, each bearing a number. Baltar himself held the number 118. The pilot straightened, holding up a single piece of paper. 'One twenty-seven.' She gazed over the anxious crowd. 'One two seven.'

In the front of the crowd, a dark-haired woman in her twenties raised her hand, holding her own slip of paper. 'Here,' The pilot waved her forward. 'Thank you, Lords of Kobol,' the woman murmured, stumbling toward the Raptor. She dropped the slip of paper into the hand of the injured male copilot as she passed him. 'Thank you. Thank you,' she muttered over and over, softly, as if unable to quite believe her good fortune.

Baltar watched her darkly as she walked up the ramp into the ship, then shifted his gaze as the pilot pulled out another slip. 'Last one.' She stood up, scanning the crowd. 'Forty-seven. Four seven.'

There was a stirring, as people throughout the crowd looked disconsolately at their own numbers and shook their heads in despair. Baltar looked unhappily at his own, his heart sinking. And then, almost like a gift from Heaven, a white-haired old woman touched his arm and said, 'Excuse me.' Her skin was wrinkled, and her clothes were worn and faded. 'I forgot my glasses, I must have left them somewhere. Could you please . . . read this for me?'

Baltar glanced at the glasses neatly resting on top of the old woman's head, and took the slip of paper from her. Even before he read the number, he had a deep, gut feeling of what it was going to say. He felt no surprise, but only vindication, when he read, *47*. Unbelievable. So this was how God – such a silly notion – was going to save him? By sending an old woman in his place? A woman who would probably die from the stress of takeoff? No, it defied all reason to see it that way. The woman would believe whatever he told her. And what future did she have, anyway? He was just fumbling with his paper and hers, when he heard, 'Hey!'

He looked up with a start, hiding both slips in his closed hand. It was the male copilot, pointing straight at him. 'Aren't you Gaius Baltar?'

Panicky, but covering, he answered, 'Why, I haven't done anything.' Why would that man be singling him out? Did the man suspect what he was about to do? Frantic, Baltar raised his hand and called out, 'This lady has ticket number forty-seven.' He pointed to his left. 'This lady here!'

'Would you come up here, please?' the military man said.

Bewildered, Baltar glanced at the old woman, whose face was beaming – and together with her, moved through the crowd toward the two pilots.

Sharon, too, was bewildered. Why was Helo calling that man forward? She could see the crowd stirring at this sudden change, and she had a knot of uncertainty in her own stomach. Stepping closer to Helo, she said, 'What are you doing?'

He half-grinned awkwardly, and closed his eyes, swallowing hard. It took him a moment to get the words out. He reached out and took her hand. 'I'm giving up my seat.'

Her stomach clenched, and her jaw. 'Like hell.'

Helo squeezed her hand. His head bobbed as if he couldn't control it. 'A civilian should take my place.'

'*No!*' She spoke with as much force as she could muster. 'You're *going.*'

Helo gave her a moment to control herself and listen. His gaze was resolute. 'Look at those clouds. Sharon, look at those clouds, and tell me this isn't the end of everything.'

She glanced away, and against her will, found herself taking in the view of the mushroom clouds in the distance. She looked back. 'Helo—!'

'Whatever future is left is gonna depend on whoever survives. Give me one good reason why I'm a better choice than one of the greatest minds of our time.'

This is wrong! 'Helo—'

'You can *do* this without me. I know you can. You've proven it.' His face was so earnest, imploring her. She didn't know what to say. Was it possible he was right?

Sharon struggled to control her face, to hold back tears. Her partner, her friend . . . leave him on this doomed planet . . . ? *Is he right? Maybe not . . . but it's what he wants.* He squeezed her arm one last time, then released her. He had made up his mind, and there would be no talking him out of it.

Baltar and the old woman had emerged at the front of the crowd and were standing, gazing at them expectantly. The woman was smiling, and Baltar was looking tentative and uncertain. Sharon closed her eyes for an instant, and made up her mind. 'Get on board,' she snapped, gesturing to both of them to move quickly. She turned to watch them board, then spun back to Helo.

The crowd were crying their disapproval of this sudden

development. 'Wait, wait, wait!' 'What about us?' 'Hey, wait!' Helo was already hobbling forward, arms spread wide, to keep them at bay. 'Stay back. Stay back!' He glanced sharply back at Sharon. 'You'd better go!'

Feeling as if she had a knife in her heart, Sharon turned from him for the last time and hurried onto the Raptor.

Gaius Baltar wondered if he were dreaming. It was far too good to be true. Had he actually been given a seat on this ship? The angry crowd certainly seemed to bear that out. They were shouting, protesting the arbitrary decision to let *him* on board. He hadn't waited to think about it, but had gallantly helped the old woman on board, and then gotten inside as quickly as possible himself.

He stood in the open doorway, staring out at the crowd of hopeless, doomed people. Standing in their midst was someone who hadn't been there a moment ago. A gorgeous blonde in a stunningly low-cut, red spaghetti-strap dress, watching him with the kind of gaze a woman reserved for just one man. *Natasi.* His heart nearly stopped, then started pounding twice as hard as before. Was he hallucinating? *Natasi's dead. I saw her. She can't be here.* He stared in disbelief. He blinked and looked back. There was no sign of her. She had never been there. *I hallucinated her.*

Haunted by that momentary vision, and tormented by the sound of the crowd, he stumbled back into the craft as the military man yelled to the crowd, 'Stay back! Stay back! It's over!'

Something was surely over, but Baltar wished he knew what it was.

*

Sharon fought her way to the cockpit, not so much through the crowd of passengers as through the resistance of her heavy heart. She grunted instructions to everyone to buckle in. A boy, maybe ten years old, had taken the right-hand seat. Sharon buckled into the left seat. She snapped on the fuel valve and masters, started the pumps, and powered up the engines. The down-thrusters began kicking up dust from the ground.

Outside the cockpit, she could see Helo hobbling, still holding his sidearm, driving the crowd away from the ship. *You're leaving your best friend to die.* Tears began streaming down her face, and she had to look away. *Just do your job.* She focused on the flight controls, and drew a deep breath. Applying power, she began lifting the Raptor from the ground. It strained, with the full load of passengers.

At the edge of the crowd, a man suddenly broke free and ran to the ship and threw himself onto the side platform. Sharon felt the Raptor lean a little, and compensated with the thruster control. She saw Helo turn and point his weapon at the man. Helo shouted something, inaudible to Sharon – then fired his gun. There was a flare, and the man spun, falling from the side of the ship. Relieved and horrified at the same time, Sharon applied more thrust. The ship rose more quickly.

From the swirling cloud of dust, Helo looked up at Sharon and raised a hand in farewell. She pressed her own hand to the windshield. *Good-bye, Helo.*

Then she pushed the throttle forward, and the Raptor lifted quickly away from the hillside and began its climb back into the skies of Caprica and the deep darkness of space.

CHAPTER

26

In the cockpit of the transport Laura Roslin and Captain Lee Adama listened, riveted, as the wireless broadcast replayed. Captain Russo reached above his head to fine-tune the signal. Out the window was darkness, and the stars, and the distant orb of Caprica.

'*This is an official Colonial government broadcast. All ministers and officials should now go to Case Orange. Repeat: This is an official Colonial government broadcast. All ministers and officials should now go to Case Orange.*'

There was a sharp intake of breath from Laura. Lee and the two transport pilots turned to her, as she struggled to maintain her composure. Sitting on a jump seat behind the copilot, she still had the blanket wrapped around her shoulders; she looked worn and very tired. 'It's an auto-mated message,' she said, answering their unspoken ques-tion with a low, even voice. 'It's designed to be sent out in case the president, the vice president, and most of the cabinet are dead or incapacitated.'

Lee stared at her, stunned.

Laura, however tired or overwhelmed she might have felt, continued without missing a beat. To Russo she said,

'I need you,' and she paused for a heartbeat, 'to send my ID code back on the exact same frequency.'

Russo barely managed to voice his response. 'Yes, ma'am.'

'D as in dog, dash—'

As she recited the code, Captain Russo punched the keys on the comm unit.

'—four-five-six, dash, three-four-five, dash, A as in apple.' Laura swallowed. 'Thank you.'

Lee followed her with his gaze as she got up and left the cockpit.

After a minute, he left the cockpit himself and walked slowly back through the cabin. It was an eerie sensation. It was like being on any passenger liner, in the quiet of night, except that this passenger liner was witnessing the end of the world as they knew it. He walked until he found the row where Laura was sitting, alone, in a backward-facing leather seat. Out the window, the universe seemed eternal and changeless. *Eternal maybe; but not changeless.* Lee took the position facing her, and sat on the edge of the seat, resting his hands between his knees. He took a deep breath, and let it out, meeting her gaze as she opened her eyes. Her sense of shock was almost physical, surrounding her like an aura.

He gathered his thoughts for a moment, then asked, 'How far down?'

She answered quietly. 'Forty-third in line of succession. I know all forty-two ahead of me, from the president down. Most of us served with him in the first administration.' Resting her head back, she seemed to leave the hopeless present for a moment. 'Some of them came with him from the mayor's office. I was there with him on his first campaign.' She wrinkled her nose. 'I never really liked politics. I kept telling myself I was getting out, but . . . he had this way about him.'

Lee smiled faintly. He wasn't sure why, but he felt humbled that she would be confiding in him.

'I just couldn't say no,' Laura concluded with a pained chuckle. She shifted her eyes to look up at Captain Russo, who had just appeared, bearing a printout. He handed the octagonal piece of paper to her without a word. She looked at it, nodded, and handed it back to him. 'Thank you,' she whispered.

She pulled the blanket off her shoulders and began putting her wine-red jacket on. Lee followed her movements with narrowed eyes as she said to Russo, 'We'll need a priest.'

Elosha, the priest who had officiated at the decommissioning ceremony, was among those passengers returning – as they had once thought – to Caprica. She stood in the center of a small knot of news reporters, who were also among those returning from their coverage of what had seemed a soft news story, the transformation of a fabled fighting ship into a museum. Now they had their cameras and microphones trained on Elosha and Laura Roslin, to witness the transfer of presidential power.

Elosha was a handsome, dark-skinned woman of about forty, wearing a deep blue dress and a matching blue headband. She held one of the sacred scrolls in her hands, and pulled it open. Soberly, she said, 'Please raise your right hand and repeat after me . . .'

Laura raised her hand, with a great sense of weight and sadness. Lee Adama stood just behind her, to her right, watching with what she suspected was disbelief. Billy stood behind her, to her left, lending silent support, as did Captain Russo, behind Elosha. Aaron Doral was a frowning presence, several layers of people back.

'I, Laura Roslin . . .'

She echoed, her voice quavering, 'I . . . Laura Roslin . . .'

'. . . do now avow and affirm . . .'

Her voice steadied a little, as she repeated the words.

'. . . that I take the office of the President of the Twelve Colonies of Kobol . . .'

'. . . that I accept the office of th—' Her voice broke on that, and she had to stop and gather herself again. 'That I accept the office of the President of the Twelve Colonies of Kobol . . .' and she continued, following Elosha, 'and that I will protect and defend the sovereignty of the Colonies . . . with every fiber of my being.' Her voice strained on those last words, as the weight of the responsibility she was taking on hit her like a mountain avalanche.

She paused, waiting for Elosha to offer the concluding words. She pushed her hair back nervously with her raised hand, and glanced momentarily at Lee Adama. Did she have his support? She thought she did. He seemed solid, intelligent, capable, and uneager for personal power. She wanted to trust him, and she prayed that there were more like him. She was going to need all the help she could get from people like that. They all were going to need help. From the Lords of Kobol, and from each other.

CHAPTER
27

GALACTICA, FIRE-GUTTED HOLDS OF DECK D

Chief Tyrol could barely keep his emotions in check as he watched the men carry out the bodies of the dead, and begin the cleanup of the devastated compartments. The stink of smoke and death filled the air. Tyrol's stomach was churning. He couldn't have said which was the target of his worst fury – the Cylons or the XO. Those people who were being carried out were all good men and women; many of them were his personal friends. None of them deserved to die. They had put their lives on the line freely – but to what purpose? So that the XO could snuff them like so many candles? *We could have gotten them out! It didn't have to be this way!*

In the CIC, Commander Adama stood under the main bank of monitors, listening to the XO's report. He had a lot of information on the pieces of paper spread out on the planning table, but he wanted to hear it directly from Tigh. The bottom line was that the ship was safe – for now. Hull breaches were being repaired, buckled supports could be straightened or replaced, and the landing bay would soon be able to receive the returning Vipers.

What he hadn't heard yet was the cost in human life. He put on his glasses. 'What was the final count?'

'Twenty-six walked out,' Tigh said grimly. 'Eighty-five didn't.' And that didn't include the three Viper pilots lost in this battle – or the CAG's entire squadron wiped out before it could return to them. Tigh took a breath and, hefting the munitions-supply notebook, continued, 'There's a munitions depot in the Ragnar Anchorage.'

Ragnar. Deep in a storm cell in the atmosphere of a gas giant planet. 'Boy, it's a super-bitch to anchor a ship there,' Adama said.

Tigh was undeterred. 'Well, the book says that there are fifty pallets of class-D warheads in storage there. They should also have all the missiles and small-arms munitions we nee—'

'Go verify that.'

Tigh straightened. 'Sir.' He handed the munitions-supply book to Adama and strode away.

If we can verify anything it'll be a miracle, Adama thought, hefting the book in his hand. *But a miracle is just what we need. That and some ammunition.*

Tyrol continued his walk-through, knowing that he probably hadn't seen the worst yet. He was right. It was confirmed when he stepped through a bulkhead door and found Specialist Cally in her yellow fire-fighting suit, slumped against a wall, cradling Specialist Prosna's burned and blackened body. She was weeping, unable to speak, Tyrol didn't try to speak to her, didn't know what to say. Cally and Prosna, besides being his two best crewmembers and friends, had been a close-knit couple. He knelt in front of her, laying a hand on her arm, trying to give comfort where none could be given.

Cally looked at him beseechingly, for just one moment her eyes asking him to make it different somehow. In that moment, his thoughts fled to the other battle, the one none of them had seen, but had only heard through Sharon's garbled transmission: an entire Viper squadron destroyed. And then the ominous silence following Sharon's report that she too was under attack. He held no hope for changing that outcome *or* this one.

Finally, he lifted Prosna's lifeless weight from Cally, and let her get to her feet. Weeping with nearly silent shudders, Cally helped him lower Prosna to the deck and lay him straight. There he would have to lie, until the stretcher teams came to remove him with the rest of the fallen.

Tyrol gave her shoulder a tight squeeze, then urged her out with him. She needed to be somewhere else, and he needed to make his report to Commander Adama.

Tyrol's voice was hoarse as he said to the commander, 'Do you know how many we lost?'

Adama's response was abrupt. 'Yes.' No emotion showed on his face, as he studied the planetary maps laid out on the strategy table. 'Set up a temporary morgue in Hangar Bay B.'

Tyrol stood trembling, trying to form the words of protest. Finally he managed, 'Forty seconds . . . sir. All I needed was . . . forty seconds.' He drew a ragged breath. 'Eighty-five of my . . . people . . . and I told . . .' He swallowed and tried to control himself but couldn't. 'I told that sonofabitch . . .'

Adama swung around to face him straight on, eye to eye. In a low, iron-hard voice he said, 'He's the XO on this ship. Don't you dare forget that.'

Trembling, Tyrol nodded.

Adama continued, his voice low and hard. 'Now, he made a tough decision. Had it been me, we would have made the same one.'

Tyrol struggled to keep from shaking. In a near-whisper, he implored, 'Forty seconds . . . sir.'

Adama held his gaze a heartbeat longer. 'Resume your post, Chief,' he said, and walked past Tyrol and on across the CIC.

Tyrol stood in shocked disbelief for a fraction of a second, then strode away to return to the cleanup. On his way out of the CIC, he passed Colonel Tigh just entering. He swerved around him with a dark, silent look and hurried on to make himself as busy as possible.

Adama watched as Tyrol departed. Sympathy would have to wait. They had something more important to worry about, which was defending their civilization against catastrophe. He needed Chief Tyrol as much as he needed Tigh, and he had confidence in the man – hell, he had brought Tyrol onto the ship at a time when no other skipper would, because of a single mistake in the past that had cost lives. He'd brought him aboard because Tyrol was the best spacecraft mechanic he had ever met, and a good leader. But right now there was no room for anything but absolute respect for authority. Saul Tigh was facing a similar test – and appeared to be passing it.

Tigh was standing across the table from him, giving him the latest information. Adama brought his attention back. 'Munitions depot confirmed, but we have two problems,' Tigh said. 'One, the Ragnar station is at least three days away at best speed. Two, the entire Cylon fleet is between here and there.' Tigh shook his head.

Adama absorbed that for a moment, then called out into the quietly bustling center, 'Specialist!'

'Sir,' answered the voice of Navigation Specialist Johnson, behind him.

'Bring me our position.'

'Yes sir.' Johnson appeared at his side, laying a sheet of paper in front of him.

Adama picked it up and studied it. Across the table, Tigh was eyeing him, and starting to shake his head. He had guessed what Adama was thinking. 'You don't want to do this,' Tigh said.

'I know I don't.'

'Because any sane man wouldn't. It's been, what – twenty, twenty-two years?'

Adama placed the piece of paper on top of the chart, studying the figures. 'We train for this,' he said without looking up.

'Training is one thing,' Tigh said, leaning over the table toward him, and continuing in a low voice, 'but . . . if we're off on our calculations by even a few degrees, we could end up in the *middle of the sun*!'

Adama finally looked up. 'No choice. Colonel Tigh, please plot a hyperlight Jump from our position to the orbit of Ragnar.'

Tigh capitulated, but not happily. 'Yes sir.' And he moved off to plot the Jump. Adama watched him, with a twitch of a smile.

No sooner was Tigh gone than Petty Officer Dualla was at his side, delivering yet another printout. Her eyes were wide, her face tense, her usually melodic voice hoarse. 'Priority message, sir.' She stood at attention, waiting, as he read it. *Lords of Kobol*. He felt the blood drain from his face. He pulled off his glasses, working through the implications in his mind.

At another station, he could hear the XO giving orders, 'Engineering – spin up FTL drives one and two.' As the engineering officer acknowledged, Colonel Tigh continued, 'Lieutenant Gaeta, break out the FTL tables and warm up the computers.' To the CIC at large, he announced, 'We are making a Jump!'

The crew had barely begun to absorb that when Adama raised his voice to make his own announcement. 'Admiral Nagala is dead. Battlestar *Atlantia* has been destroyed. So has the *Triton, Solaria, Columbia* . . . the list goes on.' He lowered his head.

Tigh walked toward him. 'The senior officer. Who's in command?'

By way of answering, Adama turned to Dualla. 'Send a message . . . to all the Colonial military units, Priority Channel One.' Dualla wrote on a clipboard. 'Message begins: Am taking command of fleet . . .'

CHAPTER
28

COLONIAL ONE

President Laura Roslin peered over Captain Russo's shoulder as he called, 'Geminon liner Seventeen-Oh-One, this is Colonial Heavy Seven-Niner-Eight.' Captain Russo looked back over his shoulder at the newly sworn-in president and amended his call. 'No, strike that. This is Colonial One.' Laura registered that with a slightly stunned expression. Clearly, this was going to take some getting used to.

'*Go ahead, Colonial One.*'

'We have you in sight, and will approach your starboard docking hatch.'

'*Copy, Colonial One. Thank the Lords of Kobol you're here. We've been without main power for over two hours now.*'

Lee Adama, meanwhile, was bent over the secure message console, watching something come in. He tore it off and read it silently. He pursed his lips thoughtfully.

'What is it?' Laura asked.

Lee held it out and read dryly, 'To all Colonial Units, am taking command of fleet. All units ordered to rendezvous at Ragnar Anchorage for a regroup and counterattack. Acknowledge by same encryption protocol.' Lee hesitated, mouth half open, then concluded, 'Adama.'

Laura pulled the printout from his hand and looked at it soberly. She thought a moment, then lifted her chin and turned to Lee. 'Captain Apollo. Please inform Commander Adama that we are involved in rescue operations and we require his assistance.' She felt a smile twitching on her lips. This was going to be interesting. Would he obey his new commander-in-chief? 'Ask him how many hospital beds they have available, and how long it will take him to get here.'

Lee looked stunned once more. 'I, uh—'

'Yes,' she said.

After taking a long time to consider her words, Lee said, 'I'm not sure he's going to respond very well to that request.' A smile touched his lips, too, matching hers.

'Then tell him,' she said, 'it comes directly from the President of the Twelve Colonies, and it's not a request.' She let her voice sharpen ever so slightly on the last words.

The two transport pilots swiveled their heads in surprise, then went studiously right back to what they were doing.

'Yes sir,' said Lee. As she started to leave the cockpit, he continued, 'And sir?' She paused to listen. 'Apollo's just my call sign. My name's Lee Adama.'

'I know who you are.' She smiled, this time letting a moment of genuine warmth come through. 'But Captain Apollo has a nice ring to it, don't you think?' Without waiting for an answer, she headed back to the passenger cabin.

GALACTICA, COMBAT INFORMATION CENTER

Throughout the CIC, tension was growing as the enlisted crew ran through checklists and startup procedures for the FTL Jump, with Gaeta and Tigh overseeing their work. Commander Adama was sidetracked from his study of the planetary and tactical charts by Petty Officer Dualla handing him a printout. 'It's from Colonial One, sir,' she said.

'Colonial One? What the hell ship is Colonial One? The president's dead, isn't he?'

'Yes sir,' said Dualla evenly. 'The new president, by succession, is former Education Secretary Laura Roslin. That's the first part of the message.'

'The first part? What's the second part?' Adama put his glasses back on and read the printout. He squinted at the message in disbelief, and as he reread it, his jaw tightened with anger. 'Is this a *joke*?' He looked at Dualla. 'Are they within voice range?'

'Yes sir,' said Dualla. She already had her headset on, and she sidled around a corner of the console to the transmission panel. 'Colonial One, this is *Galactica* . . .'

Lee Adama was sitting in the copilot's seat in the transport cockpit, awaiting the call from *Galactica*. He knew it wouldn't take long. Of all the conversations in the universe he could imagine, this was probably the one he least wanted to have. The thought of it was crowding all other thoughts from his mind, including ones that kept *trying* to come back, such as, were all his friends on Caprica dead now, and what about his mother and her fiancé? These things weighed heavily on the back of his mind – and yet, the scratchy voice on the wireless drove them once more out of his thoughts.

'*Colonial One*, Galactica . . . Galactica *Actual wishes to speak with Apollo*.'

He had to struggle to get his breath. What was his father going to say? As if he didn't know. 'This is Apollo.

Go ahead, Actual.' He pursed his lips and waited for a reply.

It was a minute or so in coming. Captain Russo fiddled with the wireless tuning, as if worried that they were missing the signal. Finally they heard Commander Adama's voice:

'*How are you*' – they could hear the commander clearing his throat – '*is the ship all right?*'

Lee could not keep the sarcasm out of his voice. 'We're both fine. Thanks for asking.' Captain Russo glanced over at him, but said nothing.

'*Is your ship's FTL functioning?*'

Lee glanced at Russo, who nodded. 'That's affirmative.'

'*Then you're ordered to bring yourself . . . and all your ship's passengers . . . to the rendezvous point.*' Pause. '*Acknowledge.*'

Lee hesitated. 'Acknowledge . . . receipt of message.'

'*What the hell does that mean?*' the distant voice thundered.

'It means, "I heard you," ' Lee said impatiently.

His father's voice sharpened. '*You're going to have to do a lot better than that, Captain.*'

'We're engaged in rescue operations. By order of the president.' *Your commander-in-chief.*

'*You are to abort your mission immediately.*'

Lee winced. 'The president has given me a direct order.'

'*You're talking about the secretary of education. We're in the middle of a war! And you're taking orders from a schoolteacher!*' Adama's voice shook the little wireless speaker; his anger practically jumped out into the cockpit of the transport.

Lee was aware of the president coming back into the cockpit, and listening to the conversation. But before he could either gauge her reaction or reply to his father, a beeping sound from the dradis display interrupted the argument.

'We've got trouble,' Captain Russo said.

'Uh, stand by, *Galactica*.' He leaned toward Captain Russo. 'What?'

Russo tapped the dradis screen. 'Inbound Cylon fighters.' He reached and pressed a series of switches. 'Spinning up FTL. We have no defense against the fighters. Eduardo, give me a plot.'

At that, President Laura Roslin came forward, putting her glasses on. 'How long till they get here?'

Russo looked startled at her reappearance. 'ETA, two minutes.'

'He's right,' said Lee. 'We have to go. Now.'

'No,' said Laura, shaking her head.

'Madame President, we can't defend this ship—'

'We're not going to abandon all these people.'

'But sir – if we stay—'

'I've made my decision, Captain.' She spoke clearly and unemotionally, her eyes focused outside the cockpit, searching for the Cylons.

He stared at her in disbelief for a moment. She was as pig-headed and irrational as his father. 'You're the president,' he said, peeling off his headset and climbing out of his seat to squeeze past her.

She looked startled at his sudden departure. Eduardo moved quickly from the jump seat back into the copilot's seat. 'All right, then,' she said.

'Permission to go below?' Lee asked, on his way out. He didn't wait for an answer. He had less than two minutes to act before the Cylons would destroy them. She might think that he was jumping to his Viper – probably even hoping that – but he had another idea. A ridiculously long shot, but what other choice did they have?

He made his way at a run, down to the cargo deck. He had seen a small control panel down there . . .

In the CIC, an enlisted man darted from the remote sensor console over to where Lieutenant Gaeta was working on the FTL solution. After a hurried conference, Gaeta darted just as quickly to Commander Adama's side. Tigh followed his movement with concern. 'Sir,' said Gaeta, 'we have remote Sensor telemetry from Captain Apollo's position, and two enemy fighters are closing in on her port . . .'

Oh frak no. Adama grabbed the headset he had torn off in disgust a minute ago, and tried to reach Colonial One. 'Colonial One – this is *Galactica*! Apollo – you have inbound enemy fighters coming toward you! Get out of there! *Apollo! Lee – get – Lee—!*'

The bloom on the dradis screen told him he was too late.

In the cockpit of the transport, Laura saw and *felt* a blinding blast that hurled her against the back door of the compartment and took the world away.

In the CIC, the dradis display flickered, sorting through static, then went clear, showing no signal returns from the area where a minute ago there had been two civilian craft and two hostiles. Then the screen went dark, as the remote sensors were caught by the blast. They were all gone. Sensors, ships, everything.

Adama watched in disbelief, and finally bowed his head. He could say nothing. He could only fight to keep the pain from showing on his face. *Lee. Gone. Why? Why Lee?* He stood that way for a very long time.

Finally he heard Gaeta's voice through the inner static of the pain: 'Estimate a fifty-kiloton thermonuclear detonation.'

Nuke. Fusion bomb. Your only hope was to Jump out of there. Why didn't you? Adama's face creased with pain. But he could not, dared not, show any more emotion in front of the crew. Not now.

Gaeta's voice continued, 'Cylons moving off. Sir.'

Around him, everyone was silent. Everyone wishing they could help, wishing they could change it, wishing they could just say something. Eventually Tigh came up behind him and rested his hands on Adama's shoulders. And stood with him. Just stood.

The others slowly returned to their posts.

Adama, bracing himself on the plotting table, forced out the words, in a low, tortured voice: 'Resume . . . Jump . . . prep . . .'

As everyone moved, slowly, Tigh raised his voice and snapped the command: 'Resume Jump prep!'

Soon the attention-tone sounded, and Dualla's voice echoed throughout the ship. 'Attention all hands. Jump prep underway. Set Condition Two throughout the ship. Set Condition Two throughout the ship.'

Chief Tyrol watched on a monitor, holding his breath, as the last of the Vipers came in for a landing. There was no way this could be an easy landing, not with all the buckling in the landing bay caused by the nuke. But this particular approach was heart-stopping; it was Starbuck, and her ship was not controlling properly in slow flight. She was yawing wildly, nearly hitting the side of the bay. It bounced and skidded as she hit the deck. Finally the Viper came to a stop on top of the hangar elevator, and Tyrol's crew wasted no time bringing it down for servicing.

When Tyrol got a close look at the condition of the fighter, he was beside himself. 'Lieutenant! What did you do to my Viper?'

Starbuck was just coming down from the cockpit, yanking her flight-suit jacket open. She looked exhausted; her flight-suit was soaked with sweat; her face was an angry scowl. Squinting up at the tail section of the Viper, she saw what the chief was so upset about. 'I wondered why the engine gave out,' she said matter-of-factly. A big chunk had been torn out of engine number one, the topmost engine in the cluster, and along with it a good part of the vertical stabilizer. It was a miracle she and the whole craft weren't a cinder now.

Chief Tyrol circled around behind. 'We're gonna have to pull the whole mounting. Get the high-lift.' He stepped up to Lieutenant Thrace. 'How did you manage to even fly this thing, much less land it?'

She seemed to be getting angrier by the moment. She yanked off her gloves. 'That's not something I want to think about right now. Where's Prosna? He has to get that frakking gimbal locked, or I'll have his ass.'

Chief Tyrol looked at her. 'He's dead . . . sir. He died in the fire.'

Suddenly she was a lot less like 'Starbuck' and more like a stunned Kara Thrace. 'How many did we lose?'

'Eighty-five.'

Kara absorbed that shocking figure for a second, and her face narrowed and seemed to harden. 'Right.' She turned and strode away.

'Oh, Lieutenant,' Tyrol called.

She turned darkly.

With difficulty, Tyrol said, 'I don't know if you heard about Apollo, but—'

She looked completely defeated. 'What?'

He couldn't say it. He could only look down, imagining how the Old Man must be feeling right now. His last son . . .

She suddenly got it. The blow, oddly, made her stand a little straighter, as though in defiance against the stream of bad news. 'Right,' she said. Swallowing, she began again to leave, then once more turned back. 'Any word on Sharon?'

This time it was Tyrol who felt utterly defeated. He knew the score, even if no one was willing to say it. 'No, sir,' he said, looking up to examine the tail section of another Viper.

Kara hesitated, nodded, then headed off to the ward-room.

Tyrol suddenly felt paralyzed, surrounded by people, machines, things that urgently needed to be done. He could barely stand up straight, much less lead the crew. Specialist Cally, who had observed the exchange, stepped closer. 'You okay, Chief?' she asked in a strained voice. She had only just hauled herself back together, after losing Prosna.

Tyrol couldn't answer. *No, I'm not okay. Neither are you. None of us is.* Finally he found his voice enough to whisper, 'Get back to work.' And he turned and walked quickly away.

CHAPTER
29

Sharon Valerii, too, seemed less like a 'Boomer' just now and more like a sorrow-weary young pilot. In order to conserve fuel and avoid attracting unwanted attention, she had cut propulsion once she'd achieved a transitional high orbit from which escape velocity was just a short burn away. There was little flying to do at the moment, but she couldn't help fiddling and checking.

When a scan of the area revealed no Cylons nearby, she decided to risk launching a communications drone. The ten-year-old boy she'd brought aboard was still sitting in the right-hand seat, watching her every move. Her hand on the launch button, she counted down, 'Three . . . two . . . one . . . launch.'

There was a little shudder through the deck, and a momentary flash of light as the drone streaked out from the bottom of the hull and twinkled off into space. 'Drone deployed . . . and transmitting,' she said to the boy, watching the drone's stats.

'Now they'll come find us?' he asked in a small voice.

'Hard to say. There's a lot of interference around here,' she said, lifting her voice a little to sound more optimistic than she felt. 'A lot of noise. It keeps my wireless from

177

working.' She fiddled with the electronic controls, then added, 'Hopefully, once that communications pod I launched gets far enough away from here, a Colonial ship will pick up the signal and start looking for us.'

The boy was silent for a bit. Then he asked, 'Is everyone on Caprica dead?' He looked at her with imploring eyes, asking to be corrected.

'I don't know,' Sharon admitted, in a muted voice. A lump swelled in her throat as she thought about Helo.

The boy seemed to accept that. 'My dad's in the Colonial fleet,' he said. 'His name's Colonel Wakefield. Maybe you know him?'

Sharon hesitated a moment, then shook her head.

'He's a diplomat. He goes sometimes to that station where the Cylons are supposed to meet us.' The boy looked very thoughtful, very vulnerable. 'They never did, though – did you know that?'

Sharon nodded.

'They told me he's missing. But I think he's dead, too.'

Sharon smiled briefly, despite the sharp pang the boy's words gave her. 'What's your name?'

'Boxey,' he said matter-of-factly.

She nodded, offering him another tiny smile. 'You know something? Both my parents died when I was little, too.' Another pang, as that memory resurfaced for the second time today. The terrible accident on the mining colony of Troy, which had destroyed the dome that was the only thing keeping two hundred thousand people safe from Troy's toxic atmosphere. They had all died, including her parents. Sharon had survived only because she was away at the time, en route to Caprica and her admissions interview at the Colonial Academy.

'Where do you live now?' he asked.

With an effort, she shook off the memory. 'With a bunch of other people on a ship called *Galactica.*'

'Isn't that a battlestar?'

'That's right,' Sharon said. She thought a moment. 'Hey, I have an idea. Maybe you could live there, too . . .'

In the rear compartment of the Raptor, Gaius Baltar sat huddled with all the other refugee passengers. He was cold, miserable, and lonely. He had never felt so alone in his entire life. No one was speaking. He could hear nothing except the throb of pumps and the hum of equipment in the compartment surrounding him. Until . . .

'You know what I love about you, Gaius?'

The voice was familiar; so familiar, for a moment he thought it was right inside his head. He looked up and started to look around – until he froze at the sight of Natasi, seated directly across from him, wearing that red, low-cut spaghetti-strap number that drove him wild with lust.

'You're a survivor,' she said softly, huskily, leaning forward until he could feel her breath.

Natasi? Here? No, that's not—

He blinked and averted his gaze for a moment, shaking his head like a dog. None of the other passengers seemed to have noticed. They were all sitting, huddled as he was, in a state of shock. The nearest one was the old woman he had helped to get on board. He shifted his gaze back to Natasi. But there was no one there. Just the old woman, and the others. *Not real. I'm hallucinating.*

But it sure had seemed real – Natasi had looked as real as—

He suddenly came down hard on his own thought. *No, it was not Natasi. Even Natasi was not Natasi – she was a frakking Cylon. Model number six of twelve models.* He began to tremble, thinking about it. *Model number six. Maybe that's what I should have called her: Number Six, She didn't deserve a real name.*

The old woman was looking at him curiously now, and that's when he realized he'd been starting to talk to himself. He managed a slight, tortured smile, rubbed his stubble-covered chin. And turned his thoughts back to the inside, back to where someone was trying to drive him mad . . .

CHAPTER
30

GALACTICA

The ship was closing up as though readying itself to spin a cocoon. All the Viper patrols had returned, and the launch bay and landing bay doors rumbled closed and locked into place. In the engineering bowels of the ship, great gears and magnetic sequencers ground into action, and the entire port and starboard launch pods began to retract into the great hull of the ship. The entire procedure took ten minutes and forty-three seconds. When they were finished, *Galactica* looked noticeably leaner.

In the CIC, the Executive Officer was going around the horn with final checks: 'Nav?'

'Go.'

'FTL?'

'Go.'

'Tactical?'

'Go.'

'Flight ops?'

'Go.'

'Sublight?'

'Go.'

'Helm?'

'Go.'

Satisfied, Colonel Tigh spoke this time to Commander Adama. 'The board is green, ship reports ready to Jump, sir.'

Adama was standing at the plotting table, glasses on, mood subdued. He was showing no emotion, no sign of the blow he had just suffered. He spoke without wasting a single word: 'Take us to Ragnar.'

Colonel Tigh turned toward the FTL console. 'Lieutenant Gaeta, execute the Jump.'

The attention-tone sounded as Gaeta spoke into the shipboard PA. 'All decks prepare for immediate FTL Jump.' Gaeta reached down to the FTL console, gripped the handle of the FTL safety interlock, and pulled it out of its repository. On the end of the chrome handle were two long, bright-glowing blue crystals. He lifted it clear of the Safety slot and inserted it carefully into the Jump slot. Once it was in place, he twisted it firmly ninety degrees to the right. The mechanism clicked into place, and several lights came on across the board.

Gaeta spoke into the PA again. 'The clock is running. Jump in ten . . . nine . . . eight . . .'

On the hangar deck, everyone was scrambling to find a seat for the Jump – not because the transition would be bumpy or jerky, but because it could be so disorienting. Chief Tyrol clapped his hands, trying to get everyone moving. Specialist Cally sat uneasily on a toolbox right next to the nose of a Viper. She winced with each second of the countdown. As the count reached two, she murmured to anyone listening, 'I hate this part!'

No one answered; no one needed to.

*

In the CIC, Adama and Colonel Tigh stood ramrod straight, facing each other across the plotting table.

As Gaeta's count reached zero, the room surrounding them seemed to flex, all the angles changing at once, like a four-sided prism distorting and flattening, and finally folding in upon itself. The moment itself seemed to stretch out, as the fabric of space-time bent and folded . . .

If an outside eye had been looking closely and quickly enough, it might have seen the ship twisting in upon itself, for a fraction of an instant – before it vanished with a diamond flash . . .

And half a solar system away, it reappeared in the same way, and unfolded into the sky above the gas giant planet of Ragnar. Directly below, in the upper atmosphere of the planet, was the whirlpool of a massive storm, a reddish-tinged mark against the dreary olive green of the rest of the clouds.

Adama looked around at the monitors, but the information he needed was not there. 'Report,' he called quietly.

Gaeta ran quickly from the FTL console to the nav, where he worked with the nav officer. 'Taking a bearing now.' Frowning at the readouts, he finally straightened. His face was sober, but by the time he had finished delivering his report, he was grinning. 'We appear to be in synchronous orbit, directly above the Ragnar Anchorage.'

Shouts and hand-clapping broke out around the CIC.

Gaeta raised a hand in salute, and reached out to shake the hands of his nearest fellow officers.

At the plotting table, Adama actually smiled. *Unbelievable.* He glanced at his XO. 'The old girl's got some life in her still.'

Tigh laughed briefly. 'I never doubted it for a moment.'

Nodding, Adama called out, 'Lieutenant Gaeta – secure the FTL drive and bring the sublight engines to full power.' He turned back to his XO. 'Colonel Tigh—'

'Sir.'

'Let's update your chart for a course . . . right down into the eye of the storm.'

'Yes, sir.'

As Tigh began happily rearranging the transparent charts on the plotting table, the voice on the PA called: 'Attention, Magazine Safety Officers, report to the CIC . . .'

Preparations were underway for the rearming of *Galactica.*

In her bunkroom, Kara Thrace was finally getting out of her flight-suit, and trying not to come unglued at the news of the shocking losses of this very young war. Most especially, the loss of Lee Adama. It was like being hit with Zak's death all over again. As she opened her locker, revealing a small mirror on the inside of the locker door, her gaze fell on a photo she'd kept stuck in the mirror's frame – a photo of herself with Zak, laughing and hugging, taken just a couple of weeks before Zak's death. Though he was a shy man, laughing was always easy for Zak to do; he had eyes that just naturally seemed joyous, full of life. It was one of the reasons she loved him.

Kara let out a long breath. She stretched the picture out

to its full original length, revealing the third person who had been folded out of view: Lee Adama, the serious one, the born pilot and ace student. For all their bickering, she'd loved Lee like the brother he'd almost become to her, and maybe a little more. The ache this picture produced in her heart was doubled, now.

Blinking back tears, she gazed at the picture, blurry to her now, and murmured softly, 'Lords of Kobol, hear my prayer. Take the souls of your sons and daughters lost this day . . .' She paused, swallowing back the lump in her throat, and continued, '. . . especially that of Lee Adama, into your hands . . .'

Hangar Bay B was a quiet place now, and somber. The bodies of sixty-some fallen crewmembers were stretched out in neat rows on the floor, zipped into ticketed white body bags. They weren't all there, of course; many had not been recovered – the pilots lost in battle, and the crewmen swept out into space during the emergency vent. But those who were here served as a sobering reminder of the price this ship, this crew, had paid already.

Launch Officer Kelly walked down the rows, carrying a fistful of dog tags, a grave expression on his face. He had not forgotten, nor would he ever forget, that many of those lying here might yet be alive if the XO and Chief Tyrol – and he – had not killed eighty-five people in the process of saving the ship. The fact that it was necessary did not take away the burning pain and anger.

More victims were being carried in past him. And he was certain this was not the end. He hoped there would be enough room in here for all those who would die before it was over.

CHAPTER
31

COLONIAL ONE

President Laura Roslin came to, groggily, and pushed herself painfully to a sitting position. *Where am I?* It took a moment to realize that she'd been sprawled on the deck of the cockpit. The two pilots were in their seats shaking their heads and rubbing their necks – they must have blacked out, as well. Power was just coming back on, the console lights flickering to life. *What the devil just happened? Two Cylon missiles coming at us . . .* She last remembered having about three seconds left to live – three seconds to regret her foolish stubbornness in forbidding a Jump to safety. *Because of the other ship. We would have left them to die. Instead, I stupidly decided we should all die. . .*

Except they hadn't.

'Captain Russo,' she said, struggling to her feet, her voice a raspy croak. 'Why are we still here?' She steadied herself on the back of the pilot's seat, squinting over Captain Russo's shoulder.

The captain's voice wasn't much stronger than hers. 'I'm not sure. I think the missiles' warheads went off prematurely. Maybe Captain Adama can explain. Do you know where he—?'

Laura suddenly remembered. 'He said he was heading below. You don't suppose—'

Russo cast a sharp glance over his shoulder. 'We'd better get down there. Eduardo, you have the controls.'

Racing down the staircase to the cargo deck, Laura was first to see Lee Adama sprawled on the deck unconscious, near some very large coils that had been offloaded from *Galactica*. Captain Russo grabbed a first-aid kit and was right behind her as she ran to Lee and crouched at his side. 'Captain Apollo!'

He stirred and blinked his eyes open. With Captain Russo helping from the opposite side, she brought him to a sitting position. Lee's eyes slowly came back into focus. 'That was fun,' he croaked.

Laura and Russo looked at each other, and suddenly began laughing, even though they had no idea what they were laughing about.

'I think it worked,' Lee said woozily, as he struggled to get up.

'What exactly did you *do*?' Laura asked.

Blinking, he said, 'I basically just used . . . the energy coils to manipulate the p-power of the hyper-drive.' Breathing hard, he continued, 'Captain, you . . . spun up the hyperdrive . . . before the president ordered you to stay. I used the coils to h-harness that energy and p-p' – he struggled to speak – 'put out a big pulse of electro . . . mag-magnetic energy that must have . . . disabled the warheads. Ohhhh—' He started to collapse, but Laura and Russo caught him and supported him until he could stand again. 'I'm – I'm hoping – that it looked like a nuclear explosion.'

Laura's heart leaped. 'So that's what that was!' She felt

hope for the first time in what seemed like a very long while.

He nodded. 'So, uh—'

'Will it fool the Cylons?'

His face darkened. 'I don't know. But, if – if they weren't fooled, then they'd be on top of us by now.'

Laura involuntarily looked up, as though she might see through the walls and the hull, to confirm that there were no Cylons on top of them.

Captain Russo spoke for the first time. 'Does the rest of the fleet know about this trick?'

Lee grimaced. 'I doubt it. It was just a theory we toyed with at war college, but' – he shook his head – 'it never used to work during war games. In the simulations, the Cylons would see right through it and destroy their targets anyway.' He chuckled painfully.

Laura absorbed that for a moment. 'The lesson here,' she said with a glance at Captain Russo, 'is not to ask follow-up questions, but to say, *thank* you, Captain Apollo, for saving our collective *asses*.'

Lee nodded and grinned. 'You're welcome.'

'I'll thank you, too,' said Captain Russo. 'And now, I'd better get back to the cockpit and check on the other ship.'

As they made their way back toward the staircase Lee began, 'Now, if I could suggest—'

'Evacuate the passenger liner,' Laura interrupted, 'and get the hell out of here before the Cylons realize their mistake? I'm right with you, Captain.'

Lee chuckled, falling back to let her go up the stairs ahead of him.

As she climbed the stairs, though, Laura's thoughts were very much on the need for tough choices ahead. She'd *thought* she was being tough by determining to stand by the passenger liner when the Cylon appeared. But only luck, providence, and the ingenuity of Captain Apollo had saved them. She had to assume that next time they would not be so fortunate.

CHAPTER
32

GALACTICA, AT RAGNAR

The great ship was gliding slowly down toward the dark immensity of the Ragnar atmospheric storm. It was harder than it looked: Bringing a ship down from synchronous orbit to the point directly below it was not like riding an elevator. It required careful orbital calculations, precise application of power, and a fair amount of brute force if you were in a hurry. *Galactica* was in a hurry.

In the CIC, Colonel Tigh was calling out instructions: 'Five seconds to turn three.'

'Five seconds, aye, sir,' answered Gaeta.

'And turn.'

Gaeta took over: 'Bow pitch positive one-half. Stern pitch negative one-quarter. Bow yaw negative three-quarters . . .'

They were in the outer atmosphere now, dropping closer and closer to the swirling storm.

'Passing into the ionosphere,' Petty Officer Dualla called, relaying the latest readings. Even as she said it, the ship was starting to vibrate from the buffeting of high winds in Ragnar's atmosphere.

Commander Adama picked up the phone and addressed the ship: 'All hands. Be ready for some chop.'

As the ship continued to descend, crews from the engineering and hangar decks were gathering equipment and tools near the main D Level airlock. They moved without undue rush, but with grim determination.

And outside the ship, the clouds darkened, and the winds grew stronger, threatening to blow the ship off her course down into the eye of the storm. Lightning flashed, illuminating and occasionally connecting with her hull. And far down in the mists of the turbulent atmosphere, a shape slowly emerged from the foreboding gloom – the long spindle of Ragnar Station, with three wheellike rings counter-rotating about its lower end.

Galactica approached slowly, bucking the ever-shifting winds. Dropping cautiously past the length of the station, she approached from beneath, like a submarine rising to dock with an underwater station. This was the most difficult part of the docking procedure. Tricky enough in space, without gravity or buffeting winds, it was ten times more difficult here.

And yet, still they drew nearer, closing on the docking module that protruded from the bottom end of the spindle. The great *Galactica* was the size of a toy truck compared to the immensity of the Ragnar Station. There was some final jockeying at the end, and then the magnetic locks pulled the ship's hull and the docking collar firmly together. Once soft-seal was achieved, large mechanical latches secured the two vessels with a series of *thunks* that reverberated throughout the ship.

In the CIC, Lieutenant Gaeta slid a single control

lever on the airlock panel, pressurizing the join between the two airlocks. A small mechanical gauge beside the control lever rotated into the green, and Gaeta looked up and reported, 'Hard seal.' He followed that with several other atmosphere and pressure checks, and reported them positive. 'Cleared for boarding, sir,' he said to Adama.

On Level D, in front of the airlock, Specialist Cally checked a similar gauge. She turned to Chief Tyrol. 'Hard seal secured, sir.'

Tyrol, speaking into the phone handset, reported, 'We confirm, sir.'

'Go find me some bullets, Chief,' Adama ordered.

'Understood,' Tyrol replied. He hung up the phone. 'All right! Let's move out.'

His men were already spinning the wheels to undog the hatch. The large port swung open, and the crew moved quickly through the airlock into the Ragnar Station.

The ammunition depot, inside the station, was guarded by huge, rusty doors that would not have looked out of place as castle gates. The crew forced them open on their creaking hinges, then moved in quickly with searchlights and weapons at the ready. The cavernous space within was dark except for the lights they brought with them, and it echoed with every move they made.

'All right, people, let's be quick about this,' Tyrol called. 'Cally, find the switches and generators and get some lights on in here.' Without waiting for the lights, they moved in through the great warehouse. Crates and larger containers were stacked everywhere, in an apparently random and hurried fashion. The crewmen flashed their beams around, finding munitions symbols and caution messages in large letters on most of the containers and caged storage areas. They were going to have to be fast but thorough, sorting out the ordnance that could be used on *Galactica* from that which couldn't.

Tyrol led the way, weaving among tall containers of unknown purpose, looking for ammunition for the Vipers, heavier cannon rounds for the ship's defensive guns, missiles and warheads . . .

Everything looked jumbled. He flashed his beam deeper into the maze. He sensed movement ahead, and was stunned to see a figure step out of a narrow alleyway. Tyrol shone his light quickly. It was a man – wild eyed, disheveled, and looking very desperate – and he was pointing a large automatic weapon directly into Tyrol's face.

Chief Tyrol nearly jumped out of his skin, but he recovered quickly. He sensed the others starting to crowd close. 'Everybody hold back!' he ordered.

The terrified man in front of him was trembling, the gun in his hand shaking, but not so much that he couldn't blow Tyrol's head off if anything spooked him. He looked like hell. He was a tall, rugged-looking fellow – but worn and ragged, his eyes red-rimmed and glassy. Though it was chilly in here, he was sweating. 'I don't want . . . any trouble,' he said finally.

'Okay, let's talk,' Tyrol replied.

'But I'm not goin' to jail,' the man barked.

'What?'

'*Do you understand me?*' He waved the submachine gun. 'I am *not* . . . going to jail.'

'Nobody's taking you to jail! Just calm down.'

For a moment, neither of them spoke. The man was pinned by about six flashlight beams against some large storage cases. 'Frickin' right, you're not.'

Tyrol knew he had to keep the man talking, keep him from losing control. 'We're not the police. We're not here to arrest you. Now put your gun down.'

'Yeah. Maybe. So who the hell are you?' the man gasped.

'We're from Colonial Fleet.' *You know – the one trying to save your ass for you?* 'We just came . . . to get some equipment from the station,' Tyrol said. He gestured with one hand for emphasis. 'You know – to get back in the fight.'

The man laughed cynically. 'What fight?'

Tyrol blinked at him in astonishment. 'You don't know.'

'Know what?'

'There's a war on,' Tyrol said, trying to keep his voice calm. He held out a hand. 'Give me . . . your weapon.'

'You think I'm stupid or something, is that it?' the man snarled. 'You think I'm stupid, you expect me to believe that?' He suddenly started shouting. 'I want passage out of here! I want a safe transport ship! With an untraceable' – he paused, abruptly sounding calm – 'Jump system. Okay?' Then the calm vanished, and his shaking grew worse. '*Now!!*'

'Look.' Tyrol answered in a tight voice. 'I don't have time to argue with you. So here's the deal. We've got over two thousand people on that ship.' He hooked a thumb over his shoulder. 'Now, if you think you can shoot every single one of us, fine. But if not . . . *get the hell out of my way!*'

The man looked startled. He backed up against the boxes, and lifted his hand slightly off his weapon, appealing for restraint. Slowly, very slowly, he lowered the gun to his side.

Three and a half hours later, the Raptor was parked in the cargo deck, directly behind Lee Adama's Viper. Lee stood at the bottom of the Raptor's entry way, helping the refugees step down off the craft. They looked ragged, weary, and frightened. A woman about Lee's age stepped down, anxiously looking for someone in authority. 'Excuse me,' she said in a thick accent. 'My husband – he's in the Colonial Fleet. In Geminon?'

Lee assisted her down. 'I'll see what I can do. If you'll just head right this way . . .' He guided her to one of the other helpers, who was taking names and steering people toward the passenger cabin.

'Have you heard anything of Geminon?' The woman's voice trailed off in the distance, as she continued to ask anyone who might listen.

'Come on,' Lee urged the next person.

'Captain?' The hand at his elbow belonged to Boomer, Sharon Valerii. She seemed to need to talk, so he turned his spot over to a transport crewman and walked with her. A boy, maybe ten years old, was with her. She introduced him as Boxey – then launched straight into her tactical situation. 'I've got two communication pods left, sir. But that's it. No sparrows, no jiggers, no drones, no markers – nothing.'

'Well,' Lee said, 'at least you've still got your electronics suite.' He gestured at his father's old Viper. 'That old crate of mine can barely navigate from A to B.'

Sharon contradicted him at once, and rather vehemently. 'That old crate may have saved your life, sir.'

Startled by her sharp tone, Lee said, a little sharply himself, 'How's that?'

'The Viper Mark Sevens? The Cylons just shut them down, like they threw a switch or something – then wiped them out. All of them – including CAG – my whole squadron. Helo and I were just lucky to be far enough away.' Sharon's voice caught, and she had trouble continuing. 'When I was out there waiting . . . for someone to find me . . . I picked up comm chatter way off. It sounds like the same thing everywhere. Even the battlestars. The only ships having any success at all are either old, or in need of some major overhaul.'

Lee blinked, trying to absorb that. He remembered his father's insistence, bordering on obsession, about keeping networked computers off the *Galactica* . . . Suddenly, out of the corner of his eye, he saw a lean-faced man with shoulder-length dark hair stepping down from the Raptor. He indicated the man with a tilt of his head. 'Is that *him*?'

Sharon looked over. 'Yeah.' She suddenly raised her voice. 'I hope he's *worth* it!' She turned back to Lee, anger and hurt on her face. 'Sorry, sir.'

That's the man who took Helo's seat. 'Don't be,' Lee said. 'I hope he's worth it, too.' As the man passed behind him, Lee whirled and put a hand to pause him. 'Doctor Baltar – Captain Lee Adama. The president's asked to see you, sir.'

Baltar looked confused, and then hopeful. 'President Adar's alive?'

'No,' Lee answered. 'I'm afraid Adar is dead.' Baltar's face fell. 'President Laura Roslin was sworn in a few hours ago.'

'Oh' said Baltar, suddenly less interested.

'If you'll come with me. She's this way.' Lee nudged him on toward the stairs to the cabin.

Laura was concluding a meeting with the captain of the liner they had recently docked with. Its passengers were now on board Colonial One, along with all the supplies they could move quickly. Reluctantly, they had abandoned the liner itself, which had exhausted its fuel while evading reported Cylon positions. The captain was just saying, 'If there's any way we can help, ma'am, any way whatsoever . . .'

'Thank you so much,' Laura replied. She turned, spotting Apollo walking into the cabin with the female pilot of the Raptor, and a shell-shocked Gaius Baltar. She recognized him easily, despite the blood and grime on his face. Laura stepped forward. 'Doctor Baltar, it's a pleasure to meet you,' she said, extending a hand. 'We met, at last year's Caprica City Symposium.'

Baltar nodded with a sort of hollow, practiced graciousness – and an obvious lack of recognition. 'Oh yeah, of course, uh' – he gestured helplessly – 'you'll have to forgive me, I'm bad with faces.'

'Oh, no,' she reassured him with a laugh. 'It's perfectly all right. I'm sure I wouldn't remember me, either.' She smiled, wincing inwardly at her self-deprecation, and soldiered on. 'Doctor, I need you to serve as my chief scientific consultant and analyst, regarding the Cylons and their technology.'

He shifted position uneasily. 'I'd be honored . . . Madame President.'

Laura wasted no time in shifting gears. With a nod to Baltar, she turned and shook hands with the Raptor pilot, a beautiful young woman with epicanthic folds at the corners of her shining dark eyes. She looked tired and vulnerable. But sleep would have to wait. 'Lieutenant Valerii? Is that right? Valerii?'

'Yes sir.'

'You've just come from Caprica, yes? Tell me your impressions of the situation there.'

The pilot drew a breath. 'Well, sir – from what I could see, the Cylons were targeting every population center with nukes. I doubt there's a major city left, at this point. Helo – Helo and I stopped counting the number of mushroom clouds over Caprica City.'

Baltar seemed to stir uncomfortably at that. Laura turned back to him. 'Doctor, would I be correct in assuming that an attack of this magnitude will trigger a planet-wide nuclear winter?' *Strangling and starving pretty much everything still living.*

'Uh, yes!' Baltar said, seeming suddenly to return to his senses. 'Yes, fallout clouds are already drifting across the continents. And the dust thrown in the atmosphere – yes, they're probably already altering the global weather patterns . . .'

Laura nodded, and for a moment bent to look out the windows at the battered, distant globe of Caprica. Settling the situation in her mind, she straightened and said to Lieutenant Valerii, 'I understand that your ship has a limited faster-than-light capability?'

'Yes sir,' Valerii replied. 'The Raptor's designed to make short Jumps ahead of the fleet, scout for enemy ships, then Jump back and report.'

'I want you to go out there and find as many survivors as you can and bring them back to this position,' Laura said. 'We will then form a convoy. We will guide them out of the combat zone and into safety.'

'Yes sir,' replied Valerii.

But Apollo was frowning, and she knew what he was frowning about: *Guide them out of the combat zone and into safety. And just where do you think is safe?*

Two hours later, Baltar was sitting alone in one of the

leather first-class seats, a fold-down table in front of him, littered with printouts and comm messages. He was sorting through them, pen in hand, trying to make some kind of sense of what had been happening. He didn't even know what he was looking for. But as long as he looked busy, he was halfway there.

'I see they've put you to work,' said a lilting female voice.

He looked up slowly, searching his mind for any obvious aberrations. As he raised his eyes, he saw Natasi – Number Six, he corrected himself – sitting in the seat beside him, looking gorgeous in the red outfit, a seductive smile on her face.

He looked intently back down at the papers, but barely saw them.

'Ignoring me won't help.'

'You're not here,' he murmured under his breath.

'No?' she said brightly.

'No. I've decided you're an expression of my subconscious mind, playing itself out during my waking states.'

That provoked a smile and a laugh. Tilting her head, she looked so achingly good, he wanted to jump on her right now. Except that she wasn't there.

'So I'm . . . only in your head?'

'Exactly.' He looked down. He was *not* going to look at her – at least not directly.

'Hm.' She raised an eyebrow and turned her face away for a moment. 'Have you considered the possibility that I could very well exist *only* in your head? Without being a hallucination?'

He could not resist looking at her; she was too devastatingly sexy. She was leaning forward now, the top of her outfit revealing far more than it concealed. He had to work hard not to tremble.

'Maybe you see and hear me because, while you were sleeping, I implanted a chip in your brain that transmits my image right into your conscious mind.'

The thought stung him with fear. Real, blinding fear. But he would not admit to it. 'No, no – see, that's me again.' He looked down with a smile. 'My subconscious self is expressing irrational fears . . . which I *also* choose to ignore.' He took a nervous sip from his glass of soda, and tried to return to his work.

She moved languidly from the seat beside him to sit on the table with his papers. Slowly and deliberately, she crossed her legs in front of him. 'What are you working on?'

He was struggling desperately now. 'If you were really a chip in my head, I wouldn't have to tell you that, would I?'

'Indulge me,' she murmured, leaning in closer.

He rubbed his bristly chin with one hand. Swallowing, he said, 'I'm trying to figure out how you managed to pull off this kind of attack. You seem to have virtually shut down the entire defense network without firing a shot. Entire squadrons lost power just as they engaged the enemy. The CNP is a navigation program, but you – uh – you made changes to the program, you said you were building in . . . back doors for your company to exploit later.'

'All true, in a sense,' she replied.

'That was your job.'

'Officially.' She cocked her head slightly. 'Unofficially, I had other motives. We *had* something, Gaius. Something . . .' She searched for the word, and smiled. 'Special.'

'This is insane.'

As she continued, her voice trembled with emotion. Her eyes were vulnerable, full of hurt. 'And what I want most of all . . . is for you to love me.'

'Love you?' he whispered.

'Well, of course, Gaius. Don't you understand?' She reached out and stroked his cheek, curved her hand behind his neck. 'God is love.' Using both hands, she pulled him forward and kissed him. He could no longer resist.

'No!' he cried, suddenly coming to his senses. Alone in his seat. Around the cabin, a few people looked oddly at him. He just smiled awkwardly, and drew a quivering breath, and looked helplessly out the window. Finally, with unseeing eyes, he forced his gaze back down to his work.

CHAPTER
34

RAGNAR STATION, AMMUNITION DEPOT

The munitions warehouse was chaotic with activity. Forklifts were hauling away large pallets of ordnance for
loading onto *Galactica*. Under the glare of overhead
floodlights, the crew were checking everything they could
find for possible use on the ship. A small tractor towing
carts of lightweight bombs sped past an elevated forklift
with a towering pallet of smaller explosives. 'Hey! Hey!
Hey!' Chief Tyrol shouted. 'Take it easy, guys! Just slow
down!' He looked like a nervous wreck, but he seemed to
be keeping things under control.

Commander Adama took it all in with his eyes even as
he walked across the depot floor, talking to Leoben, the
man they had found hiding in the back. He was telling
Leoben a little about what had been happening – not for
Leoben's benefit, but in hopes of loosening him up a little,
getting him to talk. Leoben had yet to give a convincing
explanation of what he was doing here. Adama had some
suspicions; but he wanted to tease what he could out of
the man before he jumped to any conclusions.

'We don't know much more than that,' Adama said
over the noise, casting his voice over his shoulder to
Leoben, who was walking with an armed guard behind

him. 'It's just imperative that we get our equipment and get out of here.' He stopped and peered up at some high shelves, then down at a bulkhead door in front of him. He pointed. 'What's in there?'

Leoben shambled up to stand beside him. He shrugged. 'Stuff.'

Adama glanced at him in annoyance. He gestured to Leoben to help, and they pulled the large hatch open. It was dark inside the compartment; he couldn't see a thing. 'Need a light.' As he reached back to take a lamp from one of the crew, he said to Leoben, 'Where's your spaceship?'

Leoben gestured awkwardly. 'Docked on the other side of the station.'

Adama gave him another sharp look. His crew had scanned the station for other ships on their way in. It was possible they'd missed one, if it was small. But not likely. In the background, he could hear Tyrol shouting, 'Be careful! Don't stack 'em so high!' Adama glanced that way for a moment, then back at Leoben.

The man was fidgeting, and sweating profusely. He held out his hands toward where the loading was going on. 'Okay, those warheads over there' – he gave a little laugh – 'okay, here's the deal. They would have brought a nice price on the open market.'

Adama just stared at him for a moment. 'So you're an arms dealer, huh?'

Leoben shook his head, not in denial but as if to ask why that should be a problem. 'People have a right to protect themselves, I just supply the means.' He spread his hands in innocence. But he was still trembling.

Adama gazed at him, trying to assess what part of what Leoben was saying might be true – if any of it. He shone the lantern in Leoben's face, which was pale and beaded with sweat. The man seemed to be breathing fast, too. 'You don't look too good.'

Leoben opened his mouth, but seemed not quite sure what to say. Before he could respond, though, Tyrol's voice cut the air. 'Be careful with that, all right? *Hey! Be careful with that! Look out!*'

Adama turned just in time to see a large, caged rack of bombs overbalance and topple. As it crashed to the deck, crewmembers scattered for cover. When it landed on its side, one of the cage doors popped open, and out rolled a single shiny metal canister with red stripes around it. Its activation light came on and it was blinking red. 'Take cover!' someone yelled.

Adama saw it coming toward them. With a yell, he grabbed Leoben and hurled him through the hatch into the dark compartment, and dove that way himself. He'd only begun the movement when the bomb exploded, throwing both of them through the opening, with a great thunderclap of light and heat.

As he hit the deck, he nearly blacked out from the concussion. But the force of the blast slammed the hatch closed, landing them both in blackness.

Chief Tyrol and Specialist Cally were the first to reach the hatch that had slammed shut on the Commander. It was flaming with residue from the bomb. 'Commander! Commander Adama!' Cally shouted outside the hatch. She couldn't get close enough to touch the hatch. The waves of heat drove her back.

Tyrol was busy trying to get around to the side. 'Stay back stay back! It's hot it's hot it's hot it's unstable!' Tyrol was yelling. He shone a flashlight down onto the hatch area, trying to find an attack point for getting the damn thing open. It was going to be tough, he realized; the heat had warped and possibly fused the metal. It was a miracle none of them were hurt out here; the bomb must have put out intense, but localized, heat. He whirled around and pointed to a couple of crewmen. 'You guys – go back to the ship! We need handlifts, fire equipment, and a plasma torch!'

'Wait – wait!' Cally was pulling at his arm. 'Chief – listen!'

Inside the compartment, Leoben was laughing maniacally, as Adama coughed, trying to clear his lungs of the smoke and the smell of welded metal. The hand-lantern still worked, thank the gods. They struggled to their feet.

Outside the hatch, Adama could hear someone shouting his name. 'Yeah!' he shouted back. He managed to get another breath. 'Anybody hurt out there?'

'No sir!' he heard. It was Chief Tyrol. 'We got some equipment coming, sir. We'll get you out of there, but it's gonna take a while. This hatch looks like it's fused pretty good.'

Adama grimaced. The last thing they needed was to spend manpower extricating him and mystery man here. 'No!' he shouted. 'Get all the bullets and equipment into the ship first! We're okay – don't waste time on us!' He squinted, trying to see where this compartment led. 'Is there another way out of here?' he asked Leoben.

'Yeah, sure,' Leoben said with a smirk.

Adama chose to ignore the smirk. He turned back to the hatch. 'Listen, Chief! We're gonna go out another way!'

'Sir, I don't think that's a wise idea,' Tyrol called back.

'You've got your orders. Tell Colonel Tigh he's in command until I return.'

There was a slight hesitation, before he heard Tyrol acknowledge, 'Yes sir.'

Adama turned to Leoben and gestured with the flashlight. 'Let's go.'

Leoben shrugged and slouched away down the dank, smoky passageway that looked as if it led much deeper into the station. In here the place looked more like a dungeon than a munitions warehouse. Water was dripping from the ceiling; evidently there was a leak somewhere, or malfunctioning environmental controls.

Adama rubbed his face with a grimace and followed Leoben into the gloom.

CHAPTER
35

Sharon Valerii frowned, completing the calculations for the short-range Jump. This would be her sixth Jump, and it would have to be her last. She had expended a lot of fuel in a mostly fruitless search for survivors. Not *completely* fruitless – she had located one small freighter with a crew of three and a cargo of fresh citrus products, and another rickety ship carrying textiles, electronic parts, and a few passengers. She'd sent both on to the rendezvous point. But it was hard to say that one of just two military ships in the growing ragtag bunch should be burning up its precious fuel searching the skies for so little.

Still, the president had given her an order.

She checked the plot, checked the spin on the FTL drive, and executed. In a moment, there was the familiar feeling of folding into herself, passing through a strange space-time boundary, and unfolding again. She blinked to clear her head, checked the dradis for Cylons first and survivors second – then, when she found nothing, turned on the wireless scanner.

Almost immediately, she heard a distant transmission in the blind. '*This is refinery vessel* Tauranian *to any Colonial ship. Is anyone out there? Please acknowledge.*'

Sharon's heart leaped for joy. A refinery ship! That meant fuel for the fleet – or at least the possibility of mining some. She checked the dradis once more, switched to a more distant scan, and saw it this time – a faint blip at the periphery of her field. She set course toward it with a short blast, conserving fuel – and as soon as she had it in sight, she keyed the wireless. '*Tauranian*, Colonial Raptor Three-One-Two. I have you in sight. What is your condition?'

There was a short delay, and then an answering voice that sounded breathless with relief. '*Raptor! Am I happy to hear from you!*'

'Same here, *Tauranian*,' she answered. And it was especially true, now that the ship was coming into view. It was indeed a full-sized asteroid-miner and refinery rig, much of it an enormous collection of fuel tanks, bound together in the shape of a huge shoe box. 'Please tell me you've got some Tylium in those big, beautiful tanks.'

'*Almost full. What's going on, Colonial? Is it true the Cylons have come back?*'

Sharon's thoughts darkened. 'Afraid so. It's bad. Real bad. There's not a lot left back on the home-worlds. Do you have functional FTL?'

'*Holy frak . . .*' There was silence for a few moments. Then: '*Affirmative to the FTL.*'

Sharon guided her Raptor alongside the ungainly but precious ship. 'Good. I'm sending you a set of coordinates. I need you to Jump at once to rendezvous with the fleet.'

'*What fleet? Who else is there?*'

Sharon hesitated, struggling to voice the awful truth. 'Everyone who's left.'

There were now fifty-some ships gathered in formation around Colonial One, five hours out from Caprica at normal flight speed. The ships were of every shape and size, from private yachts and couriers to the massive, multi-domed botanical cruiser *Space Park*, which President Laura Roslin and Billy were presently visiting. Under a beautiful clear dome, they walked through a lush garden with the skipper of the *Space Park*, a large, soft-spoken black man with bright, kindly eyes. He was dressed in a short-sleeved, white uniform shirt with gold bars on the shoulders.

'Most of the passengers are from Geminon and Picon, but we've got people from every colony,' he told Laura. They were threading their way among crowded groups of passengers, who were either moving nervously through the garden, or huddled together in shock. Many of them looked as if they had gathered here under the dome for no reason other than the hope of finding comfort in numbers. Everywhere they walked, people could be heard asking one another if they knew of any word from this homeworld or that.

'Give Billy a copy of your passenger manifest and a list of all your emergency supplies,' Laura said to the captain.

'All right. What about the power situation?' the captain asked. 'Our batteries are running pretty low.'

'Captain Apollo will be making an engineering survey of all the ships this afternoon,' she replied.

'Ah—' said Billy, behind her, causing them both to turn. 'Actually the captain said it would be more like this evening before he can coordinate the survey.'

'All right – this evening, then,' Laura said. 'But you will

get your needs tended to, Captain. You have my word on it.'

'Thank you, Madame President,' the captain said, shaking her hand.

'You're welcome.'

They continued to stroll through the gardens, savoring a moment of respite. It might well be her last chance, Laura thought, to enjoy such a moment of tranquility. They came upon a young girl, seven or eight years old, sitting by herself on a long, unfinished wood bench, beneath a canopy of low, tropical trees. The girl was holding a rag doll in her hands, twisting and kneading it. She looked up at their approach, but did not speak as Laura sat down on the bench beside her.

'Hi,' Laura said, pulling off her glasses to gaze at the girl. 'What's your name?'

'Cami,' the girl said, in an untroubled tone.

'Hi, Cami. I'm Laura.' She studied the girl with a soft smile for a moment. 'Are you alone?'

Cami nodded.

The captain spoke up. 'She was traveling with her grandmother. But the grandmother's been having some health problems . . . well, since the announcement. Not to worry,' he emphasized, gesturing toward the girl with his hand, 'we're taking care of her.'

Cami seemed to have decided that Laura was trustworthy. She suddenly spoke, in precise syllables. 'My parents are going to meet me at the spaceport. In Caprica City.'

'Spaceport. I see,' Laura replied, swallowing back a hundred things she might have said.

'We're going to dinner,' Cami continued. 'And I'm having chicken pie. And then we're going home. And then daddy's going to read to me. And then . . . I'm going to bed.'

Laura reached out with a smile, and gently smoothed Cami's hair. Then she nodded to Billy and the Captain, and rose. 'We need to be getting back,' she said softly.

COLONIAL ONE

The cabin was quiet, for which Laura was profoundly grateful as she leaned back against the headrest of the leather seat. She needed time to think, to rest. So much to be done. So few resources. Fuel shortages, food shortages, thousands of people on the thin edge of despair and panic. The weight of her responsibility as president was like nothing she had ever felt, or imagined. *I need time to absorb it all. Time to come up with answers.* But instead of answers, her thoughts were full of memories of that little girl in the park. So young, to be going through something like this. *As if it's any better to be old. Old and dying of cancer.*

'Madame President?'

She focused her eyes. 'Captain—'

Lee Adama sat in a facing seat, holding a piece of paper. 'We got a message from Lieutenant Valerii. She's found a fuel refinery ship. Filled with Tylium.' A big smile cracked his face.

Fuel for the spaceships? Her heart lifted, though she was too tired to show it. '*Oh.* Good. About time we caught a break. That brings us up to about what – sixty ships so far? Not bad for a few hours' work.'

Lee grinned briefly. 'No, sir.' He quickly became more sober. 'But only about forty of those ships have faster-than-light capabilities. We should start transferring people off the sublights onto the FTLs as soon as possible.'

'Yeah.' She closed her eyes for a moment. She opened them again, sensing that he had something more to say.

He did, and there was urgency in his voice. 'I don't think we should stay here much longer, sir. Sharon reports picking up signs of some Cylon sensor drones, probably looking for survivor ships.'

That brought her back to the present. 'They're . . . mopping up?'

'It looks that way, sir.'

Laura considered. 'Am I right in assuming that they wouldn't be . . . mopping up . . . unless they'd already' – she swallowed back her horror at the thought – 'finished off the colonies?'

Lee grimaced, and did not hide his feelings. 'That would be my assumption as well. And certainly consistent with the reports we've gotten. We know all twelve of the colonies were hit.'

Laura nodded. *Twenty-three billion people, at last count. Twenty-three billion . . .*

CHAPTER
36

THE SURVIVOR FLEET

Sharon came out of Jump with a flash, and was stunned to see the size of the fleet that had gathered in her absence. Large ships and small. It was practically an armada. She checked for the refinery ship *Tauranian*, and was relieved to see that it had come out of Jump just ahead of her. She keyed her wireless. 'Colonial One, Raptor Three-One-Two. I'm back and I brought a friend.'

The answering voice was that of Captain Russo, on Colonial One. '*Welcome back, Boomer. Got a lot of thirsty ships here eager to make your friend's acquaintance. Did you pick up any other contacts out there?*'

'Negative,' she answered. 'There's no one left.' *No one that we can spare the time and fuel to find, anyway.* She piloted in silence for a few minutes, leading the refinery ship through the jumble of vessels toward Colonial One.

As she scanned her instruments, something caught her eye – a new blip on the dradis screen. It was a fast-moving craft on the outside of the fleet. Fast-moving like a Cylon raider. 'Got a visitor!' she announced sharply.

'*I see him. Can you jam his signal?*'

'Trying,' she said, snapping switches on the panel. *Helo,*

I need you! Nothing she did seemed to have any effect on the incoming craft.

The Cylon sped into the midst of the fleet, then back out – and vanished in a flash of light. *Frak! FRAK!* 'It's gone. Colonial, I'm pretty sure it scanned us . . .'

Laura stood in an urgent meeting at the forward end of the first-class compartment, with Lee Adama, Billy, and Captain Russo. Russo said flatly, 'It definitely scanned us before it Jumped.'

Lee tensed, and when he spoke, it was in a strong voice. 'We have to go. *Now.* The Cylons will be here any minute.'

'Can they really respond that fast?' Laura asked.

'They can, and will. They are almost certainly mustering a squadron at this very moment.'

'Will they be able to track us through a Jump?' the President asked.

'No sir, that's impossible.'

'*Theoretically* impossible.'

'Theoretically,' Lee conceded.

Aaron Doral had joined the group, scowling. 'Madame President, there are still thousands of people on the sublight ships. We can't just leave them.'

'I agree,' said Russo. 'We should use every second to get as many people off the sublights as we can. We can wait to Jump until we pick up a Cylon force moving—'

'*No!* We're easy targets,' Lee said sharply. 'They're going to Jump right in the middle of our ships with a handful of nukes and wipe us out before *we* have a chance to react.'

'You can't just leave them all behind!' Doral protested. 'You'll be sacrificing thousands of people!'

'But – we'll be *saving* tens of thousands,' Lee

responded, and his voice became fast and urgent. 'I'm sorry to make it a numbers game, but we're talking about the survival of our race, here. We don't have the luxury of taking risks and hoping for the best – because if we lose, we lose everything.'

He looked squarely at Laura. 'And Madame President, this is a decision that needs to be made *right now*.'

She gazed back at him, remembering the last time she had faced a decision like this. That time she had followed her heart, not her mind. She'd opted to stay with the disabled liner, despite the fact that they had no way to defend it – and only through Lee's fast thinking, and the grace of the gods, had they come out of it alive. She dared not make that mistake again.

With a soft voice that belied the knot in her stomach, she said, 'Order the fleet to Jump to Ragnar immediately.'

If it weren't for the buzzing in her head, she would have sworn that time had come to a stop. Everyone had walked away from her – with urgency, with sadness, with anger. She was scarcely aware of their departure. Billy was still here. He must have something he wanted to say. The buzzing, though, was all she could hear.

Finally, Billy broke through, his words sounding distant, then drawing near. 'Madame President, something else you should be aware of . . .'

She stared across the cabin, seeing nothing. 'I have cancer,' she said suddenly.

For a moment, there was no answer. Then: 'I know.'

She turned her head to look at Billy in amazement.

He looked ready to explode with tension, fear, sorrow. He was carrying burdens someone his age should never have to carry. 'Little things you said or did,' he explained with difficulty. 'A couple of comments you made. I don't think anyone else knows; I haven't said anything to anyone.'

She looked away again; she could not bear to face another human being as she said, 'My prognosis is doubtful.' She paused for a heartbeat. 'I wish I could say it was the least of my worries. But the world is coming to an end, and all I can think about is that I have cancer and I'm probably going to die.' Another heartbeat. 'How selfish is that?'

Billy scarcely breathed. 'It's not selfish. It's human.' After a moment, he turned sadly and started to walk away.

Laura watched him, her gaze narrowing. 'Is there something you wanted to say to me?'

He stopped in the doorway leading to the next compartment, then turned. 'Well, I – I just thought you should know. That little girl you met earlier, Cami?' His fingers tugged nervously at the book he was holding in both hands. 'Her ship can't make the Jump.'

She heard his words, and yet did not hear them. She stood frozen with regret and remorse . . . and she could not breathe, or even change the pained smile on her face, until something in the back of her brain was able to take those words and put them into a container where, at least for a little while, they could not hurt her any further. 'Thank you,' she said at last, with a slight nod, releasing Billy from the awful spot he had just put them both into.

She turned away, then, to take a seat alone at the back of the first-class compartment. There was no room in her thoughts now for the living; there were too many dying, and she could only be with them just now.

In the cockpit, Lee was in the right seat alongside Captain

Russo, with Eduardo on the comm and nav panel at the rear. They were going through the pre-Jump checklist with grave efficiency. From the overhead speakers, voices were coming in from all over the fleet. Voices crying for help, for mercy . . .

Captain Russo gave Lee one last look of regret before letting a shield slide over his emotions: 'Set the SB trajectory.'

'*Colonial One! For God's sake, you can't just leave us here!*'

Lee determinedly ignored the voices. 'SB set.'

'Cycle cryo-fans.'

'*Colonial One, this is Picon Three-Six-Bravo. I can't believe you want to leave all these people behind . . .*'

Lee's fingers worked the board. 'Cycled.'

'*At least tell us where you're going! We'll follow at sublight.*'

Captain Russo glanced at Lee, then reached up to the comm panel to send a reply.

'No,' Lee said, reaching as though to stop him physically. 'If they're captured, then the Cylons know, too.'

'*I've got fifty people on board! Colonial One, do you copy this?*'

Captain Russo struggled for a moment with indecision, then lowered his hand, realizing that Lee was right. 'Spinning up FTL drive now.'

Lee: 'All ships – prepare to Jump on our mark. Five . . .'

The time stretched . . .

'*Colonial One, please respond!*'

'Four . . .'

'*May the Lords of Kobol protect those souls we leave behind.*'

'Three . . .'

*

Alone in the passenger compartment, Laura sat listening to the comm exchanges. Her thoughts had nowhere to go, her feelings were spun into a suffocating web, her ears were ringing with the sounds of desperation and fear, her gut was tied into a knot so tight she feared if she moved so much as a muscle, she and her world would spin apart into a thousand pieces. *Why me . . . why me . . . ? And why them . . . the innocent . . . ?*

Aboard the *Space Park*, it was a little before dinnertime, and young Cami sat on her favorite bench under her favorite tree, whiling away the time with her rag doll. A lot of the people had left the park, but she liked it too much to leave. 'Don't worry, Jeannie,' she reassured her doll, dancing her on her head. 'They'll come and get us when it's time to eat . . . they'll come and get us . . .'

In the dark of space surrounding the shifting fleet, there was a sudden change. With a series of flashes, half a dozen vessels popped into the local space. They were moving at high speed, directly on a course that would take them into the fleet.

'*I've got dradis contact – inbound targets heading this way!*'

Lee kept the count steady. 'Two . . .'

'*I see them, too. Are they Colonial?*'

Lee knew exactly what they were, and there was no way he could accelerate the count; he could only sit tight and pray. 'One.'

'*Oh my God, they're Cylons!*'

'Mark.'
'*I hope you people rot in hell for this—!*'

Laura felt the tears rising into her eyes, against all her inner bulwarks. There was no turning back.

It was done.

She could feel space begin to fold inward around her . . .

Throughout the fleet, dozens of flashes of light marked the Jumping of ships away from the fleet, away to somewhere else in space. At the same moment, a rapid-fire series of flashes came from each of the Cylon fighters. Long white streamers arced out in great, spreading bundles as the missiles painted their pretty, deadly tracers across the sky. It took only moments for each and every one of them to find their targets.

The sky began to light up with exploding spaceships.

In the garden, Cami gently smoothed out Jeannie's hair. She had noticed some flashing out in space, through the overhead dome. That probably meant that some of the ships were going home. She was happy for them; it was about time. Maybe, she hoped, her ship would go home soon, too.

And then her sky turned white, like the sun up close. And she felt nothing, nothing at all.

PART THREE
THE FINAL GATHERING

CHAPTER
37

SOMEWHERE IN RAGNAR STATION

The passageways seemed to be getting narrower and narrower the farther they walked, with Leoben leading the way and Commander Adama close behind. Rows of pipes and ductwork lined the walls, from deck to ceiling. The deeper into the station they went, the more claustrophobic it felt. Adama couldn't be sure he wasn't being taken on a long walk to nowhere. Although he had questioned Leoben about the route they were taking, it was nearly impossible to keep his sense of direction here; there were too many little jogs and turns.

They had been walking for maybe twenty minutes, when Leoben suddenly doubled over, gasping. Adama came up behind him. 'You all right?'

Leoben stood up, shaking his head. He was dripping sweat. 'Fine. It's just something about this place . . .'

He looked as if he meant to continue, but he didn't. 'What about this place?' Adama asked.

'Ever since I got here, something in the air' – Leoben gestured with his hands – 'affects my allergies.' He let out his breath and started walking again. 'You always keep me in front, don't you – military training, right? Never turn your back on a stranger, that kind of thing?' He ducked through a bulkhead opening. 'Suspicion and distrust, that's the military life, right? War? Hatred? Jealousy, revenge, cruelty?'

'So you're a gun dealer/philosopher, I take it, right?' Adama answered.

Leoben stopped to lean back against some pipes, laughing. Then he lurched off again, still breathing hard. 'I'm an observer of human nature, that's all. In my line of work, I see things that don't get mentioned in polite society. When you get right down to it, humanity is not a pretty race. I mean, we're only one step away from beating each other with clubs – like savages, fighting over scraps of meat.' He glanced back at Adama. 'Did you ever think, maybe we deserve what's happened to us? Maybe the Cylons are God's retribution for our many sins. Hubris – that's Man's greatest flaw. His belief that he alone has a soul, that he's the chosen of God.'

Adama grunted. 'You told me a little while ago you were a Geminon theist. Don't you believe God gave Man his soul?'

'Maybe. But what if' – Leoben paused to lean against the wall and wait for Adama to catch up – 'what if God decided he'd made a mistake – that Man was a flawed creature, after all? And he decided to give souls to another creature – like the Cylons.' He chuckled and lurched back into motion.

That made Adama flare with annoyance. He called after Leoben in a harsh voice. 'God didn't create the Cylons! Man did.' Leoben paused to hear him out. 'The Cylons are just *devices*. Technology that's gotten out of control. And I'm pretty sure we didn't include a soul in the programming. So there's no loss if we kill every last one of them. *Let's go.*'

Leoben laughed and cocked his head a little as he looked over his shoulder. 'You're not even interested in knowing the truth, are you? Maybe the Cylons feel exactly the same way you do, but about Mankind. I don't think they hate you, Adama – I think they fear you.' He stopped to cough again. 'How about you go first for a while?'

Adama just glared.

GALACTICA, COMBAT INFORMATION CENTER

Colonel Tigh peered over the shoulder of Lieutenant Gaeta as the younger man hung up the phone. He'd just been conferring with Chief Tyrol, on the station. Gaeta looked up at the colonel. 'The chief says we're looking at three hours minimum before we have all the warheads in our magazines.'

Tigh searched for an entry in the thick inventory book he was holding. 'The book says there's also fifty tons of bundled—'

The attention-tone interrupted him, and one of the junior officers at the dradis console called, *'Action stations! Action stations!'*

Gaeta quickly checked his own dradis screen. 'We have multiple contacts coming down through the storm, toward the anchorage.' He turned back toward Tigh. 'It looks like more than fifty ships.'

'Cut us loose from the station,' Tigh ordered, and strode toward the command post. He tossed his inventory book onto the charting table and called out, 'Launch the alert fighters.' He picked up a handset for ship-wide announcement. *'Set Condition One throughout the ship! Prepare to launch—'*

'Wait!' called Dualla, from the main comm station.

'Wait – I'm getting Colonial signals now.' She was pressing her earphone to her ear.

'Confirm that!' Tigh said. He strode over toward the comm station and barked, 'Don't just accept friendly ID.'

Just as he reached the comm station Dualla added, 'Confirmed, sir. Incoming ships are friendly.'

Amazed, Tigh picked up the nearest handset and keyed all-ship again. '*Action stations, stand down.*'

Dualla continued, 'The lead ship is requesting permission to come alongside, sir. They say . . .' she hesitated, listening closely, 'they say they have the President of the Colonies aboard.'

Tigh turned to look back at Dualla incredulously. Slowly his expression changed to reluctant acceptance, as he realized he had to assume the report was genuine. 'Grant their request,' he said, his voice overlaid with skepticism. 'Bring 'em into the landing bay.' *This had better be for real.*

'Oh, and Colonel,' Dualla continued. 'They say they also have Lee Adama . . . and Boomer. Both alive and well.'

Tigh blinked and rocked back on his heels. He tried like a sonofabitch not to break into a big grin. 'Well, I'll be damned . . .'

As President Laura Roslin stepped out of Colonial One into *Galactica*'s hangar deck, it occurred to her that it had been barely a few days since she'd left this ship, fully expecting that the next time she boarded the vessel, it would be a museum in orbit around Caprica. *And now it's the flagship of the surviving fleet of humanity.* She remembered her argument with Commander Adama over whether the museum could be outfitted with a small computer network. She shook her head at the memory. Obsessive and controlling, she'd thought him at the time. But it turned out he'd been right about computer networks. Tragically right.

There didn't seem to be anyone to greet them, except the deckhands who had brought up the stairs. She went down the steps, followed closely by Captain Apollo and Billy. The hangar seemed quiet, for a ship at war. 'Where is everyone?' she asked the deckhand at the bottom of the steps.

'Everyone except the stand-by crews are busy moving munitions aboard from the station,' the deckhand said, gesturing toward the other end of the hangar. 'Colonel Tigh said I should bring you to the officers' briefing room.'

'I see. And will Commander Adama meet us there?' Laura asked.

'I don't think so, sir,' said the deckhand. 'There was an accident of some sort on the station, and I heard the Commander was tied up with that. Colonel Tigh is in command right now.'

'Very well. Can you show me to the briefing room, please?'

Colonel Tigh arrived in the briefing room shortly after them. Laura watched from inside the room as Lee Adama met Tigh at the door. Tigh returned his salute and then just stared at him for a minute. He didn't reveal any emotion, but finally he shook Lee's hand and said, 'It's damned good to see you alive.'

'I'm glad to *be* alive,' Lee answered. He gestured toward Laura across the long table that bisected the room. 'I believe you know Laura Roslin. *President* Laura Roslin.'

Tigh walked slowly around the table and approached her, without quite acknowledging the full meaning of Lee's words. 'We've met, yes. Ms Roslin.'

'She was sworn into office yesterday,' Lee continued, 'following the protocol—'

'So I heard,' Tigh said, interrupting him. He glanced at Lee with an expression of derision, as if to say, *And you bought that? One day a schoolteacher and now the president?*

Laura decided it was time to cut to the chase. 'Colonel Tigh, we are, as far as we know, the sole surviving fleet of Colonial ships. And we need your help. With food and medical supplies.'

Tigh fixed her with an incredulous gaze. 'You can't be serious.'

'I'm not big on jokes today,' Laura answered evenly. 'May I ask where Commander Adama is?' She extended her arm, as if to ask, *Is he waiting in the wings?*

'He's *unavailable*,' Tigh said in a voice that was even flintier than usual. 'We expect to hear from him soon. In the meantime, I'm in command.'

'Then,' Laura acknowledged with a nod, 'we should be looking to you to answer our requests.'

Tigh was suddenly afire with indignation. 'We're in the middle of repairing and rearming this ship! We can't afford to pull a single man off the line to start caring for refugees!'

Laura tried to control her own temper. She averted her head for a moment while she channeled her anger into determination. She swung back and said forcefully, 'We have fifty thousand people out there, and some of them are hurt! Our priority has to be caring for—'

'*My* priority is preparing this ship for combat.' He

looked at her squarely, and more than a little condescendingly. 'In case you haven't heard, there's a war on.'

Laura drew a deep breath. *I still have to be a schoolteacher*, she thought. *He can't see the truth in front of his eyes.* 'Colonel,' she said evenly, stepping toward him. 'The war is over. And we lost.'

Colonel Tigh smirked. 'We'll see about that.'

'Oh yes, we will. In the meantime, however, as President of the Colonies, I'm giving you a *direct order*—'

'You don't give orders on this ship!'

'—*to provide men and equipment*—'

Lee stepped forward and broke in suddenly. 'Hold on, Colonel!' At that, Tigh turned around and stared at him in amazement. 'At least give us a couple of disaster pods,' Lee continued, in an even and reasonable tone.

'*Us?*' Tigh said.

'Sir,' Lee continued, ignoring the implied reproach, 'we have fifty thousand people out there. *Fifty thousand*. Some of them are sick. Some of them are wounded.' He gestured earnestly. 'Two disaster pods, Colonel. You can do that.'

Colonel Tigh answered very slowly and reluctantly. 'Because you're the Old Man's son, and because he's going to be so *damned happy* you're alive – okay. Two pods. But *no personnel*.' He turned away and circled around the table to leave the room. He met no one's eyes as he said, 'You get them yourselves and you distribute them yourselves. And you are all off this ship before we Jump back.'

Lee stood near the doorway, and Tigh walked up to him. 'You report to the flight deck,' Tigh ordered. His voice sharpened. 'You're senior pilot now, Captain.'

Lee raised his hand in a very precise salute. 'Yes sir.'

Tigh returned the salute and strode away.

Laura stood with her hands behind her back, gazing gratefully at Lee for a moment. When he finally turned and caught her gaze, she inclined her head with a faint smile, and nodded to dismiss him for the duties to which the colonel had called him.

CHAPTER
38

GALACTICA, DECK E PASSAGEWAY

Chief Tyrol walked along one of the ship's corridors with a group of men carrying a rack of small warheads. He stopped, looking this way and that, his heart pounding. Where was she? He couldn't just leave the work he was doing; he couldn't leave his post. But he knew she was here somewhere, and he needed to find her, to see her. *Now.* He spoke in a distracted tone to the gunnery specialist who was flanking him with a clipboard. 'As soon as you get the magazines loaded, I want a status report on Commander Adama's whereabouts.'

'Yes sir.' The specialist made a note and continued on his way.

Tyrol stood where he was for a minute, trying to figure out what to do. He was still absorbing the news that a civilian fleet had joined them – and that one of the ships was the Colonial transport that carried the new president – as well as two people they'd all given up for dead. Lee Adama . . . and Sharon Valerii. Boomer.

The passageways seemed quiet, with people doing their jobs despite their exhaustion, but with no energy left for outward shows of emotion. There was no talking, and practically no sound. He gazed anxiously one way and then another.

And then he saw her, coming toward him down the corridor, passing the gunnery specialist. She saw him at the same moment, and stopped. With her she had a boy, about ten years old. She and Tyrol stared at each other in disbelief. Sharon suddenly began striding quickly toward him. He felt the molasses in his feet let go, and he moved toward her, too, quickening his pace until they met mid-corridor. They fell into a powerful embrace, heedless of whether anyone saw or cared – and Tyrol lifted her off her feet and swung her in circles. Then he put her down and cradled her face in his hands, and they gazed into each other's eyes with joy, as the long-held grief melted away.

They kissed, hard, and then hugged for a very long time, swinging back and forth, as the bewildered boy ducked and danced out of their way.

Finally Sharon broke from their embrace long enough to let Tyrol study her face, grinning. 'There's someone I want you to meet,' she said, with a laugh. She turned to the boy and put a hand on his shoulder. 'New crewmember. Name's Boxey. He's gonna need some quarters.'

The boy looked embarrassed, and as happy as a kid could look under these circumstances. Maybe he was just glad he had someone looking out for him.

Tyrol couldn't stop grinning. 'We can manage that . . .'

In another corridor, Billy was trying to lead Baltar to the CIC, but he didn't really seem to know where he was going. Baltar followed him anyway, as they hurriedly strode along, turning this way and that. Billy occasionally said something like, 'Ah, this way,' but within a minute or two would be confused again.

Baltar was confused, period. This ship was the gloomiest place he had ever seen. It was dark and claustrophobic, and the walls slanted inward toward a peak at the ceiling, so that he felt like he was walking through a triangular prism, in perpetual twilight. He wondered how long it took people to get used to it.

Ahead of him, Billy suddenly straightened and quickened his step. 'Dualla!' he cried to someone in the corridor ahead. 'Hi! Um, we're kind of lost – again.'

Baltar squinted to see who Billy was talking to. A tall, striking crewwoman with exquisite olive-toned skin stopped in her tracks at the sight of them. She just stared at them for an instant, then ran toward Billy. 'We need to get to the CIC—' Billy began, and then the woman he'd called Dualla grabbed him around the neck and planted a kiss on him. A long, urgent kiss.

Noticing Baltar, she finally broke from the clinch. She looked a little sheepish. Billy simply looked shell-shocked. Dualla regained her poise first and said, 'It's this way,' and strode past the two, leading them in the direction from which they'd just come.

Billy turned, dazed, toward Baltar. 'I think she was happy to see you,' Baltar murmured. Billy nodded, then hurried to follow the impatiently gesturing Dualla.

Baltar stumbled along behind, envious and wondering what he had missed. Poor Billy. *If you don't understand it . . . don't ask me to explain it to you.*

Lee Adama was having trouble keeping a smile off his face, too, as he entered the hangar area, ready to take up his duties as chief pilot. There was someone he wanted to say hello to.

He found Kara Thrace under a Viper, on her back on a mechanic's crawl, open toolbox at her side. She hadn't noticed his approach, and he stood for a moment, wondering what the last day or so had been like for her. Rumor had it she'd had a big hand in saving *Galactica*. When she still didn't notice him, he called down. 'Hey!'

She turned her head to see who had called, and a strange look came over her grease-smudged face, as if she thought she were seeing a ghost. He smiled down as she slid out from under the Viper, and extended a hand to help her to her feet. They stood frozen like that for a moment: her hand in his, not exactly a handshake, but not that other way of holding hands, either. She was trembling, and trying to catch her breath, and looking as if she wasn't sure whether to hug him or rub her eyes and go back to work. Finally she managed to force out, 'I . . . thought . . . you were *dead*.' And for a moment, her face seemed to flicker between the grief she'd obviously been dealing with, and astonishment that he was standing there in front of her, alive.

Lee finally cracked a grin at the same time she did. 'Well, I thought *you* were in hack,' he said, remembering that indeed she'd been in the brig that last time he'd seen her. He felt an impulse to grab her in a bear hug, and guessed she was probably feeling the same way. But he wasn't sure he trusted his own feelings enough to do that – and besides, he was her senior officer now.

She laughed and nodded, and dropped her hands to her hips. 'It's . . . good to be wrong,' she said finally, with a vigorous nod.

He couldn't resist a crack. 'Well, you should be used to it by now.'

236

She grinned broadly. 'Everyone has a skill.' And then she turned sober, and they just looked at each other with clear relief on both of their faces that they were still alive in the midst of this madness.

Finally he broke the silence, with a nod to the Viper. 'So, how go the repairs?'

For a few heartbeats she didn't move. Then suddenly she made an inner transition and became more animated, if uncomfortable. 'On track. Another hour and she'll be ready to launch.' She hugged herself with her bare arms and said, 'So I guess you're the new *CAG* now.'

'Yeah, that's what they tell me,' Lee answered, a little self-consciously.

'Good!' Kara said. 'That's good. It's the last thing I'd want.' She pressed her lips together, apparently thinking hard and looked him soberly in the eye. 'I'm not a big enough dipstick for the job.'

She held a straight face for a second, as he worked his mouth, trying to think of a comeback. When he couldn't, she cocked her head to one side with a grin, and they laughed silently together. He managed to get his command face back on and said, 'I'll be in the squadron' – he choked a little – 'ready room.' And he turned away and left her grinning.

He was just rounding the end of the Viper when he heard, 'Hey!' He looked back. 'Does your father know you're still breathing?' Kara called.

Lee gave a little snort, once more at a loss for words. Finally he said, 'I'll let him know.' And this time he did leave. But he could sense Kara shaking her head behind him as he walked away.

CHAPTER
39

Although they seemed to be walking ever deeper into the
bowels of the decaying station, Commander Adama had
found a grime-covered directory marker that showed
where they were: a hell of a long way from the armory,
that was for sure. They already had missed two turnoffs
that might have taken them back. It was upon making that
discovery that Adama had taken the lead. From their
present position, they just needed to get through this
crossover section; then they could turn left and go up a
level and start making their way back out along the next
radial passageway. Damn good thing, too. Adama was sick
to death of this place, with its leaky steam pipes and
dripping condensation everywhere. It made him feel
chilled. Leoben, on the other hand, was sweating more
and more profusely, as if they were in a sauna.

They paused at a strange juncture where a couple of
dirty window-ports actually gave them a view out into the
atmosphere of Ragnar. The seemingly eternal green storm
continued to rage, with lightning flash followed by lightning flash. The great counter-rotating wheels of the station churned around in the field of view like ancient

water-wheels, endless grinding dust for masters long since forgotten.

Adama squinted for a few moments, then grunted and continued on his way. Leoben followed, with increasing difficulty and signs of illness. Adama was impatient at the pace, but did not drop his vigilance, or his awareness of where Leoben was at every moment. He was giving the 'arms dealer' a little wiggle room, and waiting to see if Leoben would take a misstep.

As they descended a metal staircase into the deepest part of the maintenance section, Leoben staggered. Adama paused and looked back. Leoben was grimacing in pain. He swayed a little, then crouched down, wincing, and sat on the stairs a few steps up from the bottom. Adama watched him grimly, almost certain now that what he'd suspected was true.

Leoben's skin was now tinged with gray and green. He screwed up his face as if the very air was poisoning him. 'Ahhh— !' he gasped, rolling his neck in pain. 'What is it about this place? What's it doin' to me?'

Adama stared coldly at him. 'Must be your allergies.'

Leoben raised his sweat-beaded head and widened his eyes as he looked at Adama. His face glistened with sweat as he suddenly broke into a grin. 'I don't *have* allergies.'

'I didn't think so,' Adama said in low, measured tones. He stepped a little closer. 'What you've got is silica pathways to the brain – or whatever it is you call that thing you pretend to think with. It's decomposing as we speak.'

Leoben didn't deny it. 'It's the storm, isn't it?' he managed. 'It puts out something – something you discovered has an effect on Cylon technology. That's it, isn't it? This is a refuge. That's why you put a fleet out here. A last-ditch effort to hide from a Cylon attack. Right? Well,

239

it's not enough, Adama. I've been here for . . . hours. Once they find you' – he paused to shake his head – 'it won't take them that long to destroy you.'

Adama stared at him, anger building up like a pressure in his chest. Now that Leoben had revealed himself, Adama suddenly felt all the rage he'd been holding back rise like lava in a volcano. He didn't know how the Cylons had come to look so much like humans, but he did know that they'd destroyed his world and killed his son and a lot of other good people along with him. And they were trying to exterminate all that was left of humanity.

As if he could read Adama's thoughts, Leoben started to smirk. 'They'll be in and out before they even get a headache.'

Adama stepped forward suddenly and grabbed Leoben by the shirt front. 'Maybe,' he growled. He pulled Leoben down from the steps and slammed him up against a pillar. 'But *you* – you won't find out, because you'll be dead in a few minutes.' *As dead as I can make you.* Through clenched teeth he growled, 'How does that make you feel? If you can feel.'

'Oh, I can feel more than you could ever conceive, Adama.' Leoben chuckled. 'But *I* won't die. When this *body* dies, my consciousness will be transferred to another one. And when that happens . . .' Leoben's voice trailed off as if he'd run out of steam, and he groaned and slid to the floor. Adama released him to sit crumpled against the pillar. Panting for breath, Leoben continued in a strained whisper, 'I'll tell the others exactly where you are . . . and I think they'll come, and they'll kill all of you. And I'll be here watching it happen.'

Adama squatted down slowly and shone his light up into Leoben's ashen face. 'You know what *I* think? I think if you could've transferred out of here, you would have done it long before now. I think the storm's radiation really clogged up your connection. You're not going anywhere. You're stuck in that body.'

Leoben showed no reaction. 'It doesn't matter. Sooner or later' – and now he grinned through the pain – 'the day comes when you *can't hide from the things you've done.*'

Adama stared at him, stunned. How the hell did Leoben know that expression? Did he know those were the exact words Adama had used to end his speech at the decommissioning ceremony, just a day or two ago – or however the hell long it had been?

Leoben's head lolled back, as if he were about to pass out. Adama watched him, still at a loss for words. Maybe this was the end of the line for Leoben.

Suddenly Leoben's hand shot out and seized Adama by the throat. It was no dying man's clutch, but a vice grip, closing on Adama's windpipe. Adama began to gasp.

Leoben straightened with a grin and stood up, raising Adama along with him – lifted him by the windpipe, until they were both on their feet. Unable to breathe, Adama whipped his lantern across in his right hand, trying to knock Leoben out with it. It barely glanced off Leoben – and an instant later, Leoben came back with a solid right to Adama's jaw. That stunned Adama, but not enough to keep him from feeling himself being lifted completely off the floor by Leoben's grip on his throat. Leoben held him there for what felt like forever. And then Leoben hauled back, and with a great roundhouse punch to the solar plexus, sent Adama flying backward to slam into a wall and land in a heap.

Adama forced himself up to a crouch. He saw Leoben walk slowly toward him, then stop at a vertical standpipe that came out of some kind of waist-high chamber. With a deliberate motion and apparent superhuman strength despite his debilitated state, Leoben grabbed the pipe and wrenched it loose from its upper mounting. Then he bent it back and forth until it broke off at the base. Steam billowed hissing out of the broken line. Leoben stepped forward and swung the section of pipe in a lethal blow.

It *would* have been lethal, except that Adama managed to duck out of the way. The force of the swing brought Leoben staggering into range, and Adama still had the lantern in his right hand. He brought it around in a sharp uppercut to the jaw. This time it connected perfectly, and Leoben staggered back. Adama was on him in a flash, with two more solid blows.

Shaken, Leoben stepped backward, to the stove with the broken pipe jetting steam. Adama forced him backward over the stove, until Leoben's back was pressed directly over the steam jet. Leoben cried out, losing strength. He managed to break away from the steam – but not from Adama, who came at him again and again, swinging the heavy lantern in savage punches.

Leoben staggered and went down, and still Adama rained blows onto him. Blood was spattering now from the blows, but if anything that only increased Adama's fury as he brought down on Leoben his vengeance for his son, and the millions of people killed, for the treachery, the death of everything he'd held dear . . .

Some time after Leoben had ceased moving, Adama finally stopped hitting him, and simply crouched over the body, glaring through the blood that spattered his face and eyes. And he rubbed his blood-slicked fingers together, shocked to realize that these twisted machines, these Cylons, didn't just look like humans. They bled real, red blood, just like his.

242

CHAPTER
40

GALACTICA, COMBAT INFORMATION CENTER

Baltar had at last found himself in a place where he might actually be able to do some good – at the nav station on *Galactica*'s bridge, where he could try to make a start at finding out just what went wrong with the programming. Or rather, what Natasi – *Number Six* – had done to make his code so vulnerable. At the moment, however, Lieutenant Gaeta, who seemed to be his liaison here with the bridge crew, was being rather chatty.

'So let me get this straight,' Gaeta said, leaning over the nav console from its back side. 'You're saying that the Cylons found a way to use *your* navigation program to disable our ships?'

Baltar winced, and tried not to show it. 'Essentially, yes,' he said, not really wanting to talk about it. 'I think they're using the CNP to infect your ships with some kind of computer virus, which makes them susceptible to Cylon commands.'

Gaeta pressed his hand to the stack of printouts he had placed here for Baltar's reference. 'Well, you can see we do have your CNP navigation program here on *Galactica*, but . . . our computers aren't networked, so it's never been loaded into primary memory or even test run.'

'Good,' Baltar said automatically, not really paying that much attention. Then he realized what Gaeta had just told him. 'That's *good*. Well, you shouldn't have any problems, then.' He thought for a moment. 'Still – I should purge all remaining references to it if they're on your memory tapes.'

Gaeta nodded. 'Right. I should probably retrofit the newer Vipers, as well – not that we have many left. Oh – here's the checklist for the CIC computer.' He lifted an open notebook across the console and handed it to Baltar.

'Ah. Thank you.' Baltar began flipping through it, as Gaeta walked away.

After a moment, he realized Gaeta was still there, looking back at him uncertainly. Gaeta finally spoke. 'It must be hard for you.'

Baltar looked up from the notebook, trying to shift gears. 'What do you mean?'

Gaeta said softly, 'Just having something you created twisted and used like this must be . . . horrible.' As Baltar stared at him, he continued, 'The guilt . . .'

Baltar blinked. He sensed movement to his right, and there was Number – Natasi – *Six* – leaning in to speak softly to him. 'I remember you telling me once that guilt is something small people feel when they run out of excuses for their behavior.'

'It is,' he said, trying to answer Gaeta, '*hard*. I feel . . . responsible . . . in a way . . .' Gaeta was nodding, his head bobbing up and down with understanding. Baltar was struggling to string words together: '. . . for what happened . . .'

'But you *don't*,' Six said, right beside him. 'That's one of the reasons I fell in love with you. You have a clarity of spirit . . .'

Baltar was going mad trying to maintain a conversation

with Gaeta, with Six whispering in his ear like this. Gaeta obviously couldn't see or hear her – *no one else could* – and her words didn't even seem to be taking any time; Gaeta was still nodding like one of those dolls with a bobbing head.

'. . . not burdened by conscience, or guilt, or regret . . .'

'I bet,' Gaeta said, leaning a little farther toward him. 'But . . . try to remember, it's not really your fault. I mean – you didn't mean for any of this to happen. It's not like you knew what they were going to do.'

Baltar was shaking his head now, sweating. He felt like a little boy, hauled on the carpet for doing something very bad, and he knew they were going to find out just *how* bad, soon. In the face of Gaeta's earnestness, he tried to ignore Six, who was leaning in close to his ear in that low-cut red gown, whispering, 'It's not like you knew you were lying, not like you were breaking the law.' She straightened up and spoke louder. 'Not like you cheat on women. Not like the world's coming apart . . .' She turned and sat on the nav desk right in front of him and leaned into him again. '. . . and all you can think about is Gaius Baltar.'

His voice was shaky as he said to Gaeta, looking past Six and her dramatic cleavage. 'No. No, I know . . . *exactly* what you're saying. I do know.'

Gaeta seemed to accept that. 'Right. Uh, just let me know if you need anything.' He nodded and this time when he turned away he actually left.

Baltar watched him go, waiting for his heart rate to subside. Unfortunately, Six was still right there with him.

'You know . . . I really do hope we make it out of here alive.' She gave him a warm, sexy smile and said in that husky voice of hers, 'I think we could have a real future together.'

'Yeah, that would be special,' he said brusquely, turning his head away. Whether she was a chip in his brain or a psychotic hallucination, his only defense seemed to be to ignore her.

Her expression darkened. 'You don't have to be sarcastic. Especially when I'm trying to help you.' She got up and walked around behind him.

'How have you been trying to help me, huh? How are you trying to do that?'

She draped her arms around his shoulders seductively. Then her grip tightened, and turning his head by his chin, she forced him to look straight ahead over the top of the console, toward the center of the CIC. 'Do you see anything there that looks familiar?'

He gazed, and saw Billy standing with a cup of coffee, near Dualla, who was working at a console. And above Dualla's head, that big ceiling-mounted, six-way rack of dradis monitors. 'No. Should I?' She didn't answer, but waited for him to look harder. In the middle of that rack, between the monitors, there was a small, pale blue object, shaped a little like the separated hemispheres of the human brain, but much flatter, and smooth.

'Well, now you mention it . . . I've seen something like it . . . somewhere before.'

She was breathing close to his face now, brushing back strands of his hair. 'Yes?'

It came back to him. 'In your briefcase.' He could picture it now, her silver metal briefcase, and always inside it she carried an object that looked very much like – no, *exactly* like – that thing up on the monitor mounting. 'You used to carry it around with you. You said it was an electronic organizer.' He looked up at her momentarily, then back at the distant object.

'That would be a lie,' she murmured.

'Then it's . . . it's a Cylon device.'

She circled around to perch in front of him again. 'That would follow.'

Breathlessly, he began, 'Did you—?'

'No.' She twisted around to look back at the thing. 'Not my job.'

'Then that means—'

She smiled. 'Say it.'

'There's another Cylon aboard this ship.'

Almost imperceptibly, she nodded.

CHAPTER
41

RAGNAR STATION PASSAGEWAY

William Adama forced himself to keep walking through the blinding pain. He was probably about halfway back to the armory now. It hurt to walk – he must have cracked or bruised a rib when that damned machine hit him – but it would hurt a lot more not to get back to his ship. Blood and sweat kept running into his left eye, and he repeatedly wiped his forehead as carefully as he could with his left sleeve. He was pretty sure he had Leoben's blood as well as his own on his face, and he didn't want any of that frakking Cylon blood in his wound. *How did it ever come to this?* he thought. *How did it ever come to this?*

Was that another directory plaque at the next intersection? He stopped to check it, squinting to make out the engraved map. Good thing – he'd been about to take the wrong route. These frakking passageways all looked the same. Time was fleeing, and he damned well didn't want his crew delaying departure while they went out looking for him. He pushed himself to move faster. Screw the pain.

His lungs were burning by the time he gasped against a heavy hatch, pushed it open, and staggered out into a much wider corridor. There was noise here, men moving pallets of explosives toward the airlock. He swung around, trying to find the chief – and sagged against the wall just as someone bellowed, 'Commander Adama! It's Commander Adama!'

GALACTICA, COMBAT INFORMATION CENTER

Baltar walked around the center of the CIC, glancing casually this way and that, trying not to be conspicuous as he peered up at the Cylon device attached behind the monitors. He was thinking frantically, trying to figure out what to do about the damn thing now that he knew of it.

He felt a hand on his shoulder. It was Lieutenant Gaeta walking past. 'Everything okay there, Doc?'

'Oh yeah, fine,' he said nervously, but getting his façade of confidence back up quickly. He hooked a thumb over his shoulder. 'I've just finished erasing the program from the backup memory. I'm just going to check it one more time, from here.'

Gaeta nodded and moved on, and he took that as his cue to get back to something that at least looked like work. He took a chair in front of a secondary computer console. But before he could so much as pull himself up to the console, Six had reappeared. She came from behind, circled around him, and nestled easily into his lap. He shut his eyes. *I do not believe this. What is happening to me?* He blinked them open to see Six smiling at him. She was fingering his collar, and shifting her weight provocatively on his lap. In frustration, he murmured, trying to keep his voice low, 'You're not helping.'

Six stopped what she was doing and looked hurt. 'I'm sorry,' she said, looking away from him. 'How can I help?'

'Well, for a start, you can tell me what that is.' He nodded toward the device.

She shrugged innocently. 'Honestly, I don't know.'

'Well, it hasn't exploded.'

'Yet?' she said. He looked up at her in consternation, and she turned back to smile mischievously at him. 'I'm just guessing.'

Feeling an increasing pressure in his chest, Baltar nodded. 'I have to warn them.'

Six laughed. 'How do you propose to do that?' Her voice shifted to mimicry, without losing its husky sensuality. ' "Oh look – a Cylon device!" "Really? Well, how do you know what a Cylon device looks like, Doctor?" "Oh – I forgot to mention – I'm familiar with their technology because I've been having *sex* with a Cylon for the last two years now." '

'I'll come up with something,' he whispered.

She leaned inward as if to kiss him. 'I love surprises.' Nuzzling him, she continued, 'Speaking of sex . . .' She reached surreptitiously down between their bodies and began stroking him.

He gasped. With difficulty, he managed, 'I don't think that's such a good idea, really . . . *really.*' He was trembling now.

'Why not?' she murmured. 'No one will know. It'll be our little secret.'

He couldn't help himself, or dredge up the willpower to make her stop touching him. As she nuzzled his neck, he began to breathe faster, to moan with pleasure. He let his head fall back in the chair. 'Ahh-h-h . . . *ahh-h-h* . . .'

'Doctor,' he heard in a sharp voice, by his right shoulder.

He straightened with a jerk, trying to get control of

himself. 'Y-yes.' He blinked, slowly regaining his composure.

It was that public relations man, Aaron Doral. Doral handed him a three-ring binder. 'You asked for a report on how many civilian ships had your CNP program?'

Baltar stared at him, trying to process what the man had just said. Report. Civilian ships. CNP. 'Right. Thank you,' he said at last.

'Are you all right?' Doral asked. 'You look a little flushed.'

Baltar jerked his gaze back up at the man. 'I'm fine. Thank you very much,' he said sharply.

Doral looked slightly taken aback. 'Okay.' But as he left, he glanced back at Baltar, as though uncertain whether to believe Baltar's assurance.

Baltar was watching Doral, as well. And he was getting an idea. 'What are you thinking?' asked Six, back in his lap as though she had never left.

Baltar felt his own voice become very hard. 'I'm thinking someone else might need to be implicated as a Cylon agent.'

Six gazed out over the center of the CIC, where Doral was now talking to Dualla. 'He doesn't seem the part,' she said, her voice softening with mock earnestness. 'And I don't remember seeing him at any of the Cylon parties.'

'Funny,' he said, raising his eyes to her as she chuckled. He focused again on Doral, his resolve hardening. 'He's a civilian. He's an outsider. And he's been aboard this ship for weeks with virtually unlimited access to this very room.' He nodded to himself, then hesitated. 'There is one problem, though.'

Six laughed quietly. 'Morally?'

He glared at her. 'Practically.' He frowned in thought. 'And that's that so far, aboard this ship, no one even suspects that the Cylons look like us now.' He gazed back at Six, but if she had an answer to his dilemma, she was keeping it to herself.

GALACTICA, DECK E, NEAR THE AIRLOCK

Commander Adama winced as the medical corpsman tightened the last stitch on the wound near his left eye. He saw movement to the right of the corpsman and turned his head to look – causing another sharp twinge, as he pulled on the untrimmed suture. 'Hold still, Commander, please,' said the corpsman, reaching to cut the suture thread. Adama grunted. It was worth the pain. He had just seen Leoben's body being carried past on a litter. Good. The men had been able to follow his directions, and they'd recovered the body in half the time he'd expected.

'This just gets worse and worse,' Colonel Tigh growled, standing off to one side of the corpsman, and also watching the body being carried past. 'Now the Cylons look just like us?'

'Down to our blood,' Adama said. Though his face and hands had been scrubbed with antiseptic wipes, he still felt the slickness of the Cylon's blood on his hands; he wondered if he would always feel it. The corpsman pressed a piece of gauze to his forehead, and Adama held it in place with two fingers of his left hand. With his other hand, he wiped again at his right eye with a small towel.

'You realize what this means?' Tigh muttered. 'They could be anywhere. Anyone.' He began pacing.

'I've had time to think about it,' Adama said.

'So what do we do?'

'I don't know.' He'd had time to think, but he hadn't

come up with any answers. Bowing his head, he changed the subject. 'How are we doing on the warheads?'

Tigh sounded a little more upbeat. 'Magazine two secured. Magazines three and four within the hour.' He thought a moment. 'Something else . . .'

Adama waited.

Tigh finally let it out. 'Lee . . . is alive.'

The commander's cabin seemed enormous, vacant, sullen as Lee walked through it, looking around. 'Commander?' he called again. His father wasn't here. Lee turned to leave; then something caught his eye. It was a framed octagonal picture, taken probably twenty years ago, standing prominently on his father's table. It was a photo of his mother with him and Zak, taken when they were maybe eight and ten years old. He and Zak were smiling, full of life and hope, and his mother was . . . beautiful. He hadn't seen this particular photo in a long time. He stared at it, lost in thought.

Funny, as a boy he had never thought of his mother as being beautiful or not beautiful; she was just his mom, his and Zak's. She was loving and dependable, but wasn't that what mothers were? He'd never really even thought of her as being his father's wife – not until the divorce, when she wasn't anymore. But she was still Mom, of course. Zak's death had hit her hard, very hard. He knew that since then, she worried twice as much about him as she had before. There were so many ways a fighter pilot – test pilot – could wind up at the wrong end of a funeral.

He'd worried about her happiness, about her impending remarriage, about which he'd felt relief and contentment, glad to see an end to her loneliness. But while she had always worried about *him* dying in the service, he'd never imagined that *she* would be the one to die in a war, with thermonuclear bombs raining down on her world. She was almost certainly dead now – though he would probably never know for sure. He'd been so busy since the attack, he'd hardly slept. And he hadn't had time to think much about those he had left behind.

His father was the only family he had left. And his father . . . His stomach started knotting, just thinking about his father. So maybe it was better that he didn't. *Put the picture down and leave.*

That was when he noticed the movement to his right. His father had quietly walked into his quarters, and before Lee could even react, was standing at his side. His face was a mess, scraped and with a blood-soaked bandage taped over his left temple; that must have been some fight he'd been in. He didn't say anything to Lee right away, just looked at him, and looked down at the picture Lee was still holding, a hint of a smile on his face.

Lee dropped his gaze back to the photo, and had to work to bottle up his feelings again. There would be another time to mourn his mother's death.

'I'm sorry,' his father said, as though reading his mind.

Lee nodded. He placed the photo carefully back down on the table. 'I, uh – gotta go,' he muttered, and turned away.

As he walked past his father, the commander's arm shot out and caught his, stopping his movement. Lee turned, surprised, not knowing what to say. Or what his father wanted to say. For a moment they both stood there, looking at each other in a kind of arrested shock. The air was heavy with things they might say to each other, things neither one of them was likely to say.

As suddenly as the last movement, his father stunned him again by pulling him into an awkward hug. Lee resisted at first. How long had it been since he had last hugged his father, or wanted to? As his father's arms tightened around him, Lee stood rigidly at attention, fighting the emotions. But the feelings were deeper and stronger than his resolve: the pain and loneliness breaking out of their prison and bubbling up. Feelings he didn't want to admit to: longing for forgiveness; love for his father, buried almost beyond retrieval . . . but not quite.

Almost against his will, he brought his own arms up to return the embrace, pressing his hands against his father's back. He could feel the contortions in his own face; he knew there were tears somewhere down there, wanting to get out. That wasn't going to happen, he was too strong for that – *wasn't he?* – but something was breaking down on the inside, because he felt a strange sense of gladness and release . . . a letting go. But of what? The years of anger? The walls he had struggled, *labored* to maintain? It was *so hard* to keep those walls up. Maybe he didn't have to do that. Wouldn't Zak have wanted it this way? Wouldn't his mother?

At last, he and his father stepped apart. His father nodded in obvious gratitude, but still couldn't quite look him in the eye. And he knew then that his father was struggling as much as he was.

Neither of them spoke as Lee left the cabin. But something had changed, and there would be no going back from it.

CHAPTER
42

Billy Keikeya looked up from the notes he was organizing, as President Roslin paced the room. Since they'd moved the two disaster pods off *Galactica* and onto a small transport assigned the task of distributing the supplies (damned meager supplies!) to the rest of the fleet, President Roslin had been acting like a caged cat. And in fact, they *were* caged; there were two armed guards outside the room, by Colonel Tigh's orders. Theoretically they were there to ensure the president's safety. But it was perfectly clear that they were there to contain the president, to keep her from wandering the ship or making any further demands.

At least they had been permitted to stay on board for a while. Tigh had rescinded his order that they get off the ship at once – probably thanks to Adama's intervention, though Billy wasn't sure *which* Adama.

President Roslin paused to peer out the door of the meeting room. 'What's *wrong* with these people, Billy? Are they so afraid to give up any power?' She turned and kept pacing.

Billy hesitated to speak, but this very question had been weighing on him. He drew a breath. 'With all due respect,

Madame President . . . I think you may have overplayed your hand with Colonel Tigh.'

President Roslin turned toward him in surprise. 'Excuse me?'

Now he was in it. But though his face burned, he plunged ahead. 'Well – when you tried to give Colonel Tigh a direct order – you know, telling him that he *had* to help us—'

'I haven't forgotten what I said,' she answered dryly, and with some impatience.

'Right. Of course.' Billy was starting to get a little flustered now, but he forced himself to finish what he had to say. 'The point is, he's second in command on this ship – and the ship's in danger – and you suddenly forced him to make a choice between you and his commanding officer. He doesn't even *know* you. He's not going to—'

'Obey *me*,' President Roslin finished. 'No . . . of course not.' She turned around, pressing her palms together in front of her face. 'Of course he wouldn't,' she repeated. 'Which I should have realized at the time.' She suddenly looked strangely at Billy. 'Have you been this smart all along, and I just never noticed?'

Billy flushed, not knowing what to say.

'I mean it,' she said, rubbing her shoulder absently under the collar of her blouse. 'Did I hire you because you were really smart?'

'Well, I—' he stammered. 'I did assume you'd read my résumé – so you would have known the work I – my background.' He looked down at his hands, completely embarrassed now.

'Well, I'm sure I did. But I have a confession to make. I was so overwhelmed, and there were so many applicants, that I let Personnel make the pick.' She chuckled. 'Is that so – *wait a minute!*' She stabbed a finger in the air. 'Are

you the kid who won a Siltzer Prize for writing a paper on
– on— ?' She snapped her fingers, trying to remember.

He finally broke down and grinned. 'Diplomacy and
Leadership Models. Yes.'

'And you've kept your mouth shut all this time?' She
was laughing and shaking her head at the same time.

'Well . . . you didn't ask. And there were a lot of other
things to think about—'

'Well, I'm asking now. You just became my most
trusted advisor.' President Roslin suddenly became serious. It was amazing; she was such a nice lady, just like his
mother. But she could be tough as a street cop. 'What do
you think I should do with these people? These . . .
leaders.'

Billy drew himself up and unconsciously straightened
his tie, even though it was loosened around his neck. He
knew exactly what he wanted to say; he'd been biting his
tongue *not* to say it for hours. 'Well – these are military
people. Things like tradition, duty, honor – they're not
just words to them, they're a way of life. You want them to
accept your authority as President, you're going to have to
make them see things in those terms.'

'You mean, wave the flag at them?' President Roslin
asked, cocking her head.

'Almost. You have to observe the protocols and tradi-
tions of the service. And . . . you have to *be the president.*
All the time. Every minute. Stand up to them. No, make
them stand up to *you.* Don't lose your temper with them.
But *demand their respect.* Demand that they honor the
constitution that put you in office. The constitution
they're sworn to uphold.'

She was looking at him with very thoughtful eyes now.
'I see.'

'And . . . one more thing.'

'Yes?'

'Don't ever let them think they're your equal. Because the minute they think they can walk over you, or think you're not really the president . . .' He paused.

'We're finished,' she said. She blinked and looked away for a moment. Then she gazed at him. 'Thank you, Billy.'

Baltar sat at the end of a small wooden table in Commander Adama's quarters, practically the only place he'd seen on this ship that, while lit in a subdued fashion, didn't seem oppressively gloomy. He was waiting for the commander and Colonel Tigh – both gruff, no-nonsense men – to talk their talk with him. He was, to say the least, nervous, and trying hard not to show it. He was praying – well, not really *praying*, but hoping fervently – that Six, or his hallucination of her, would not intrude while he was meeting with the two most senior officers on the ship. On the ship, hell – in the *fleet*. Most senior military officers left in the entire *civilization*, for that matter. And here he was, trying to pretend that he was answering the call to civic duty. Ready to help the fleet in any way he could! Just ask!

He was afraid they *would* ask. Afraid they'd ask too much.

And yet . . . at the same time, a most wonderful thing had just happened. Commander Adama had been attacked by a Cylon man, *a Cylon who looked just like a man*. They hadn't come right out and told him yet, but he just knew that was it. The truth would be out soon – that piece of it, anyway – and he, Baltar, didn't have to sweat bullets trying to figure out how to slip the information out. No, he could concentrate on implicating his fall guy, through whom he could reveal the presence of that insidious-looking Cylon device in the CIC. Now, if they asked him to do what he thought they might . . .

The commander had a sizable bandage on the side of his face, near his left eye, but he was sitting apparently at ease at the table; maybe it was because of his son, Captain Apollo, coming back from the dead. Plus, they were in his cabin, his comfort zone. Tigh, on the other hand, was pacing – and the pacing was making Baltar even more nervous. He snatched a look up and over his shoulder as Tigh paced back into sight, waving one of his ubiquitous paper printouts. 'Ship's doctor says, at first glance, everything in Leoben's body looked human' – Tigh finally slid into a seat (*thank the gods!*) and shoved the paper over to Baltar – 'internal organs, lymphatic system, the works.'

Which Baltar already knew. While the autopsy had been underway, he had been given samples of hair and skin and one hour to test them in the ship's limited laboratory. Spectrographic analysis of the samples, both before and during controlled incineration, had revealed nothing of interest. At least nothing that *he* could identify. Then again, chemical analysis was far from his specialty. He was going to have to fake it if he wanted to be able to 'prove' that Doral was a Cylon.

Baltar suddenly realized that there had been a pause, and they were both looking at him. He marshaled his thoughts and his scientific jargon. Had anyone actually *said* to him that Leoben, the man Adama had killed, was a Cylon? No. '*Right.* Well, uh, the tissue sample yielded unique chemical compounds during cremation that revealed the nature of the sample to be synthetic.' He paused, and feigned thoughtful surprise. '*So he was a Cylon!*'

'Yes, he was,' Adama said, in a gravelly voice. He paused, then added, 'And now we have a problem.'

'Big one,' Tigh said.

'If the Cylons look like us,' Adama continued, 'then any one of us could be a Cylon.'

Baltar held his look of shock. 'That . . . that's a very frightening possibility.'

Adama didn't argue. 'We need a way to screen human from Cylon. And that's where you come in.'

'Me?' *Careful, not too eager now.*

Tigh came in with a growled, 'Rumor has it, you're a genius.'

'Well, I, uh . . .' He bobbed his head awkwardly, practically shedding humility like cat hair. 'I'll certainly give it my all . . . Commander.'

'Keep this to yourself for now,' Tigh warned. 'We don't want to start a panic, or have people begin accusing their neighbors of being Cylons because they don't brush their teeth in the morning.'

Baltar nodded. 'I'll be very discreet.'

Yes, I will.

As Baltar and Tigh were leaving his quarters, Commander Adama suddenly called Tigh back. 'Colonel.'

Tigh hesitated and returned to the table. 'Sir.'

Adama scratched his forehead next to the wound, carefully. 'Colonel, the president is still aboard, is that correct?'

Tigh snorted. 'The schoolteacher? Yes, she is. Shall I have her—'

'*No.* No.' Adama turned away from his old friend for a moment, and gazed across the room to a small display case where he kept some of his medals, dating back to the first Cylon war. A long time ago. But the fight to defend the Colonies, and their rule of law, had never ended. With his back still turned to his friend, he said, 'Saul, whether we like it or not, Laura Roslin is the duly sworn-in President of the Colonies. She was the forty-third in line of succession, and she stayed to do her duty.' Adama turned to face his XO. 'She stepped up to the job, Colonel. And as long as she's legally in office, it's our duty to treat her as President. Is that understood?'

Tigh's face was strained as he held his emotions in check. 'Yes, sir.'

'That'll be all. Let me know when the magazines are ready.'

'Sir,' Tigh said, and turned smartly and left.

Adama watched him until the door was closed, then sat down, grimacing. His forehead and ribs hurt like hell. And so did his head. He wished he felt as certain as he had just sounded to his XO.

CHAPTER
43

PORT HANGAR DECK

Kara Thrace sat in the cockpit of the Viper, completing the pre-launch checklist. The Viper she'd flown last was still undergoing major repairs; this one was still shiny and clean from the museum floor. It too bore the call-sign 'Raygun' on its cockpit. But it would be flying as 'Starbuck' this trip.

It was going to be a very short trip.

'You understand the mission?' Lee Adama asked, walking up beside the cockpit.

Of course, you dipstick! We just went over it about five times! Grinning to conceal her irritation, she signed the checklist, handed it to the deck hand on the other side of the cockpit, and recited to Lee, 'Put my head outside the storm, look around, listen for wireless traffic, come home.'

'No heroics. This is strictly recon. Look, listen, return.'

She rubbed her eyebrow. 'You don't have to worry about me. My taste for heroics vanished about the time I engaged that first Cylon fighter.' She looked over at Lee and met his gaze straight on.

Lee nodded and turned away. On the other side of the

craft, the deck crew removed the access ladder. Kara straightened in her seat, ready to close the canopy. Suddenly it just came out; she wasn't planning to say it, but she couldn't hold it in any longer. 'Lee—' Still staring straight ahead, she waited until he turned. 'Zak failed basic flight.'

Lee came back to stand under the cockpit. 'What?' he asked, incredulous.

'Or at least he should have. But he didn't.' Kara finally turned her head to look at him. *Why are you telling him this now? Now, of all times?* 'Because I passed him,' she continued. 'His technique was sloppy, and he had no feel for flying, but I passed him. Because he and I . . . because *I* felt something, and I let that get in the way of doing my job. And I *couldn't fail him*.' This was so hard to say, but not as hard as it had been to keep it inside all these years.

Lee gazed at her in stunned disbelief. 'Why are you telling me this? Why . . . why now?'

She stared at him as long as she could, until finally she could meet his eyes no longer. 'It's the end of the world, Lee,' she said, in a hard-edged tone that was intended to be sardonic, to mask how much it had been weighing on her. 'I thought I should confess my sins.'

Before he could think of anything to say – indeed, he was speechless – she clamped her helmet down over her head and secured it. 'Set!' she yelled angrily over the wireless to the controller. As Lee continued to try to absorb that bombshell, she grabbed the canopy and slid it back into the shut position.

Lee had no choice but to step back out of the way, as the crew began to move her into launch position.

DECK B PASSAGEWAY

The armed security team marched quickly down the passageway, automatic rifles at the ready. Captain Kelly was in command. The order had just come, straight from Colonel Tigh, and they'd been told to be fast about it.

Their quarry was supposed to be somewhere in this corridor. And there he was, coming around the bend. Aaron Doral looked bewildered as he saw the team coming his way – with weapons pointed straight at his heart.

'Halt!' Kelly shouted. 'No sudden moves!'

Doral extended his hands. 'Whoa, whoa, wait a minute. Guys, what—?'

Captain Kelly, while his men fanned out around Doral, leveled a Previn handgun at the suspect and shouted, 'Get down on your knees and cross your ankles – *now!*'

Doral raised his hands and began to sink toward the deck, stammering in fright. 'Just, just – wait a minute! What? Wh – what do you want?'

'Hands behind your head.'

Doral complied, and the men moved in with handcuffs. And with that, the first suspected Cylon was in custody.

In the brig, manacled to the bars, Doral could only fume helplessly as Tigh and Baltar conferred over his case, just a few meters away.

'If he's really a Cylon, why hasn't the storm radiation made him sick by now?' Tigh asked, hands behind his back.

Baltar hesitated, knowing that the explanation he was

about to give would have a short shelf life. He would have to come up with something better, quickly. 'Well, I can only theorize that it takes a while for the storm's effects to become really apparent on Cylon physiology. By the time you encountered Leoben, he'd been here a lot longer—'

'I don't suppose it matters to you that I am *not a Cylon?*' Doral shouted from his cell.

'The smartest thing you could do right now would be to *shut your mouth,*' Tigh growled. After glaring at Doral for a few seconds longer, he turned back to Baltar. 'Are you sure?'

Baltar tried to sound reassuring, while acknowledging the natural fallibility of his remarkable findings. 'One can never be a hundred percent sure. But the evidence . . .' And here he stuttered a little, glancing at Doral, conveying as profoundly as he could his deep humility in the face of pure scientific evidence. 'The evidence seems conclusive. Basic – uh, basically what I did was, I expanded on – on your doctor's analysis of Leoben's corpse.' He nodded briskly, trying not to appear hyper and nervous. 'I then went around the CIC – discreetly! – taking random hair samples of people who've been working there, and subjected them to a special form of spectral analysis that I've been experimenting with for quite some time now, and . . .'

As Tigh fidgeted, glancing over at Doral, Baltar thought to himself, *My God, could I possible lay this on any frakking heavier?* Nevertheless, he continued, 'I then wrote a clinical computer subroutine to screen that for synthetic chemical combinations.' He handed the computer printout to Tigh, who was scowling in obvious incomprehension. 'His ones – his samples' – and he pointed directly at the appalled-looking Doral – 'were the only ones to register as synthetic.'

Tigh looked briefly at the printout with raised eyebrows, then handed it back to Baltar. 'I'll take your word for it.'

At that moment, Six, still dressed to kill, sashayed into view and murmured in a sultry voice that only he could hear, 'And just . . . like . . . that, Doctor Baltar invents the amazing Cylon detector.' She touched his chin, caressed his cheek. Whether the gesture was admiring or teasing was hard to tell.

'Look, gentlemen,' Doral protested, from behind the bars. 'I understand your concerns here. This is a very difficult situation.' His words started to speed up, as he became more and more frantic. 'But I think you need to take a step back, take a deep breath, and *really look at what you're doing here!*'

Tigh stared darkly at the prisoner. To Baltar, he said, 'I want everyone aboard this ship screened. No exceptions.'

Baltar acknowledged with a nod.

Doral stood up, pleading, raising his hands, which were manacled on the outside of the bars. As he did so, the guards stationed across from him raised their weapons and took aim. 'Whoa. *Whoa!* I, I – I don't know about anybody else, but I can tell you that I'm – I'm human.' His voice became more and more desperate. 'I'm from Moasis – you know, it's a hamlet a couple of stops outside of Caprica City. I grew up on the south side. I went to the Kobol colleges on Geminon, I studied *public relations!*'

Baltar had started to leave in the middle of Doral's plea, but then he swung back, attempting to be casual. 'Oh – by the way, I – I don't know if this is important – might be important, might not be important – but earlier, when I was in the CIC, I noticed that Mr Doral seemed to be doing, um—' As he talked, Six cozied up to him, putting an arm around him from behind. 'Well, I'm not exactly sure what it was he was doing, but he seemed very interested in this odd-looking device on the bottom of the . . . overhead dradis console.'

'*What?*' Doral burst out.

Baltar looked at him and nodded vigorously. 'Yeah.'

As he did so, Six was nuzzling him from behind, stroking his temple. 'We should really make a copy of your brain patterns at some point.' She nibbled his ear.

'*What device? What are you talking about?*' Doral was on the verge of becoming incoherent with rage. He pointed at Baltar. 'He's lying! He is *frakking lying!*'

Baltar looked sad, aggrieved.

Tigh was on the phone already. 'Combat, this is Tigh. Isolate the dradis console—'

'Don't listen to him!' Doral shouted.

'Nobody comes near it until I get up there,' Tigh said. He hung up the phone and headed for the door.

'No, Lords of Kobol, this isn't happening to me!' Doral pleaded.

Captain Kelly called out to Tigh, 'Colonel, your orders, sir?'

Tigh answered over his shoulder, 'If he moves, take him out.'

Doral was practically in tears as he shouted, 'You mixed the samples up! *I'm human!*'

But no one was listening.

COMBAT INFORMATION CENTER

Colonel Tigh watched as Petty Officer Dualla probed the mysterious device with a rad counter. 'It's not hot, sir,' she reported.

'Very well, remove it,' Tigh ordered.

Lieutenant Gaeta was studying some papers on a clipboard. 'I don't see anything in the maintenance records, sir. But I'm pretty sure I first noticed it about a week ago.'

Tigh shook his head, pacing with his hands clasped behind his back. 'And you didn't say anything? Didn't investigate a new piece of equipment that just appeared in CIC?'

'No, sir,' Gaeta answered somberly. 'I . . . just assumed it was part of the . . . museum.' As he spoke, Dualla removed the device from overhead and turned it over in her hands, before placing it into a metal carry case. 'I'm sorry, sir,' Gaeta continued. 'There's . . . no excuse.'

Tigh grumbled in a low voice. 'You're not alone, Lieutenant! Any one of us should have seen the perfectly obvious, staring us in the face.' His voice dropped still lower. 'Especially the ship's XO.'

Dualla locked the carry case. 'What should I do with it, sir?'

'Take it to Doctor Baltar. I've given him clearance. He's become our resident Cylon expert. Have him take it to the lab, figure out whether it's a *bug*, or *whatever* the hell it is.' He stopped pacing and fixed his gaze on Lieutenant Gaeta. 'In the meantime, I want this ship searched for any other pieces of equipment that just "appeared" in the last week . . .'

VIPER, OUTBOUND FROM *GALACTICA*

The Viper streaked upward through the billowing green clouds of Ragnar, through the layers of turbulence and lightning and fuming, toward the calm blackness of space. The real calm, Starbuck knew, would come only after she rocketed out of the uppermost layers of atmosphere. Until then, she had to hold onto her ass and fly with care. It was a complex passage, out from Ragnar Anchorage.

'*Starbuck*, Galactica. *You should be approaching turn eight.*' The reassuring voice of control in her headset was becoming more and more frakked with static as she penetrated the upper clouds.

'Copy,' she replied. 'Starting to lose wireless contact.' As if on cue, a flash of lightning crossed her path. Ball lightning danced along the trailing edges of her wings.

The next transmission from *Galactica* was indecipherable.

She called her report anyway. 'Making the final turn now.' And ahead of her, she saw the wonderful dark of space. She was almost out. '*Galactica*, Starbuck. I've reached the threshold.' After a moment, she called, '*Galactica*, do you read me?' Pause. '*Galactica*, do you read me?' No answer, only static.

Never mind. She focused her attention on the task at hand. Make a good thorough sweep of the area, and verify that they had not been followed by the Cylons.

The first scan looked good. Or did it? Squinting at the dradis screen in front of her, she felt a sudden chill. The rotating hoop of the scanning sensor had been showing no contact of any sort. But now, there was a flickering of something there. Not clear, but . . .

'That can't be right,' she muttered. *It should be clear.*

But it wasn't.

The dradis screen was coming into sharper focus now – and what it showed was a blizzard of small contacts, and a strange shading behind them. Looking up through the canopy over her head, Starbuck saw the last of the clouds dissipate. She cut her engines to idle. She would coast in a suborbital trajectory while she checked the situation.

'Oh frak!' she yelled, looking up and left and right.

She had emerged just below a huge swarm of Cylon raiders. 'Lords of Kobol,' she breathed, trying to get a rough count. It was impossible; they were everywhere. Instinctively, she flicked on her weapons systems. Then, upon deliberation, she shut them down again. She wasn't here to take on a flock of raiders; she was here to discover and report.

As she looked up again, she realized she had not seen the worst of it – not by far. Shockingly close, so close overhead that she'd almost missed it, was the vast, menacing, starfish shape of the worst enemy she could imagine: a Cylon base star. Not just an almost invulnerable dreadnought, which it most certainly was, but the mother ship to hundreds of raiders.

Frak, frak, frak . . .

There was only one reason that base star would be here. It was lying in wait for its prey to emerge. It was lying in wait for *Galactica*.

CHAPTER
44

Commander Adama strode toward the conference room door. The two armed guards saluted. 'As you were,' he said. One of the guards pulled the hatch door open, and Adama stepped over the lip of the coaming and into the room President Roslin and her aide had set up as a temporary office. Colonel Tigh had practically made this a prison for them, but Adama had loosened the restrictions and allowed her to conduct business here.

The young aide was sitting at the conference table with his back to the door, apparently going over a list of concerns with the president. Roslin herself was behind the table, facing the entrance, with a lot of papers spread out in front of her. Her eyes shifted enough to note Adama's entrance, but her attention never wavered from her aide, who was in the middle of a report: 'Medical supplies running low in the outer half of the fleet. The disaster pods never made it that far, Madame President.'

'Not surprising,' she said. 'What else?'

'Three of the ships are reporting engine trouble and want to know when they'll be getting engineering assistance from *Galactica*.'

Roslin's eyes shifted to Adama. 'That's a good question.

Hello, Commander. Have a seat. I'll be with you in a moment.' To the aide, who had started to rise to give up his seat, she said, 'Keep going.'

The young aide – Billy? – looked uncertain for a moment, then sat back down. There was a certain tension in the air. *Is she trying to make a point?* Adama wondered. He said nothing, but took a seat beside Billy. *All right. I'll play along.*

Billy cleared his throat. 'Ah – the captain of the *Astral Queen* wants you to know he's got nearly five hundred convicted criminals under heavy guard in his hold. They were being transported to a penal station when the attack happened.'

Roslin's face clouded. 'Oh, great.'

'He wants to know what to do with them.'

Roslin leaned forward. 'What to *do* with them?'

Billy shrugged, twitching his pencil. 'Well, with food and medical supplies being what they are, I think he's considering just—'

'No – *no.*' The president's gaze sharpened. 'We're not going to start doing *that.* They're still human beings.' Roslin drummed her fingers for a moment, glancing only momentarily at Adama, who was doing his best to maintain an impassive expression. He didn't appreciate being placed on hold, but neither was he going to reveal any annoyance. Nor did he have any intention of being drawn into a political debate.

Roslin continued, 'Tell the captain I expect daily reports on the well-being of his prisoners. And if there are any mysterious deaths, the *Astral Queen* may find herself on her own, without *Galactica*'s protection.' She glanced again at Adama, perhaps checking for a reaction; he refused once more to betray any emotion.

'Yes, Madame President.'

'Thank you, Billy.'

The aide rose to leave, taking a sheaf of papers with him. Roslin tapped a pen against her hand, following Billy with her gaze until he had left the room. The hatch clanged shut. President Roslin turned at last to Commander Adama.

Laura Roslin knew, as she and Commander Adama met each other's gazes across the table, that the power struggle was not over, just because he had acquiesced to waiting while she finished less urgent business with Billy. But neither of them wanted to say so. There was a dark suture line near his left eye, but the wound was no longer bandaged; he looked strong, recovered, and fully in command.

Maybe the best thing was to come right out with her biggest concern. 'Are you planning to stage a military coup?' she asked.

Adama was no doubt taken aback, but he hid his surprise well as he studied her. 'What?'

'Do you plan to declare martial law? Take over the government?'

Adama maintained an expression of military dignity. 'Of course not.'

'Then' – she hesitated to be so blunt, but she really had no choice – 'you do acknowledge my position as President, as duly constituted under the Articles of Colonization?' It was a mouthful, but it needed to be said.

Adama, to her disappointment, didn't answer the question. Instead he looked exasperated. 'Miss Roslin . . . my primary objective at the present time is to repair the *Galactica* and continue to fight.'

How noble. And how futile. Roslin pressed him. 'Correct me if I'm wrong, Commander, but isn't *Galactica* the last surviving battlestar?'

'We don't know for sure how many other elements of the fleet may have survived,' he said.

'Come on now. Do we have any reason to think there are *any* other survivors? The rest of the fleet was being systematically destroyed, was it not – because the Cylons were infiltrating their computer networks?'

Adama stirred, his eyes betraying nothing. 'That was how it appeared, yes.'

'Commander, the only reason this ship survived – the only reason *any* of us survived – is that *you refused to allow any computer networking on* Galactica. Despite the efforts of some people to change your mind.' Roslin paused, allowing a hint of genuine chagrin on her face. 'For which we owe you incalculable thanks. But at this moment, there are *fifty thousand* civilian refugees out there who won't stand a chance without your ship to protect them.'

'We're aware of the tactical situation,' Adama insisted. 'I'm sure that you'll all be safe here on Ragnar after we leave.'

'After you leave?' Laura cleared her throat and suddenly felt very much like a schoolteacher once again – trying to help a student who misunderstood a question. 'Where are you going?'

'To find the enemy. We're at war. That's our mission.'

She struggled to keep her expression neutral – resulting, she knew, in a strained smile, more like a grimace. 'I honestly don't know why *I* have to keep telling *you* this,' she said with painstaking deliberation. 'But the war . . . is over.'

He narrowed his gaze, and she could see an iron

hardness settling into his craggy face. 'It hasn't begun yet,' he growled.

She refrained from throwing up her hands. 'That's insane.' *It's your testosterone talking. I wish you could see that.* 'You're going to fight a war that's already been lost . . . with one ship? Our *last* warship?'

'You would rather that we run?'

She answered instantly. 'Yes. Absolutely. That is the only sane thing to do – exactly that. Run. We leave this solar system and we don't look back.'

Adama looked down for a moment, then back up at her. 'And we go where?'

'*I* don't know. Another star system, another planet. Somewhere the Cylons won't find us.'

His back was clearly up, despite his calm, military demeanor. 'You can run if you like. This ship will stand, and it will fight.'

Lords of Kobol, she thought. *Right sentiment for another time.* 'Commander Adama, let me be straight with you here. The human race is about to be *wiped out.* Yesterday we numbered in the billions. Today we have fifty thousand people left, and *that's it.* Now . . . if we are even going to survive as a *species* . . .' She paused to let that thought sink in. 'Then we need to get the hell out of here, and we need to *start having babies.*'

Adama raised his eyebrows. *Start having babies?* she could see him thinking. He didn't seem to have an answer – but it was clear that this conversation had gone too far for his taste. He pushed himself up from his seat. 'If you will excuse me,' he muttered.

Laura nodded. 'Think about it,' she said, as he pushed the hatch open.

After he was gone, she sat a while and wondered, *Did I get through to him? Or did I push too hard – again?*

CHAPTER
45

COMBAT INFORMATION CENTER

The signal from Starbuck was coming out of the overhead speakers with a lot of static. Adama had to listen carefully to make out her words: '*I didn't get an accurate count, but it looks like two base stars with at least ten fighter squadrons and two recon drone detachments patrolling the area.*'

Colonel Tigh was on the comm with a headset and mic. He replied, 'Starbuck – were you followed?'

'*Negative. No sign of pursuit. By the way they're deployed, I'd say they're waiting for us to come to them.*'

Adama called to Dualla, 'Bring her home.'

Dualla's voice came from the speaker much more clearly, '*Thank you, Starbuck. Continue present course. Return to visual contact, then stand by for instructions.*'

'*Roger, Galactica. Starbuck out.*'

'Captain,' Adama said, beckoning to his son, who was also listening closely. 'Lieutenant Gaeta, stay, please.' Adama, Tigh, and Lee joined Gaeta at the plotting table, where the most current chart of the Ragnar storm was laid out as a backlit transparency.

'How the hell did they find us?' Tigh growled as they gathered around the chart.

'Maybe that thing we found on the dradis display was some kind of transponder,' Gaeta said darkly.

'Or,' Lee suggested, 'either Leoben or Doral might have gotten a signal out.'

'It doesn't really matter,' Adama said. 'They've got us.'

'Why aren't they coming in after us?' asked Gaeta.

Tigh answered in a cynical voice. 'Why should they? They can just sit out there and wait us out. What difference does it make to them? They're machines. We're the ones that need food, medicine, and fuel.'

Adama turned from looking at the nearby vertical situation board and looked around among the three of them. 'I'm not going to play their game. I'm not going to go out there and try to fight them.' He paused for a moment, then looked at Gaeta. 'Can we plot a Jump from inside the storm?'

Tigh looked incredulous. 'With all this EM interference mucking up the FTL fix?'

'I tend to agree, sir,' Gaeta said. 'I don't think we should even attempt a Jump until we've cleared the storm threshold.' He indicated one of several concentric circles on the vertical board.

Lee spoke up. 'If we're going outside the storm, we'll have to be quick about it. They'll launch everything they have, first glimpse they get.'

'We could stick our nose out just far enough to get a good FTL fix, and then Jump,' Tigh said. As the colonel spoke, Adama was momentarily distracted by the sight of the young presidential aide, Billy, crossing the CIC and speaking to Dualla. It didn't look like a business conversation; he looked like a shy teenager approaching a girl to say hello.

'And what about the civilians?' Lee asked, drawing Adama's attention back.

'Oh, they're probably safe for the time being,' Tigh said.

This time it was Lee who looked incredulous. 'You mean leave them behind?'

'The Cylons might not even know they're here in the first place,' Lieutenant Gaeta said. 'They're probably only after us.'

'Now, that's one hell of an assumption,' Lee retorted.

As Adama listened to his officers arguing the possibilities, his gaze wandered back across the CIC, to where Dualla and Billy were, quite obviously, attracted to each other . . .

Billy, whose heart rate had doubled when D. smiled and said hello, was trying to put words to a very awkward situation. 'I – I'm getting ready to head back to the transport.' He cleared his throat and shrugged, feeling that he should say something more than just *that*, but not sure what.

Dualla's eyes conveyed disappointment, but with a heart-stopping intensity. She could not have looked more beautiful. 'Oh,' was all she managed.

Billy struggled to muster the words. 'I know this is awkward . . . but what happened in the passageway . . .'

'Yeah,' Dualla said, with a sheepish grin. 'I don't know why I did that. Sorry.'

Sorry for what? Billy thought. *Don't be. Don't ever be . . .*

Colonel Tigh responded somewhat indignantly to Lee's persistent questions about the civilian fleet. 'We can't very well cram fifty thousand men, women, and children aboard this ship,' he growled.

'I'm not suggesting that, sir.' Lee was adamant in making his point. 'I'm just saying, we cannot leave them behind. They should Jump with us.'

Gaeta replied, 'I just don't see how we can manage that without jeopardizing the ship.'

Lee looked impatient. 'We pick a Jump spot. Far enough outside the combat zone that—'

'What the *hell* is outside the combat zone at this point?' Tigh interjected.

Adama, only half listening to his senior officers, had been watching Dualla and Billy. He couldn't hear a word they were saying, but everything about their demeanor and their body language suggested that he was watching two young people falling in love. His thoughts flashed, back to his recent conversation with President Roslin, and in that moment he realized what a fool he'd been. 'They'd better start having babies,' he said suddenly.

That drew a startled gaze from Colonel Tigh, and then from Lee and Gaeta. One by one, they turned to look across the room to see what Adama was watching. Tigh asked in a dry tone, 'Is that an order?'

'It may be before too long,' Adama said wryly. 'Okay, we're going to take the civilians with us. We're going to leave this solar system and we're not going to come back.'

Tigh shot him an accusing look. 'We're running.'

Adama drew a deep breath and faced his old friend. 'This war is over. We lost.'

'As far as we know, we're the last surviving battlestar,' Tigh said. 'If we flee from the system, the people left behind don't stand a chance.'

'They don't stand a chance anyway, Colonel,' Adama replied. 'We can't save them.'

In the face of Tigh's disbelief, Lee suddenly said, 'My father's right. It's time for us to get out of here.' His assertion was clear and firm.

My father's right. Adama could scarcely believe he'd just heard those words. But he didn't have time to dwell on it. He had just proposed a bold move, and he wasn't entirely sure how to pull it off.

Colonel Tigh clearly knew he was overruled. 'So where are we going, Commander?'

Adama reached under the table and pulled out a wide-view star chart. He studied it for a moment, then pointed to a cluster of stars thirty or so light-years away. 'The Prolmar Sector.'

'That's *way* past the Red Line,' Tigh protested.

The Red Line. The distance beyond which their calculations were considered too uncertain, too risky for a single Jump. And yet, how else to get beyond the reach of the Cylons? No one knew where the Cylons were based, but the Prolmar Sector was at least in the opposite direction from Armistice Station. So in a game of wild guesses, it seemed a better bet than many they might choose.

Adama turned to Gaeta. 'Can you plot that Jump?'

'I've never plotted a Jump that far, sir,' Gaeta said worriedly.

'No one has. Can you plot that Jump?'

Gaeta took a moment to think about it. 'Yes, sir.'

Adama nodded. 'Do it . . . by yourself.'

Gaeta acknowledged, took the chart, and headed for the FTL station.

Tigh looked very worried. 'The margin of error at that distance . . .'

'I know. It's a big risk. We could be way off, we could land inside of a sun. But at least we won't be here with the Cylons.' Adama turned to the vertical situation board and changed the subject. 'This is a bad tactical position. We'll pull the *Galactica* out . . . five klicks. Send out the fighters.' He traced on the board with his hand. 'The civilians will come out behind us, cross the threshold, and make the Jump – while we hold off the Cylons.'

He turned back and faced Lee. 'Once the civilians have made the Jump, every fighter is to make an *immediate* combat landing. We won't have much time.'

'I'll tell them,' Lee said.

'I want *all* my pilots to return.' He fixed Lee with his gaze. 'Understand?'

Lee stood unmoving for a moment. 'Yes, sir, I do.' Every muscle in his neck seemed taut. Then he turned and headed off to the pilots' ready room.

Adama and Tigh both watched Lee go. Then Tigh leaned across the table and said, 'So could I ask what changed your mind?'

Adama felt about six layers of emotion pass through his face, then clear away. 'You can ask,' he said, with a straight face. Tigh finally let out a wry chuckle, and Adama matched it.

Tigh's next question was a lot more sobering, though.

'So what do we do about our prisoner?'

RAGNAR STATION, INTERIOR

'What? You can't – you can't – you can't do this!' Doral's cries echoed through the metal-walled chambers of the Ragnar Station. Tigh accompanied a crew of two guards and two crewmen carrying cases of supplies, as they force-marched Aaron Doral into a huge, unused compartment within the Ragnar Station.

'*You can't just leave me here to die!*' Released by the

guards, Doral spun around and shouted his desperate plea.

Tigh answered in a steely voice. 'You've got food, water, all the luxuries of home.' Even as he said it, he was turning to go back to *Galactica*. The guards and crewmen followed.

'I'm – I'm begging you! Don't do this! I'm not a Cylon!' Doral cried behind them.

'May be, but we just can't take that chance,' Tigh said with finality. 'For all we know, you could be the one who gave them our position.'

'*I'm not a Cylon!*' Doral screamed.

The guards, backing out of the entrance, pulled on the heavy steel doors. '*What kind of people are you?*' Doral shouted, as the heavy doors shut with a thunderous boom. There were two further clanks as locks slid into place.

Through the heavy steel doors, they could still hear his shouts:

'*Don't leave me . . . !*'

CHAPTER
46

LEAVING RAGNAR ANCHORAGE

'*Action stations! Action stations! Set Condition One through-out the ship!*'

The warning voice echoed repeatedly as Commander Adama turned off the main corridor, went down a set of steps, and strode into the CIC. The place was afire with tension. The crew were doing their jobs with deliberation overlaid with urgency. Colonel Tigh met him. 'The fleet is ready to Jump, sir.'

Adama nodded. 'Lieutenant Gaeta,' he said, crossing the center of the CIC.

'Yes, sir.'

He handed Gaeta an octagonal paper bearing a complex series of numbers. 'Disperse to all the fleet. Final coordinates.' He'd had two other people plot the Jump independently, and used their results as a check on Gaeta's calculations. Gaeta's work was confirmed. The start-point coordinate was still missing; that would have to await their emergence from the storm.

'Yes, sir.' Gaeta took the paper and went at once to the nearest comm station. He would be transmitting the coordinates not by wireless, which the Cylons might intercept even through the storm, but by short-range ship-to-ship laser transmission. If they'd been at sea, they might have used blinker lights, in a cascade from one ship to another.

Adama spoke quietly to his XO. 'Stand by to execute battle plan.'

The fleet was moving. *Galactica* led the way out through the maelstrom of Ragnar's atmosphere, taking a carefully chosen course that would keep as much of the fleet hidden as long as possible from the Cylons. The green clouds swirled their toxic dance. Lightning flashed along the edges of the ships.

It was an armada such as humanity had never launched before, except perhaps in the days of the exodus from Kobol, in the distant past. There were ships of every size and description: small freighters and transports, enormous passenger liners, private yachts, tankers, a ring-ship, one of just about every kind of ship known to the Twelve Colonies. It was motley, it was ragtag, and it looked as though it couldn't possibly stick together in a coordinated fashion. And yet it did.

Galactica was now approaching the outer limits of the storm, close to the point where they could take their final reading and make the Jump – and also close to where the Cylons would detect them with ease.

As they reached the outer fringe of the atmosphere, the battlestar began a slow turn, bringing herself broadside to the expected position of the Cylons. *Galactica*'s purpose was to defend the Ragnar storm exit point. If she could protect the civilian fleet from the Cylons even for a few minutes, it would give the fleet the precious seconds it needed to make the Jump.

Only a matter of moments, now.

'Weapons grid to full power,' Colonel Tigh ordered, striding through the CIC. 'Stand by enemy-suppression barrage.'

On the outer hull of *Galactica*, forty-eight gun batteries swung into position, both rapid-fire cannon and longer-range heavy cannon. In the last battle, there'd been no ammunition for these guns, but now their magazines were full. On the other hand, they'd faced only a few raiders before; now they were up against a much more fearsome enemy, the Cylon base stars.

As the gunners made ready to fire, *Galactica* emerged at last from the interference of the storm, into what should have been the calm of space.

Gaeta, on the short-range dradis, saw what most of the crew could only imagine with dread: Cylon raiders swarming away from the nearby base star, like bees from a hive. They were too many to count by sight, but the dradis console told him the news. 'Incoming seventy-two Cylon fighters, closing at one-two-zero mark four-eight!'

'FTL, get your fix and transmit to the fleet!' Adama ordered, watching on the overhead dradis monitor. He hated to give the Cylons time to disperse for attack, but they were still out of range. Until . . . *closing, closing* . . . now. 'Enemy suppression fire – all batteries execute!'

His command was echoed by Colonel Tigh, on the all-ship: '*All batteries, commence firing.*'

The outer hull of *Galactica* came alive like a manic fireworks finale. The long-range cannon pounded out heavy fire against the enemy, *thud-thud-thud-thud*, relentlessly.

The rapid-fire cannon erupted in streaming volleys, creating a jet stream of deadly fire raining outward at the incoming raiders.

The emptiness of space was filled with swarming killers, the scythelike Cylon raiders breaking in seemingly random zigzags, the hail of fire from *Galactica*, and then the white-hot streaks of the fast-boosting Cylon missiles, aimed at the battlestar and the fleet behind her. For a few moments, it looked as if the suppression fire was doing nothing. And then the Cylons started to explode, repeatedly, in great blossoms of fire . . .

From within the ship, it sounded like a continuous drum-roll, over the bass-drum pounding of the heavies. Adama watched, grateful for every gunner who managed to pick off an incoming missile or an approaching fighter. Finally, Gaeta called out, 'Perimeter established!'

The suppression-barrage had created a bubble of relative safety immediately surrounding the ship; now the Vipers were to widen the bubble and keep the raiders at bay. 'Launch Vipers,' Adama ordered.

The voice of Dualla called out over the all-ship, '*Vipers, cleared to launch.*'

In the port launch bay, Captain Kelly gave the word, and Vipers sped down multiple launch tubes, flung into space by the magnetic catapults . . .

In the lead squadron, CAG Lee Adama, call-sign Apollo, led his wing of Vipers in a sweep, starting by getting them the hell out of the line of fire of *Galactica*'s gun batteries. His call went out to all the Vipers; '*Broken formation,*

Razzle-Dazzle, don't let 'em use their targeting computers! And for frak's sake, stay out of Galactica's *firing solution!*'

In another Viper, Starbuck nodded, keenly aware of just how difficult that was going to be. Cylons everywhere, freewheeling dogfight – and pull it off without getting directly between *Galactica* and the enemy.

From *Galactica* came the final instruction, Dualla's voice calmly passing on the order: '*Vipers engage fighters only. Leave the base star to us.*'

'*Okay, people, let's do it.*'

At Apollo's signal, the Vipers shot outward in irregular formation, opening fire on the approaching raiders. In moments, all was chaos again, as fighters dodged and swerved, engaging the enemy. Some Cylons exploded, but so did some Vipers.

Apollo was hard pressed to track the immediate adversaries, keep a watch on the squadron at the same time – and do so without the aid of onboard computers. He was flying the way he had not flown since his last war games: spinning, twisting, flying tight and fast, and mostly by the seat of his pants. To his right, he saw one of his wingmen explode, hit by a Cylon missile. Cursing viciously, he dodged a raider, brought another into his sights, and let loose a burst on the cannon. It exploded. But there were so many more, far more of the Cylons than of the Vipers. He made a hard pitch up and a left turn, just in time to see another of his wingmen explode. *Frak!*

No time to think about it; three more raiders were buzzing around him. He kept turning, flipping, shooting. Another enemy gone. Several more coming in . . .

*

Colonel Tigh's command went out to the fleet: 'Galactica *to all civilian ships. Commence Jumping in sequence.*'

As still more Cylon missiles streaked in, some this time aiming for the civilian ships that were beginning to emerge from the storm, bright flashes of light signaled the departure of one ship after another through the folds in space that would take them to safety.

Galactica was holding the perimeter, but just barely. The Cylons were pressing the attack inward, and the Vipers could not avoid giving up ground. It was only a question of time until the Cylons broke through.

The Cylon missile tracks were getting closer, overwhelming the ability of the gunners or Vipers to stop them. In the CIC, Gaeta's voice shouted a warning: 'Incoming ordnance!' An instant later, the CIC shook from an explosion on the outer hull – then another. More than one screen shattered or went dark. The hits were probably not nukes, but were bad enough.

Tigh was on a handset at once. 'Damage control—!'

Apollo's jaw set with grim determination as he and his crewmates fought against the steadily turning tide. *How many ships away?* His thumb squeezed the trigger, and another burst bracketed a Cylon above, below, then dead center. He veered out of the explosion path.

As he came back around, he saw another flash, and another of his shipmates died.

A flash, a different kind, and another civilian ship was away.

His headset was filled with chatter from the other pilots, warning each other, giving breathless encouragement, cursing with rage. Apollo remained silent except for the occasional barked order. All of his attention was on flying, shooting, and keeping an eye on *Galactica* and the fleet. Another ship away – a big one, too, just before a Cylon missile streaked right through the spot the ship had occupied an instant before.

Another target in sight. *Kill the frakking thing.* He squeezed a long burst, longer than he should, but it ended in a blossom of exploding Cylon.

Still another coming in, though, and he couldn't come around quite fast enough. He saw the streak out of the corner of his eye, then felt the bone-crushing *SLAM* of the impact, and his Viper spinning out of control. *Frakking hell!* He fought to stabilize it, but his left wing was gone, the engine on fire, and all he had left working was a handful of thrusters.

Somewhere dimly he heard Starbuck's voice: '*Apollo! Do you read me?*' He had no time to answer.

Using the thrusters, he gradually succeeded in slowing the spin. He saw a Cylon coming around, and his spin brought it directly into his sights. A quick squeeze, and another blossom. But the Viper was still gyrating, and there were plenty of enemies left.

Oh damn.

At his ten o'clock, he saw the white trail of a missile seeking its target. And its target was him. There was absolutely nothing he could do now except hold his breath and say good-bye . . .

The missile closed – and exploded in a hail of cannon fire, as a Viper shot past him. And Starbuck's voice screaming with delight, '*Wheeeee! C'mon, bassstard!*' And arcing right, then left, she destroyed the Cylon that had launched the missile. She turned back toward him, '*Looks like you broke your ship, Apollo!*'

'I've had worse!' he lied, not knowing whether to laugh or cry. 'But thanks!'

His joy was cut short, though, as he looked to his left and saw another white streak – and the fiery blaze of a direct hit on *Galactica*.

CHAPTER
47

GALACTICA, COMBAT INFORMATION CENTER

Commander Adama wasn't sure how much longer the ship could take this kind of pounding. The CIC was shaking as if an earthquake had struck, and consoles and wiring were flaring and sputtering. Colonel Tigh was making his way across the center. 'Function check on the damage control panel!' he shouted to the two nearest crewmen.

Tigh reached Adama's side as another hit threatened to crush the ship. Grimacing in pain, Adama pulled himself up as Tigh reported, 'We've got multiple hull breaches. They're targeting the landing bays. We've got to get the fighters back on board, retract the pods, or we won't be able to Jump.'

'Fleet status!' Adama shouted.

In the monitor, one last large ship vanished in a flash of light. Gaeta turned. 'Last civilian ship's away!'

'Recall all fighters! Stand by to secure landing bays!' Adama ordered.

Dualla's voice rang out, 'Galactica *to all Vipers, Break off, come on home. Repeat! Come on home!*'

*

Apollo's call reinforced the message. 'All Vipers, this is the CAG! Return home at once! Starbuck, that means you, too!'

'*Frak that, I'm coming after you!*' answered Starbuck.

'Starbuck, shove the heroics and get home!'

'*Save your breath! We go back together!*'

Starbuck's fighter continued to maneuver protectively around Apollo's disabled craft, raking one Cylon after another with her cannon fire as they came too close. The other Vipers of the squadron were obeying the come-home order and were flocking back to *Galactica*.

In the port landing bay, wave after wave of Vipers came in hot, holding together in shaky formation. With a thunderous, rhythmic pounding spread along the entire length of the landing bay, they slammed down in emergency combat landings. They all came down hard; many of them bounced and some collided. But in they came, wing after wing of fighters, half of them with battle damage. The last few came in hotter than the rest, and had to brake-thrust violently to keep from plowing into the Vipers ahead of them.

Many of them broke something in landing. But their pilots came home alive.

In the CIC, Gaeta and Dualla were frantically tracking the IDs of the returning Vipers, getting a count.

Gaeta straightened up with his clipboard. 'Forty-three. Ship reports ready for Jump as soon as landing bay's secure, sir.'

Adama squinted up at the monitor, his stomach in knots. All back. All that were alive. Or were they? In the monitor he saw a spread of Cylon missiles, too fast for the gunners to handle. The ship quaked from the impact.

Dualla called, 'Two Vipers still out there, sir! Starbuck and Apollo!'

Colonel Tigh strode past Adama, reaching for a microphone. 'We can't stand toe to toe with those base ships.' He grabbed the mic. '*Retract the pods!*'

Adama picked himself up from where the last impact had thrown him against a table, and looked anxiously from one monitor to another. Pods retracting, and Starbuck and Lee still out there? They'd lost Lee's signal, but Starbuck was still out there with him. 'I can't leave them here,' he muttered. Raising his voice, he called, 'Stand by on that pod retraction!' and to Dualla, 'Patch me through to Starbuck!'

'Yes sir.'

He picked up a slender headset and held it to his ear and mouth. 'Starbuck! What do you hear?'

The universe was going insane. Starbuck had shot up more Cylon raiders than she could count, and still they kept coming. She continued maneuvering around Apollo, keeping him alive until he could troubleshoot his machine, kick it in gear, and head back home. As another raider exploded at pointblank range, she heard a voice in her headset: '*Starbuck*, Galactica. *What'd*' you . . . 'ere . . .'

'*WHAT?*' she shouted, over the intense cockpit noise, with just about everything running or firing at once.

The next time it came in clearer. It was Commander Adama, astoundingly calm. '*Good morning, Starbuck. What do you hear?*'

At that instant, her canopy was pelted by a hail of tiny bits of debris from a shattered Cylon. Another time, she might have been worried about being holed. But just now she could only grin crazily and answer, 'Nothing but the rain.'

'*Then grab your gun and bring the cat in.*'

The pelting continued. 'Aye-aye, sir! Comin' home!' She pitched up and over, potting another Cylon on her turn. 'Let's go, Apollo! Can you move that crate yet?'

From the Viper behind, she heard Apollo's voice: '*I'm losing power. I'm not gonna make it, Starbuck! It's over. Just leave, damn it – that's an order!*'

'Lee, shut up and hold still!' Frakking hell with his orders. Starbuck fired her nose and belly thrusters and launched her ship up and over, in a completely reckless flip into an inside loop. '*Whhaaa-HAAAAAHH!*' Watching Apollo pass by her in an inverted position, she gave it one more second, then yanked back on the stick and repeated the maneuver and rolled sharply to complete the loop. She was now in front of Apollo's ship, aiming straight at his nose.

'*Oh no,*' she heard Apollo murmur.

Starbuck kicked in power, hard, then eased back. She had to do this exactly right, or she'd kill them both. Apollo's ship loomed in front of her. '*YAHHHHH-HHHH!*' She tickled the yaw ever so slightly to the right, banked a hair – and slammed into Apollo's Viper, nose beside nose, jamming the root of her left wing hard against the tip of his nose. She threw the mag-lock switch, praying that it would help hold the ships together.

'*You are beyond insane!*' he shouted as he flew backwards toward home, propelled by her engines. His canopy was maybe half a dozen meters ahead of hers, and she could see him gesturing and trying to look around behind him.

'Kickin' in the burn!' she cried gleefully, hammering in full power. Together, one forward, one backward, they screamed through space toward *Galactica*.

They were not the only thing screaming through space. Cylon missiles arced past in dizzying succession. The enemy fighters, which until now had been standing off from *Galactica*'s firepower, were closing in for the kill. Only a little farther away, the Cylon base star was unleashing volley after volley of missiles. A lot of them were being stopped by *Galactica*'s suppression fire; too many of them weren't. Explosions flashed all along *Galactica*'s hull.

Commander Adama's fists were clenched as he watched their progress on the screen. He could see them approaching. The ship rocked with explosion after explosion. The shattered glass of broken screens and lights was everywhere. Tigh had his hands wrapped around the microphone, waiting for the order to Jump. Adama knew what he was thinking: *Leave them behind! You have to leave them behind or you'll lose the ship!*

'Come *on!*' Adama muttered under his breath, gaze fixed to the overhead screen. He was going nowhere without his son and Starbuck. He counted the seconds silently, calculating their progress. When he judged they were close enough, he barked the order, 'Close the landing bay doors!' They could make it, in the time it would take the doors to close. He knew they could.

They'd better.

The missiles were flying everywhere, and cannon-fire from *Galactica* was spraying outward. Starbuck could do nothing but stay her course, and pray that nothing hit them. *Galactica* loomed in front of them now; she could see the lights of the landing bay, the beautiful landing bay. She was still maneuvering at high speed, *way* faster than any normal, or even combat, approach speed.

Apollo shouted to her: '*We're coming in a little hot, don't you think?*'

'No-o-o?' she answered, craning her neck to try to see past Apollo's ship, which was obstructing her view. She hadn't meant it to come out as a question, but she winced as she saw how fast they were closing on the landing bay. 'Not really,' she gulped. *Oh frakking gods, I can't land at this speed.*

Ahead of them, she could see the landing bay doors starting to close.

Another explosion shook the CIC. Adama pulled himself to his knees and looked up at the screen. '*Come on . . .*'

Across the room, Dualla reported coolly, '*They're coming in.*'

Adama looked around in desperation, ignoring Tigh's glare. Was he killing all these people to try to save his son?

Just a few seconds longer . . .

'HANG ON-N-N-N-N-N-N-N!' Starbuck yelled, as they screamed straight toward the narrowing entrance to the landing bay. She struggled to get the bank just right, and the pitch, and popped the thrusters down just a little. In the other cockpit, Apollo was looking desperately left and right, trying to see what she was doing.

Do these doors always close that fast? She popped a little thrust to the left, got the aim just right, and cleared the doors by a breath. 'HYAHHHHH!' She slammed on full braking thrust as they came in over a landing strip that was littered with the rest of the squadron. *My God, I'm gonna hit somebody! There's no way I can avoid them—!*

The instant the Vipers cleared the doors, Dualla reported breathlessly, '*They're aboard!*'

Standing beside Adama, Tigh called, 'Stand by for Jump!' They were going to Jump with the landing pod extended. They had no choice.

Adama's fists were still clenched, his gaze hard on an interior video of the landing pod. He could see the crumpled duo coming in over the tops of other Vipers, flying way too fast. *Put her down. You've got a space there. Plant it!*

He watched as Starbuck did exactly that. When a patch of empty deck opened beneath her, she brought it down hard. The Vipers skidded, sparks flying, out of the range of the camera.

Lieutenant Gaeta looked up from his console. 'Landing deck secure.'

Another camera picked up the Vipers, as they slammed into the interior side of the landing deck and careened to a stop.

'Jump!' Adama commanded.

A hailstorm of missiles and raiders converged on the lumbering battlestar. There was no way it could survive this final firestorm unleashed by the base stars. It had just seconds to live before the knockout blow, the final killing punch.

With a flash of white light and a wrenching twist of the space-time continuum, the battlestar vanished. The Cylon firepower converged on nothing, and vanished into the turbulent clouds of the planet below.

CHAPTER
48

RENDEZVOUS POINT

Space seemed silent again. Peaceful. The peace of the
dead, and of the living. The survivor fleet was gathered
around the scorched and battered, yet comforting, bulk of
the last battlestar, the one named *Galactica*. Where they
were, no one really knew. The Prolmar Sector. They knew
the coordinates, but beyond that, it was unknown, uncharted space.

Where they were going, no one really knew, either.

But the time for that would come.

GALACTICA, STARBOARD HANGAR

What had once been the hangar deck of a warship, and
then the floor of a museum, was now a place of mourning.
It was filled to capacity with both the living and the dead.
The bodies of those who had fallen on *Galactica* were
lined up with military precision at the front of the great
room. Each was draped with the flag of the Twelve
Colonies. A row of helmets represented the pilots and
others who had died in space, their bodies unrecoverable.

At the very front, standing at the same lectern where

Commander Adama had not so long ago delivered his speech at the decommissioning of this ship, was Elosha, the priestess. Her words, songs, and prayers were being carried by live video feed throughout the fleet. But standing before her in person was a multitude assembled from the crew of *Galactica* and representatives from many of the other ships. At front row center, side by side, stood Commander William Adama and President Laura Roslin, leaders of the surviving free people of the Twelve Colonies of Humanity. Flanking them on one side were Lee Adama, Kara Thrace, Sharon Valerii, and Gaius Baltar; and on the other, Colonel Tigh, Lieutenant Gaeta, Captain Kelly, Chief Tyrol, and Petty Officer Dualla.

The President and the Commander had already spoken in tribute to those had given their lives. Elosha had led them in song and scripture. And now, with the seventh scroll of Kobol unrolled before her, her dark face a strong and captivating presence, she led them in prayer:

'With heavy hearts we lift up their bodies to you, O Lords of Kobol, in the knowledge that you will take from them their burdens and give them life eternal.' As she spoke, those gathered were utterly silent, focused with rapt attention on her words. 'We also pray that you will look upon us now with mercy and with love, just as you did upon our forefathers many years ago. Just as you led us from Kobol and found the Twelve Worlds, so now we hope and pray that you will lead us to a new home, where we may begin life anew.'

Elosha looked out over the gathered company. 'So say we all.'

The company murmured in response, 'So say we all.'

Commander Adama turned around to look in stern dissatisfaction at the assembly. *Is that the best you can do?* He strode out in front of the gathering again, looking up and down the rows. Finally he repeated, in a firm but controlled voice, 'So say we all.'

The assembly echoed his words, just a little louder. Even President Roslin and the staff officers seemed to have little heart for it. They had found victory in battle, but now looked as if they had found defeat in the quiet after the battle.

Adama tried again, louder. He had more than a little annoyance in his voice. 'So . . . say . . . we all!'

A better response this time. But still not good enough.

He shouted: '*So say we all!*'

That finally provoked what he was looking for. The voices rose together in solid refrain: '*So say we all!*'

Commander Adama walked up alongside the first row of the fallen, gazed down at the flag-covered bodies, and looked back at his people. 'Are they the lucky ones?' he asked, his voice booming through the big room. He continued walking along the row. 'That's what you're thinking, isn't it?' He spoke as he continued along the outer edge of the funeral row toward the front. 'We're a long way from home. We've Jumped *way* beyond the Red Line into uncharted space.' He rounded the front end of the row and faced the gathered crowd again, from near Elosha. 'Limited supplies! Limited fuel! No allies! And *now* – no hope?'

He began walking back down the center, between the rows of bodies. He had their attention, and he kept it. 'Maybe it would have been better for us to have died *quickly* back there on the Colonies with our families, instead of dying out here, slowly, in the emptiness of dark space.' On the faces of his officers, he saw somber agreement. Many of them *did* feel that way; and who could blame them? They blamed themselves for feeling it. He could see that in their faces, as well. They envied the dead, and they felt guilty for being alive. He had brought their darkest feelings into the open.

He called out the questions: 'Where shall we go? What shall we do?'

There was some stirring, as people considered his words. Some of them were probably thinking *forward* for the first time since the war had begun. They needed something to think forward *to*. Maybe he could help them.

' "Life *here* began out *there*," ' he quoted.

He paused to see how they would respond to the familiar words. 'Those are the first words of the sacred scrolls, handed down to us by the Lords of Kobol, many centuries ago. And those words made something perfectly clear: We are not alone in this universe.' He turned around toward the priest. 'Elosha – there is a Thirteenth Colony of Humankind, is there not?'

Elosha responded clearly, but with perhaps a note of uncertainty in her voice. 'Yes. The scrolls tell us the Thirteenth Tribe left Kobol in the early days. They traveled far and made their home upon a planet called Earth . . . which circles a distant and unknown star.'

Adama let that last phrase hang in the air for a moment, before saying, 'It's *not* unknown! *I know where it is! Earth!*' For the next several heartbeats, no one in the room drew a breath. Everyone, including Elosha, stared at him in astonishment. 'It's the most guarded secret we have,' he continued. 'The location is known only to the senior commanders of the fleet. We dared not share it with the public – not while there was a Cylon threat upon us. And thank the Lords of Kobol for that. Because now we have a refuge to go to! A refuge that the Cylons know nothing about!'

Giving them all a moment to absorb his words, he

continued, 'It won't be an easy journey. It'll be long, and arduous. But I promise you one thing: On the memory of those lying here before you, we shall find it. And Earth . . . will become our new home.' He looked out over the stunned and hopeful faces. 'So say we all!'

'So say we all!' they echoed, still a little uncertain.

Louder: 'So say we all!'

And the response came louder.

Finally he shouted the words, as he walked toward them: '*So say we all!*'

At last it sounded as if they meant it: '*SO SAY WE ALL!*'

Commander Adama resumed his position in the front row again, facing forward to Elosha. This time he said it calmly, in benediction: 'So say we all.'

Elosha echoed his words, and his tone.

Satisfied at last, Adama stepped once more out of line and turned to face the assembly. 'Dismissed!'

An enthusiastic cheer went up, as the tension was finally released. Many of the crew hugged one another, or shook hands, or simply shook with relief. Some, a few, stood thoughtful and uncertain, wondering just what this new revelation meant.

One of those wondering thoughtfully was President Laura Roslin. Her smile was tentative and brief. But whatever it was that troubled her, she said nothing about it then; let the moment be what it was, her eyes seemed to say.

CHAPTER
49

PILOTS' QUARTERS, DECK E

Kara Thrace wrenched off her boots with the jerky
strength that comes from deep weariness. She sat motionless on the edge of her bunk for a little while, silently
reliving the events of the last day or two. It seemed
impossible to believe that they had gotten through it all,
and the worst was over. At least she *thought* it was – for
now.

With a long, luxurious sigh, she stretched out full-
length on her bunk to rest. She was wound so tightly, she
couldn't relax, though. She reached over her head to grip
the headpiece of the bunk, and she pulled, trying to
stretch her body. She wished she were a cat; then she
could stretch properly. She was exhausted, physically *and*
emotionally. The battle, the crazy rescue of Lee, the after-
math. Following their hair-raising landing, she and Lee
had climbed out of their broken Vipers, and then simply
clung to each other – she in relief and he in gratitude.

After a minute or so, the discipline had kicked in – and
they'd gone all awkward again, not daring to do something as radical as hug each other. But she knew one thing:
Commander Adama had risked the ship, holding it for
the two of them, and she knew that Lee knew that, too.

Maybe things were finally on the mend between the two of them, Lee and his father. That alone would be cause for celebration.

'You look comfortable,' one of her roommates said teasingly, on her way to answer a knock on the door.

'Yeah, if no one bothers me, I may sleep for a week,' Kara answered, shutting her eyes.

There was a brief silence, then, 'Kara – Colonel Tigh to see you.'

Bloody hell. She pushed herself up out of bed and into a posture vaguely resembling attention. She made no effort to remove the scowl from her face, though.

Colonel Tigh entered the little cabin area. 'As you were.'

'I'm just trying to avoid another trip to the brig, sir,' she said tiredly, tilting her head in question. *What the hell are you doing here?*

Tigh let out a breath. He seemed very uncomfortable. 'Lieutenant Thrace,' he began. His gruff expression softened a little. 'Kara. What you did out there today with Lee Adama . . . it was, uh . . . a hell of a piece of flying.'

Did he come here to compliment me? What's wrong?

Tigh nodded, and there seemed to be a slight tic in his cheek as he struggled to make nice with Kara. Well, too frakking bad. Kara didn't feel like making nice with him.

In his trademarked growl, Tigh continued, 'The commander has always said that you were the best pilot he's ever seen, and . . . well, today you proved it.' He just looked at her for a moment, and she looked back at him. She didn't give him an inch.

'Now . . . about the other day . . . during the game . . .' He was struggling now. He looked as if he were about to pop a blood vessel in his head, trying to force the words out. 'Well, maybe I was out of line, too.

And I just . . .' He tried to force a smile. The tic in his cheek was getting worse. 'I just wanted to say, um . . . I'm sorry.'

Kara allowed a slight, sarcastic smile onto her face.

'Well, don't you have anything to say?'

She felt an urge that she knew she should resist. She couldn't, though. 'Permission to speak off the record, sir?'

'Granted.' He shrugged.

She allowed a long moment to pass. Then: 'You're a bastard.'

He began trembling, and shaking his head. 'You just don't know when to keep your mouth shut, do you? I'm offering you a clean slate here.'

'I'm not interested in a clean slate with you,' she said, with a silky smooth edge to her voice. She was starting to feel cocky, and she let it show. 'You're dangerous. You know why?'

His expression darkened. 'This'll be good.'

She laughed softly. 'Because you're *weak*. Because you're a drunk.'

'You done?' His eyes were filled with anger again.

She thought a moment, angling her eyes momentarily upward in contemplation. She cocked her head. 'Yes, sir.'

'You're returned to flight status,' Tigh growled. Turning to walk away, he added, 'Let's see how long that lasts.'

Kara watched him leave, torn between wanting to laugh and wondering why the hell it was she *couldn't* keep her mouth shut around that man.

COMMANDER ADAMA'S QUARTERS

Laura Roslin knocked on the metal hatch door to the Commander's quarters. 'Come in!' she heard from the far

307

side of the wall. She pushed the hatch open, stepped through, and secured the hatch again from the inside. She wondered how long it would take to get used to the awkward system of doors on this ship.

Walking slowly into the room, she glanced curiously around Adama's living space. It was very neat, with mementoes of service attached to the walls, and a surprising number of books. Old books. She didn't know why that surprised her. She hadn't pegged him as the reading type. And yet, why not?

Commander Adama was dressed more casually than she had ever seen him; his formal service coat was unbuttoned, and he was wearing it more like a robe. He was kneeling on the floor at a wide coffee table, eating dinner from a bowl. Noodles and salad. He looked up at her thoughtfully as he sorted stacks of paper on the table. God, didn't the man ever rest? 'I hope I'm not disturbing you,' she said.

'Not at all. Have a seat.'

She sat, a little stiffly, on a bench sofa beside the table. She was aware that she was wearing the same maroon business suit she'd had on since before the start of the war. *I wonder if there's a laundry on this ship somewhere.* She shook her head and brought her thoughts back to her reason for coming. 'First thing, I suppose I should thank you for deciding to bring us—'

'Listen, you were right,' he said, interrupting her. 'I was wrong. Let's just leave it at that.' He put down the papers in his hand.

Startled, she nodded slowly. 'All right.'

He turned away for a moment to lift some books off the floor.

She suddenly voiced the thought that had been on her

mind for hours. '*There's no Earth*,' she said, a faint smile on her face. 'You made it all up.'

Adama didn't say anything. He took off his glasses and turned to face her again, wearily.

'President Adar and I once talked about the legends surrounding Earth. He knew nothing about a secret location regarding Earth. And if the *president* knew nothing about it, what are the chances that you do?' She said it, not accusingly, but matter-of-factly.

He straightened a little, his expression as impenetrable as ever. 'You're right,' he admitted finally. 'There's no Earth. It's all a legend.' He put his glasses back on and turned to his stack of books once more.

'Then why—?'

'Because . . .' Adama suddenly looked to her like everybody's favorite grandfather or uncle, passing a nugget of wisdom on to the next generation. 'It's not enough to just live. You have to have something to live *for*. Let it be Earth.'

Laura felt a grin she could barely subdue sneak onto her face. She stood up and walked around, many emotions warring for control of her expression. She didn't know precisely what she felt just now, but she certainly had to admire his guts. 'How long can you keep it up as a pretense?'

'As long as it takes. Until we find a planet that can sustain us, and start life over.'

She nodded and smiled tightly. 'They'll never forgive you for lying to them.'

'Maybe.' He looked up at her. 'But in the meantime, I've given all of us a fighting chance to survive. And isn't that what you said was the most important thing? Survival of the human race?'

Did I say that? Maybe I did. 'Who else knows?' she asked, arms crossed.

'Not a soul.'

She nodded thoughtfully. 'All right. I'll keep your secret. But I want something in return.'

Leaning one elbow on a pile of books, he said, 'I'm listening.'

'If this civilization is going to function, it's going to need schools, hospitals – however limited. Manufacturing and repair. Agriculture and mining. Service industries. Police. An economy. It's going to need a *government*.' Her voice was soft, but her tone was adamant. 'A civilian government run by the President of the Colonies.'

Adama stood up slowly and began buttoning his coat. He looked down at the books, then slowly raised his eyes to her. 'Run by the president, huh? So you'd be in charge of the fleet's civilian concerns. Military decisions would stay with me. Is that what you're saying?'

She nodded. 'Yes.'

Finished neatening up his jacket, he took off his glasses. 'Then . . . I'll think about it . . . Madame President.' And he extended his hand to her, and after a moment, she extended hers in return.

DECK C STARBOARD CORRIDOR

Gaius Baltar strode along, not really sure where he was going. He was still waiting for his heart to slow down. He still couldn't believe that the fleet had escaped the Cylon attack. Whatever happened now, it would have to be better than what *almost* happened, back there at Ragnar.

Of course, they would still be expecting him to come

up with a Cylon detector, which was not an easy problem, not an easy problem at all . . .

Rounding a corner, he found Six waiting for him. His heart sank. She was, of course, dressed in the red outfit that was clearly calculated to drive him mad with desire. Not this time, though. He was too tired physically, and too tired of her games.

She greeted him with a smile that seemed more sardonic than usual. 'Your escape is a temporary one at best,' she said, in a tone that now seemed insufferable. 'We will find you.'

'Yeah, you can try.' He pushed past her. 'It's a big universe.'

She followed him. 'You haven't addressed the real problem, of course.'

'Yes, yes,' he answered with an impatient glance back. 'There may be Cylon agents living among us, waiting to strike at any moment.' He kept up his pace.

'Some may not even know they're Cylons at all,' she said. 'They could be sleeper agents programmed to perfectly impersonate human beings until activation.'

He wheeled to face her. 'If there are Cylons aboard this ship, we'll find them.' He nodded and turned to continue on his way.

'We?' She came around in front of him, causing him to stop. 'You talk like you're one of them, now. You must know that you can never be one of them – not really. Not anymore.' She reached out, as though to touch him, but didn't quite. 'My sweet Gaius, you have no idea how important you are . . . how important your *mission* is.' She lowered her head slightly, and her voice became a little sterner. 'You're not on their side, Gaius.'

He tensed at those words, and as she moved as though

to embrace him, or maybe even kiss him, he answered through clenched jaw, 'I am *not* . . . on anybody's *side*.'

That seemed to take her by surprise, even to hurt her. He walked past her again. But this time she made no attempt to answer, or to follow, as he continued on his way.

CHAPTER
50

GALACTICA, AT THE END OF THE DAY

Colonel Tigh strode into his private quarters, grim determination on his face, determination fueled by rage. Indignation. Shame.

He loosened his jacket, taking the familiar steps over to the top right drawer of his desk. As he had done so often in the past, virtually every day of his life for years, he lifted out the bottle of whiskey and raised it to the light. It was a fairly new bottle, three-quarters full. If he were going to follow the usual pattern, he would take out a glass and pour. And the fire as it went down would dull, somewhat, the pain of all the years, and the pain of his absent wife, now almost certainly dead.

This time, to his own surprise, he did something different. He carried it over to the wastebasket, half full of crumpled papers – and he dropped it in. It hit the bottom of the basket with a *clunk*. He walked away from it, scowling. But he felt a little happier, a little prouder.

Boxey Wakefield still felt uncertain, finding his way around the area of the enlisted quarters. He really didn't know where to go, or what to do with himself. But there was one room he knew how to find, and that was the pilots' lounge. He hesitated outside in the corridor for a minute, peering in through the open hatch. He could see Sharon in there – Boomer, they called her.

She glanced over and caught his eye with a wisp of a smile. She was playing cards with some of the other pilots. With a motion of her head, she invited him in. He entered, feeling his heart pound, his shyness suddenly overwhelming. These looked like serious people, these pilots – and they were all looking at him with what seemed like amusement. Never mind that, Sharon's expression seemed to say. She gestured to him to come around and take a seat beside her.

Sharon put a hand on his shoulder, and passed him a plate of cookies. Or rather a plate that *had* had cookies, and now had just one. He reached out for that last cookie and took a bite.

Sharon grinned at him, and he grinned back. Suddenly, for a moment anyway, he didn't mind being just a kid here.

Kara Thrace was finally unwinding, hanging her uniform shut in her tiny closet. As she did so, she noticed once more the photo of Zak and her, with Lee folded behind, tucked into the mirror frame. When she'd thought Lee was dead, she'd flattened the picture so that she could mourn the two brothers together. When he'd come back to life and become her senior officer, she'd felt funny about it and had refolded the picture. Now, she flattened the photo once more and replaced it in the mirror frame, smoothing the crease with her finger. That felt right now, and she didn't think she'd be changing it again.

She reached up onto the shelf and felt around until she

found one of her few remaining cigars. Lighting it, she flicked her lighter shut and puffed a few times in satisfaction, gazing at the photo. Then she walked over to her bunk and stretched out, puffing, contemplating the day.

Not a good day, certainly. But she, and many of the people she loved, had come through it alive. There was that to be said for it.

And there was Earth, somewhere in their future, and so there was that, too.

For a long time she lay there puffing, surrounded by a thick cloud of pungent blue smoke.

Throughout the ship, life was returning to . . . not normal, because normal could never again describe the lives of these people of *Galactica* . . . but something that *felt* more like life, something sustainable.

Repair work proceeded everywhere throughout the ship. In the landing bay, Captain Kelly was overseeing the removal of Vipers from the landing area, in some cases untangling craft from each other before they could be moved to the elevator pads and lowered to the hangar deck for servicing. The landing pod itself needed substantial repairs – not just from the Ragnar battle, but from the nuke that nearly took the ship out in the first engagement.

Below decks, Chief Tyrol was hard at work pulling together a flyable squadron of Vipers. They'd lost eight fighters at Ragnar, and another fourteen were seriously bent, bashed, or busted up. The CAG's Viper, Apollo's, was the worst trashed of any that had come back; but Tyrol was damned if he was going to let the CAG lose his ship. His crew was working industriously – some, like Cally, working extra hard to fill a space in themselves that would otherwise be devastating.

In the Combat Information Center, Lieutenant Gaeta was gearing up to juggle just about everything: repairs to the battle-shattered CIC, formation operations with the fleet, constant vigilance for Cylons, and plans for the next Jump. He was tired, but he figured he could manage a little longer on caffeine; let the ones who had been on the first line of the fight get their rest first.

Dualla, on the other hand, knew she needed a break, and she wisely took it. Let the superheroes be the superheroes. She walked the corridors of the ship, just glad to be alive. Still, she was definitely surprised to find Billy in the passageway, surrounded by eager female crewmembers, a big grin on his face. D. didn't stop to say anything; she just walked by with a beaming smile. And her smile grew broader when Billy saw her, and came running after her, calling her name.

Colonel Tigh sat in his quarters, studying the three-quarters full bottle of whiskey that he had retrieved from the trash can. He hadn't drunk any. But it was a damn good bourbon, and who knew when he would have a chance to acquire more. It seemed a sin to waste it. To waste his fine whiskey – his poison, the thing that would destroy him if he didn't destroy it. He stared at it, his hands clasped over his belt, his thumbs twitching nervously. He had done pretty well this last day without it; the XO had returned. But would he stay?

Didn't he, after all, deserve a little reward?

Commander Adama and Lee walked together toward Adama's quarters. They were both bone-tired, but this was a good end to the day, to talk with his son whom he thought he had lost – twice in the space of twenty-four hours. It was good to talk, even if the talk was entirely about the work, the ship, the command. As Adama opened the hatch to his quarters, Lee concluded his report:

'Tomorrow I'll begin a formal combat patrol around the fleet.'

'Good,' Adama said, turning to say good night. 'I'll see you in the morning, then.'

Lee hesitated. He clearly wanted to say more, but it just as clearly was very difficult for him. 'I – listen, it's just I – it's been so long—'

Adama gazed at him, feeling emotions he had practically forgotten. How long had it been since he had looked his son straight in the eye? So many thoughts in his mind, and too much weariness to sort it all out. He finally just nodded. 'Let's save this for another time, son. I think we've pulled off enough miracles today, don't you?'

Lee took a moment to react to that, and returned the nod. 'Maybe so. Good night, Commander.'

'Good night, Captain.'

As Lee turned away, Adama closed the door and breathed a sigh of relief and satisfaction. He was finally ready to think about sleep. He didn't think he had ever felt so ready.

And then he saw the small, folded piece of paper on his side table. Someone had left a note for him. He put on his glasses and picked it up. It was a single sentence, typed on *Galactica* printout paper. It was unsigned. It read:

THERE ARE ONLY 12 CYLON MODELS.

Adama stared at the note for a long time, stunned. *Twleve Cylon models – and all indistinguishable from humans? Who would have left such a note? And why anonymously? And what could he do about it?*

317

Not a damn thing that I can think of.

In the end, he refolded the note and put it away in his wall safe, all thoughts of sleep effectively banished.

We haven't escaped from them yet.

CODA

The gaseous green storms of Ragnar continued to swirl, as they had for millions of years, and probably would for millions of years more. But around the Ragnar Anchorage, a fleet of ships had gathered: a looming Cylon base star and a buzzing horde of its attendants.

Inside the station, in a large storage room, a man sat huddled in misery. He was not lacking for food, or air, or water. But he *was* lacking for company. And he was lacking for even the remotest semblance of comfort.

The place smelled of rust, dankness, emptiness, and fear. Most of the gloomy light, such as it was, came from a weird shaft that went up through the ceiling of the room at the end where he sat. It looked a little like a gigantic coil spring, or a cylindrical cage, with a vague column of orange light going up its center. It was the most prominent feature of the room, but he had no idea what it was, nor did he care. Aaron Doral just sat in front of it, right where the soldiers of *Galactica* had left him to rot. *The bastards. The inhuman bastards.*

He was sweating profusely, though the room was, if anything, chilly. His skin color was pallid – greenish – and he was shaking. Something about this place was making him ill.

He started at the sound of a sudden crash at the other

end of the room. A flare of light blazed through the crack in the heavy doors. Another crash, and more light. Smoke and steam billowed out into the room. Someone on the outside was using explosives or torches, or both. Finally the doors began to spread apart, with a screech of metal on metal. Outside he saw only bright light and fog. It was difficult to focus, but he squinted and finally saw what was coming in.

Two late-model Cylon centurions clanked into the room, shining stainless warriors with clawed hands and red-glowing Cyclops eyes scanning side to side. Doral tensed, feeling a strange confusion. He didn't quite understand what was happening to him. He should be terrified. Why wasn't he more frightened?

The centurions strode forward only a little way, then stepped aside. Apparently, they were here to guard the doors. So more Cylons would be coming. Yes, of course. It was starting to become clear. Even through the haze of the fog and the sickness, he was starting to understand.

A series of figures emerged from the light-haze, following the centurions into the room. They slowly became clear to him as they approached. There were three Cylons who looked exactly like Leoben, the agent whom Adama had killed. They were dressed identically in casual, almost sloppy shirts and pants. There were three of the . . . Number Six model. Yes, he recognized them now. Blonde, gorgeous, all three dressed in crimson skirt-suits. And there was one of the . . . Aaron Doral model. Him. His double. Dressed in an electric-blue suit, the way he often had dressed, when he was working on *Galactica*.

It was like a window opening in his mind, as he suddenly understood his relationship to all of the Cylon models. He knew now that he should speak, without waiting for them to speak. 'We have to get out of this storm. The radiation . . . it affects our neural relays.' He stood up to confer with them.

'Where did they go?' one of the Leoben models asked.

'I don't know. They were preparing for a big Jump,' Doral answered.

'We can't let them go,' said his identical model.

The first Number Six model, in a silken voice, agreed.

'If we do, they'll return one day and seek revenge.' That was the second Leoben. The remaining Cylons spoke in turn.

'It's in their nature.'

'We have no choice, in any case. We must find them. The Mission, the Project, require it.'

'If they've Jumped out of known space, it could take decades to track them down.'

A new figure entered the room at that moment, emerging from the haze outside. It was a female Cylon – brunette, petite, and beautiful. The easy smile on her face revealed her utter confidence. 'Don't worry. We'll find them. And it won't take *nearly* that long.'

It was the Sharon Valerii model. The Boomer model.

'By your command,' murmured a Number Six.

With that, they turned. And with the ailing Doral model, they walked out of that place, followed by the steel warriors.

Minutes later, the base star detached from Ragnar Station. It rose, at once majestic and malign, wheeling up through the swirling clouds. Once free of the atmosphere, it accelerated at high speed into the dark emptiness of interstellar space.

The hunt for the remnants of humanity had begun.

Here's a sneak peek at the next exciting
Battlestar Galactica novel

THE CYLON'S SECRET

BY CRAIG SHAW GARDNER

TWENTY YEARS LATER

THE EDGE OF
EXPLORED SPACE

Saul Tigh looked at the crisply pressed sleeve of his Battlestar uniform – the uniform that had saved his life. Well, he guessed the uniform and Bill Adama were equally responsible.

It wasn't the first time Adama had pulled Tigh's fat from the fire. Frak, he remembered the first time they met, at a dive of a spaceport bar. Tigh had gotten in a bit over his head with some of the jerks he had been shipping out with.

'He's a real-deal war hero,' one had said. The other had called him a 'freight monkey.' The second one had laughed. 'No high and mighty Viper pilot no more.'

Tigh had seen this kind of jealousy before. He got up to leave. But the scum wouldn't let him.

'War's over, soldier boy,' one of them said in his face. 'Why you gotta keep going on and on about the war all the time?'

Tigh had had enough. 'You're the one who can't stop talking about it,' was his reply.

The other guy stared at him. 'What's that supposed to mean?'

And Tigh let him have it.

'You didn't serve because your rich daddy got you a

deferment. That's why you're always trying to prove you're a man – but you're not. You're a coward.'

Tigh meant every word. And as soon as he said them, he knew he was in for a fight. He ducked the first guy's fist, and got him spun around into a hammer-lock.

That's when the bartender pulled the shotgun on him.

Tigh swung his crewmate between himself and the gun as another man came out of the dimly lit side of the bar to knock the gun from the barkeep's hands.

Maybe, Tigh thought, he had somebody on his side for a change. He added a little pressure to the grip on his opponent. It reminded him, in an odd sort of way, about fighting hand-to-hand with the Cylons all those years ago.

'See,' he said very softly, close to his crewmate's ear. 'You wouldn't know this, but although Centurians are tough, their necks have got this weak joint. Not very flexible. Add pressure in just the right direction and it snaps. Human neck's more resilient. Takes a little more force.'

The man who had grabbed the bartender's gun stepped fully into the light.

'You flew Vipers?' the man asked.

And that was the first time Tigh saw Bill Adama.

'Yeah, that's right,' Tigh replied.

'Me, too,' Adama said. 'So what's your plan here?'

Tigh looked down at the man still in his grip.

'Don't really have one,' he admitted.

Adama glanced first at his rifle, then back at the other men in the room. 'Well, let's see,' he mused. 'I've kind of committed myself here, so – you pop that clown's neck, I have to shoot his buddy here and probably the bartender too . . .'

'Sweet Lords of Kobol,' the bartender whined.

'Shut up,' Adama snapped. He turned his attention back to Tigh. 'After that, well – I don't know what we do. Personally, I tend to go with what you know until something better turns up.'

Tigh eased up on the man's windpipe. 'Safe play is to let them go, I imagine.' Maybe, Tigh realized, he had let things get a bit out of hand.

'Probably,' Adama agreed.

Tigh let his guy go. Adama uncocked the shotgun. He looked at the bartender.

'I'll keep the pepper gun for now.'

Adama introduced himself then, another veteran kicked out of a military that no longer needed him, and told Saul he'd just signed on to the same crew that Tigh was shipping with.

Bill Adama and Saul Tigh clicked from that moment on. They traded war stories and watched each other's back on three different cruisers – each one a little better than the one before – over the course of a couple years they went from taking whatever loose cargo small shippers wanted to haul to working with one of the premier shippers in the Colonies. Bill was good at getting both of them to nicer berths, talking up their experience and pushing up their wages. Before Adama had shown up, Saul was sure that piloting those runs from cargo ship to backwater planet and back again was the most dead-end job anywhere. But as the ships, the cargoes, and the destinations improved, so did his view of the future.

Eventually, the two had gone their separate ways, with Adama wanting to stay closer to Caprica and his new family, but they had never lost touch. Tigh stood up for his friend when Adama got married, and had visited Bill on Caprica after the birth of each of Adania's two sons. But Adama had done more than find a life beyond the shipping lanes. Adama had gotten himself back into the service, with a captain's rank on a Battlestar. Without Bill talking up the team, Saul found the shipping jobs weren't quite so good. So his best friend kept moving up, while Tigh found himself shipping out on one lousy freighter after another.

Not that Tigh had expected to be in that situation for long. When Adama got himself back into the military, he promised to bring Tigh along. All of a sudden, Saul had had big hopes for his future. The Battlestar brass had turned him down three times for reenlistment, sure; but they had turned Adama down twice. Not enough positions open in a peacetime navy, was the official line, even for the most honored of veterans.

But then, despite every door that had been slammed before them, his best friend was back in uniform. Adama had stayed on top of the news, kept in touch with an old Battlestar crony or two, listened for the first mention of an expansion of the fleet, and – bang – had talked himself back into a job. With Bill Adama, Saul realized, anything was possible.

Anything but keeping close. Saul realized Bill was busy now, what with a full-time military career and a family back planetside. Tigh hadn't wanted to bother his old buddy unless he had to – reminding Bill of unkept promises just wasn't his style. Tigh even stopped sending those short, joking missives they had usually used to keep in touch. The messages had stopped coming from Adama as well. He hadn't heard from his best friend in the better part of a year.

When the two of them had been close, it had given Tigh a reason to keep going, a reason to hope. But all these months of silence had led Saul back into his bad habits. He always drank, he guessed, but back with Bill he had kept his carousing to off-hours. Now he drank all the time.

It had cost him his job. As crappy as the last freighter had been, they couldn't harbor a drunk. They had canned him halfway through their run, and left him to rot on Gemeinon. Maybe even Adama couldn't talk his superiors into taking a middle-aged man – an old lush, really – like Tigh back in the service. Saul still thought Bill's offer had been a nice gesture, but it had been far too long since he had put on a uniform. Who would look at him now?

So he sat for a month in his rented single room, using up the last of his money, cut off from the stars. Without somebody like Adama around, Saul had been drifting, lost. He had thought about wiring his old mate one more time, to see if there was any hope. He had decided to spend the money on alcohol instead. Saul was already fresh out of hope.

He could only see one option – to end it all. He'd drink himself into a pleasant stupor. Liquid courage, that was what they called it. Then he would pour the rest of the bottle over his clothes and strike an open flame.

He had always wanted to go out in a blaze of glory. He was ready to burn.

And then the knock came on the door. When Tigh had been at the lowest of the low, he'd opened the damned door and seen – not Adama – but a couple of men in uniform, informing him that he was back in. Adama had been promoted. They needed someone to fill his old position. Saul Tigh had been William Adama's personal recommendation.

In two weeks, he'd be Captain Saul Tigh, serving on a Battlestar.

Now Saul was convinced Bill really *could* do anything.

He had been back in the service now for a little over

two months. He had been surprised at how easily he had slipped back into the military routine, how natural the rhythms of a ship seemed, even though he had been away from them for close to twenty years.

Before that? Well, maybe that was better forgotten. For years he had tried to forget what had happened in the war. Why not forget his own little war with the bottle?

He was a captain now, assigned to train all the new pilots who shipped on board the last time they stopped on Caprica. Twenty-three pilots, nineteen of them green recruits – nineteen youngsters who would learn to eat, drink, and sleep with their Vipers before he was done.

They were a good bunch of kids. He just hoped they never had to be tested in battle.

The Cylons had almost broken humanity. Humanity would never allow anything like that to happen again.

Tigh sighed and hauled himself off his bunk. Enough of the introspection. The last time he had gotten this deep in thought, he'd ended up looking to light himself on fire.

He was on duty in twenty minutes. He'd stroll up to CIC, see if anything was happening, before he chewed out the troops. These days, he liked to get out and stretch his legs. Saul just wanted to walk down the corridors of the Battlestar – his Battlestar.

He looked up at the sound of Klaxons. A voice came over the shipboard wireless, instructing all senior staff to report to Combat Information Center at once.

That meant they'd found something – something serious.

Well, so much for the stroll. He shut the door behind him and quick-marched down the corridor.

It was time to do his job.

Today he had a purpose. Today somebody else could look over the edge.

*

Colonel William Adama looked up from the star charts spread before him. A dozen others busied themselves in other parts of the CIC, the huge, central space that served as the beating heart of the Battlestar. He was surrounded by stations that handled navigation, communication, air filtration, artificial gravity, and every conceivable line of supply, both for ship functions and the needs of the crew – every piece of that complicated equation that kept a starship alive and running. Each of the many tasks was overseen by a member of the operations crew, working with their own individual computer designed to perform that specific assignment. Before the war, they had net-worked the computers together to run all the ship's functions. But the Cylons had learned to subvert those networks and turn them against their human crews, shutting down life support, exploding fuel tanks, even plunging whole spacecraft into the nearest stars.

The CIC was still filled with gray metal panels and a thousand blinking lights. But each panel had a living counterpart, men and women who specialized in each individual task and shared their knowledge with those around them. Rather than let the machines do their work, they were forced to network the old fashioned way, as human beings.

And all of those specialists reported to Bill Adama.

Adama looked quickly about the room before glancing back at his map. He allowed himself the slightest of smiles. Everyone around him seemed engrossed in his or her different job, a dozen different pieces of the great human machine that ran this ship.

He was still trying on the fit of his new executive officer position. In the two months he had held this position, the

Battlestar had certainly run well enough, even though, on some days, he didn't feel quite up to speed.

'Sir!' the dradis operator called. 'We have a large ship, just within range, moving erratically!'

Adama turned to the comm operator who controlled the ship-to-ship wireless. 'See if you can raise them.'

'Aye, sir!'

Some days, the XO position came with a few surprises.

These last two months, *Galactica* had been exploring the edges of what they called 'known space,' hopping from one solar system to the next, looking for worlds, moons, even asteroids where humans had been before. Until now, they hadn't found much at all.

Before the Cylon rebellion, humanity had spread far and wide, each of the Colonies claiming their own little corner of space and defending those claims against all others. Some of those territorial disputes were what had brought on the inter-Colony wars of a century past – battles that had also led to the invention of the original war machines, the Cylons.

Back before the Cylon conflict, humanity had lived under an uneasy truce. Every Colony pushed at the limits imposed on them. Some built secret installations to give them an advantage over their Colonial foes. Some secrets were so deep, even the Colonies' own citizens knew nothing about them – hidden installations run by a few individuals in government or the military; it varied from world to world.

And then the Cylon War came to dwarf all their petty disputes – a war that almost killed them all.

'Any luck with that comm?' Adama asked.

'No sir. No response at all.'

They hadn't found much of anything at all this far out – until now.

'Let's take the *Galactica* in a little closer. See if we can find out anything else about this ship.'

Maybe they had really found something this time.

With the Cylon conflict fresh in their minds, the Twelve Colonies had been eager to cooperate, and the Battlestars had been able to repair much of the immediate damage from the war, cleaning up asteroid fields that had been littered with mines, reopening supply stations and mining operations, even relocating survivors. But years had gone by now since the Cylons had disappeared. A whole new generation was growing up – a generation which had never seen a Cylon.

They were lucky to have the Battlestars out here at all. Sometimes, Adama wondered how long the Colonial alliance would really hold. The Cylons, after all, had never really been defeated. The Colonies had to stay united. But the politicians, eager for the approval of each separate world, already seemed to have forgotten. If the Battlestars wanted to keep exploring the edges of space, they needed to find results. This exploration of the outer reaches, delayed though it was, was the last piece of putting all the far-flung pieces of the Colonies back together.

'Sir, I'm getting some strange readings here.'

Adama looked over at the technician. 'Explain, Lieutenant.'

'I'm seeing bursts of radiation out of this new ship. I think their engines have been breached. We've got a very unstable situation on our hands.'

'Sound the alarm,' Adama said. 'Let's get the senior staff up here.'

The Klaxons rang out around the room.

The first thing they had found out here was about to blow up in their faces.

Saul Tigh showed up first. The ship's doctor and head engineer were right behind him.

'I was on my way to the morning briefing. What have we got?'

'Admiral on deck!' The shout rang out before Adama could even begin to explain. The crew snapped to attention.

'At ease!' Admiral Sing announced as he strode into the room, then stopped to return their salute. He was a compact man with skin that looked like aging parchment. But while the admiral might look ready for retirement, Adama often thought his superior's energy rivaled that of a raw recruit.

'Colonel Adama, please report.'

'We've picked up the signal of an unknown ship, a potential hazard. It seems to be leaking radiation, sir.'

'Are there any signs of life on board?' Sing asked.

'We've attempted to establish contact, but we've gotten no response.'

'We're close enough to get a visual, sir,' one of the techs called.

'Put it up on the forward screen,' Sing ordered.

'It's an old B-class freighter,' Tigh said with surprise in his voice. 'Bill – Colonel Adama – and I shipped out on one of those when we first met. Just looks sort of dead in space.'

Sing frowned at the still image in front of them. 'Could the ship have been damaged in a fight?'

'It doesn't look like it has a scratch,' Tigh replied.

'And it's leaking radiation?'

'Intermittently.' The tech checked the dials before her. 'Sometimes, there's hardly any reading. At others, the sensors are going wild.'

'Captain Frayn.' Sing addressed the ship's engineer. 'What could cause those sort of readings?'

'It has to be the engines. They must have been stripped of most of their shielding. That sort of damage had to have been done internally.'

'Sabotage,' Adama added. 'They wanted to blow up the next people to board her.'

'Quite possible,' Frayn agreed. 'Without getting close enough to get blown up, I think it's a reasonable assumption.'

'This isn't the friendliest of gestures,' Sing remarked. 'Who do we think is responsible?'

'We've been trailing scavengers for some time,' Adama replied. 'I've mentioned it in my reports.'

The few abandoned Colonial sites they had managed to find had been well picked-over.

'I recall,' Sing replied. 'Seems our scavengers don't like being followed.'

'They're probably trying to cut out the competition,' Frayn ventured.

'Won't they be surprised when they find their competition is a Battlestar?' Tigh asked with a smile.

'And I think we need to find these folks before they leave any more gifts.' The admiral looked to Tigh. 'Let's get some pilots out there to take care of this, shall we?'

'Yes, sir!' Tigh saluted and left for the flight deck.

'Colonel Adama, you believe the scavengers are exploring the same area we are?'

'The evidence suggests that we've crossed paths half a dozen times. I'm guessing they have the same intel that we have.'

'Knowing how difficult it was for us to get the intel out of the Colonies, they may have more.' Sing shook his head in disgust. 'Let's increase our speed, do a sweep of the area. Maybe we can pick these characters up.'

'And if we find them, sir?' Adama asked.

'A bunch of crazy scavengers who leave bombs behind as gifts? We may just have to blow them out of the sky.'

ABOUT THE AUTHOR

Jeffrey A. Carver is the author of fifteen popular science fiction novels, including *The Infinity Link* and *The Rapture Effect*. His books combine hard-SF concepts, deeply humanistic concerns, and a sense of humor. His last novel, *Eternity's End*, was a finalist for the Nebula Award. He is currently completing *Sunborn*, the long-awaited fourth volume of *The Chaos Chronicles*, a cosmic-scope series inspired by the science of chaos.

Carver has taught science-fiction writing to young authors both as an educational television host and as the author of *Writing Science Fiction and Fantasy*, an online guide to the craft of storytelling and writing. The guide is now available online, free, at *www.writesf.com*.

A native of Huron, Ohio, Carver graduated from Brown University with a degree in English. He has been a high-school wrestler, a scuba-diving instructor, a quahog diver, a UPS sorter, a private pilot, and a stay-at-home dad. He lives with his family in the Boston area.

Discover more at www.starrigger.net.